Created by
WARREN MURPHY
and RICHARD SAPIR

THE

Destr⊕yer™

PROPHET OF DOOM

A GOLD EAGLE BOOK FROM
W⊕RLDWIDE®

TORONTO • NEW YORK • LONDON
AMSTERDAM • PARIS • SYDNEY • HAMBURG
STOCKHOLM • ATHENS • TOKYO • MILAN
MADRID • WARSAW • BUDAPEST • AUCKLAND

First edition May 1998
ISBN 0-373-63226-6

Special thanks and acknowledgment to James Mullaney and Daisy Snaggers for their contribution to this work.

PROPHET OF DOOM

Printed in U.S.A.

To Father John Connell.

And the Glorious House of Sinanju.

PROLOGUE

She brought the goat as payment.

Some people brought jewels or perfume. Those who were poor brought food or even wine to Delphi. Gold was an offering worthy of a god. But without any of these things available to her, Nausicaa brought the goat that had been her responsibility ever since she had gone to live with her father's brother in Thebes.

Her uncle would be angry when he learned that the animal had been used in sacrifice at the temple in Delphi, but it was the only thing Nausicaa possessed that would be acceptable to the god of the smoke.

Not that the Pythia itself was a god. The Pythia of the Temple of Apollo was a servant. Within the vapor—the *knisa*—that flowed from the living rock inside the temple, there dwelled a spirit who infected any who sat above it. When the vapor was inhaled, the servant would become in its very essence the spirit of the Pythia. Whoever was fortunate enough to become Pythia was given the gift to prophesy.

As a result of its mysterious Oracle, Delphi attracted pilgrims from every corner of Greece who wished to see into the future. Because of this, the spirit of the Pythia was granted special status as a conduit to the gods.

But the Pythia served a greater master, the sun god Apollo, who daily led his flaming chariot across the heavens.

It was the powerful Apollo, son of Zeus, to whom Nausicaa silently prayed as she made her way up the well-trampled road to the temple on the hill.

Her question for the Pythia would surely seem petty to some. Her uncle had arranged for her to marry the son of a prosperous neighboring farmer, but Nausicaa was opposed to the union. She would slaughter the goat before the Pythia and then ask the Oracle if the marriage was her true destiny. If the Pythia foretold this was her future, she would surrender herself to the will of her uncle and return with her slave, Tyrtaeus, to Thebes. Reluctantly.

When Nausicaa finally laid eyes on the magnificent Temple of Apollo, she was awed by the sight. The building was huge. Bigger than any other man-made structure Nausicaa had seen in all of her fifteen years.

The walls were towering vertical sheets of the smoothest quarry rock. Creamy white marble statuary dotted the landscape along the path up to the main entrance of the temple. Gleaming bronze likenesses of Apollo, carved with painstaking detail by the finest craftsmen in Greece, stood watch over the huge archway into the temple. Particular attention was paid in many of the statues to Apollo's defeat of the mighty serpent Python near Delphi, when the sun god was only an infant. The Pythia was named thusly because of this event in the young god's life.

At the entryway Nausicaa was confronted by one of the white-robed temple priests who demanded the customary fee before he would allow her entry. Meekly

Nausicaa offered him the cloth sack that she had brought. In the bag she had placed the *pelanos,* which was a type of cake, for payment to the lesser priests.

After inspecting it, the man seemed satisfied with the gift and he pulled the drawstring closed on the bag. Putting the sack aside, he led Nausicaa into the bowels of the temple.

Once inside, Nausicaa noticed the other priests, who stood in the darker recesses of the temple, motioning excitedly toward her. Some nodded and whispered among themselves as if some momentous decision had been made.

The hungry looks they gave her as she was led through the inner chambers made her uncomfortable. As they walked through chamber after massive chamber, the stares from Apollo's priests became more intense. She realized with growing concern as they negotiated the labyrinthine corridors that the world outside was getting farther and farther away.

Nausicaa began to feel uneasy. Her mouth felt dry.

When they at last reached the entryway to the Pythia Pit, the slave, Tyrtaeus, was made to remain behind. Alone and with a feeling of deep foreboding, Nausicaa followed the priest into the Pythia Pit.

Inside, the room was filled with a choking yellow smoke. Nausicaa knew that the Pythia divined the future by inhaling the noxious sulphur fumes, but she hadn't expected the smell to be so strong. A fine yellow film of sulphur powder coated the floor and walls of the inner chamber. Nausicaa began coughing uncontrollably as another priest came forward and led her goat up to the platform on which the Pythia sat.

The temple had been constructed around the rocky

fissure through which the breath of Apollo had first appeared, and so the floor of the Pythia Pit resembled the hillsides of the region.

The goat left tiny hoofprints in the yellow sulphur powder as the priest led the unwitting animal to the top of the hill. There, he held the creature firmly in place as he removed a ceremonial dagger from his belt. With a practiced motion the priest swiftly slit the animal's throat. The goat squirmed in pain and fright as a fountain of thick red blood erupted from its throat and poured out into the cleft in the mountainside.

As she watched the ritual from the floor of the chamber, Nausicaa grew more fearful. Perhaps she should have stayed at home and married the farmer's son. Since the death of her father, her life had been one of hardship, and the young farmer could offer her a warm home and freedom from want for the rest of her days.

There was something else that had troubled her since entering this inner chamber. If the Pythia was to predict Nausicaa's future—then where was the girl through which the Pythia spoke?

For the stool on which the young female servant of Apollo was meant to sit was vacant.

This, above all else, filled Nausicaa's heart with fright.

Nausicaa resolved to return to Thebes, to surrender to the life her uncle had arranged for her. She would leave the oracles of the Pythia to generals and kings.

She turned to hurry from the temple—but a group of priests barred her way. She hadn't even heard them enter the room behind her. Now they blocked her path.

She pleaded with them to let her pass, but the priests didn't listen. They took up a low, lyrical chant.

Nausicaa tried to go around them, but they grabbed her arms and held her fast. As she screamed and struggled, they carried her slowly, almost reverentially up the incline to the rocky crevice. Nausicaa saw through frightened tears the yellow smoke pouring out of the mountainside in steadier bursts, keeping time with the chants of Apollo's priests.

For the first time she saw that the flat top of the tiny hill was moving in a strange, undulating pattern. She realized in horror that the entire upper platform was covered with squirming, wriggling snakes. The serpents slid atop one another, across the bare feet of Apollo's priests and in and out of the giant cleft in the earth through which the noxious smoke issued.

The stool on which the Pythia interpreted the oracles sat vacant. Nausicaa wept openly as many powerful hands forced her upon the small wooden tripod. The thick smell of sulphur wafted up through the rock, filling her nostrils, overpowering her reeling senses.

The chanting of the priests grew louder, more frenzied.

Nausicaa's head felt as though it had filled with the yellow smoke. Slick brownish bodies of dozens of slithering snakes moved with sickening slowness across her sandals, coiling up around her naked ankles.

She attempted a last scream, but the ecstatic cries of the priests muffled her voice so that only a whimper escaped.

Terror clogged her throat.

She felt the snakes tighten about her ankles. Cool,

flicking tongues were exploring her knees, her thighs. She could feel dry, scaly muscles sliding slowly across her neck—but it no longer seemed to matter.

Something terrible was happening inside her head.

The smoke continued to pour out of the crevice, surrounding her with its nasty old-egg stink. She became dizzy and fatigued. Nausicaa tried to blink at the sensation, but her eyes no longer worked. She thought hard on this, and realized that her eyes still worked. It was only that they no longer worked for her.

Through a strange, shifting haze, Nausicaa saw the temple priests surround her body, ankle deep in slithering snakes, but she was no longer in her body. She was beyond it, above it.

Somewhere from a distant, indistinct place her father was beckoning her to join him, and she left the temple and its chanting priests along with her body as she moved into a place of light and warmth.

As her thoughts fluttered free, a strong alien presence that had taken root somewhere in a far-off place within her mind told her that the events of this last day in her young life would have resonance down through the ages, and that the chain that began here would end as it was foretold.

The words spoken in her mind foretold that when East met West, a god of the past would meet a god of the distant future.

There was only one word in the prophecy Nausicaa did not understand, and as her essence vanished into the ethereal nothingness, that single word and its significance—along with all the troubles of her earthly self—vanished behind her.

The word she did not understand was "Sinanju."

1

This day the Prophetess foretold a great fire that would wash down from the mountains and scorch the valley below. The ground would quake beneath a stampede of mighty beasts, and the earth would give up its dead.

There was much excited discussion among the new arrivals upon hearing of the catastrophe that would soon befall mankind. They looked up and around as if the end were at hand, which it was, according to the pamphlets they had received upon passing through the high steel gates.

The sky was a warm pastel haze, the Wyoming sun a small spark of yellow white against the sea of ice blue. There wasn't much in the way of apocalyptic activity at present, but the Prophetess insisted it was on the way, and they had been assured that the Prophetess was never, ever wrong.

"Will the seas turn to blood, like in Revelations?" someone asked fearfully.

The Prophetess considered. "Like the blood of a thousand times a thousand souls," she intoned.

There were gasps.

"Will the sky darken?"

The Prophetess allowed that it would. "The sky will turn the color of death for seven days, and on the seventh it will be torn asunder and a hail of holy fire will pelt the valley below.'' Pelt? She'd have to reconsider that word. It didn't sound sufficiently lyrical, let alone apocalyptic.

The crowd was enraptured. ''When will this come to pass?'' they chorused.

The Prophetess held her right hand to the heavens, as if the sun's rays against her palm were the source of divine inspiration. Her hand made an arc through the still air as she thumped the heel of the long hickory staff clutched in her left hand against the ground three times, making tiny circular marks in the dirt of the compound. Puffs of reddish dust rose and fell as she considered the question.

Those gathered held their breath as the seconds slipped away.

The Prophetess stepped up onto the broad wooden porch of the ranch house so that the crowd, clumped together at the end of the long road leading up from the main gate, was a full head-length beneath her. It was a well-rehearsed move and one that placed her in a clear position of authority.

She suppressed a shudder as the air-conditioned coolness poured out through the open door of the house onto her back.

At last the Prophetess spoke. ''It will happen in the time of which I have spoken and in the manner in which I have foretold.'' She said it with certainty. Her blue eyes, like azure pools, held each of theirs in turn.

There was power in the eyes. And wisdom. Those determined, unwavering eyes had converted many a disbeliever, leading the new faithful over to the Church of the Absolute and Incontrovertible Truth like

Moses leading the Hebrews through the parted waters of the Red Sea.

At least that was how the faithful saw themselves. Esther Clear-Seer, the divine Prophetess, was nick-named "Yogi Mom" by her followers. As founder and Beatific Head of the Church of the Absolute and Incontrovertible Truth, and possessing a mystifying gift of prognostication, she saw her followers less as Levites than as lemmings. They streamed willingly to Esther's wilderness church and flung themselves off the cliffs of reason with an almost violent eagerness.

This new group was no exception. They had been driven by bus from the nearby town of Thermopolis, Wyoming, to the Truth Church ranch for religious indoctrination. Esther could see from their naive, hopeful expressions that they were ripe for the picking.

There were about a dozen of them, men and women in their twenties and thirties. They stood there in the dirt of the arrival center of Ranch Ragnarok—duffel bags, knapsacks and third-generation suitcases bursting open at their feet—and Esther knew that they were all hers.

She had seen their type before. Despondent, lonely, downtrodden. These were her flock: people with an emptiness in their barren lives. They looked to Yogi Mom for deliverance. Many such converts were toiling on the grounds of the ranch or in the concrete bunkers beneath her gold-sandaled feet.

Some in this latest batch thought it odd that heaven could be achieved by sheer brute force, for that was the impression one got upon seeing the well-armed squads of Truth Church disciples who milled about at the periphery of the indoctrination area. It seemed that everyone on this side of the Ranch Ragnarok gates carried some kind of pistol or rifle or machine gun. The new faithful were told in no uncertain terms that force was sometimes necessary to ensure harmony of spirit. They learned, soon enough, to adhere to this dictum, lest they find themselves staring down a 700-rounds-per-minute barrel of divine retribution.

Thus, surprisingly few questioned the wisdom of Esther Clear-Seer. Most who had joined the Church of the Absolute and Incontrovertible Truth had nowhere else to turn. These were society's outcasts, desperate for something to cling to. Esther Clear-Seer gave them hope, family, community. A future. Her assurances that they would be the survivors of the coming Dark Times made them somehow special. And in the end, special was all they had to cling to.

These new arrivals were no different. Failure showed through the glazed look in their eyes and sat across their slouched shoulders. The world had dealt them many harsh blows, they believed, and they longed for some deus ex machina to alleviate their troubles.

At Ranch Ragnarok in the piney woods of Wyoming, they were promised the secrets of the future and protection from the things that were to come.

Of course, nothing was ever given away, free of charge.

On the steps of her sprawling ranch house, Esther Clear-Seer addressed this latest motley collection of human flotsam and jetsam.

"You all realize that you must suspend your belief in the external. For to become one with truth is to forsake all that is false. Beyond those walls—" with her staff she indicated the high hurricane fence and gun towers surrounding the ranch "—lies falsehood. Within these walls you will find safety and contentment. And spiritual knowledge. When the world as you know it has turned to ash, only those of us inside this fortress will be spared the ravages of the Dark Times." Her voice became a husky threat. "And you can only pass through to salvation when you have been stripped of all worldly trappings." With that she beckoned with her staff and, with a solemn bow of the head, backed through the open door behind her.

When she was gone, some of the older faithful, the few who had been around since Esther Clear-Seer had founded the Truth Church, descended like pack animals and began the inevitable shake-down of the new recruits. Cash was taken, credit cards impounded, bank books signed over, personal belongings searched. It only took a matter of minutes before the worldly trappings of the newly converted became the worldly trappings of Esther Clear-Seer.

Esther sighed inwardly as she watched the scene through the large bay window in the air-conditioned coolness of her Meditation Chapel.

Just another day in the God game.

Of course, the line she had fed this group was nothing new. She had predicted the whole "mountain, fire, burning valley, stampeding death" scenario before. In fact, she had given this particular prediction to every new arrival since Day One.

And when these events failed to come to pass, she reminded the skeptical that she had never mentioned what mountain or which valley, and if someone had the temerity to press further, she invariably ducked the question and accused the questioner of heresy in shrill, demanding terms.

Heresy was always a good dodge, Esther Clear-Seer held. You could get away with nearly anything by calling someone a heretic.

But Esther didn't much care for heresy. She felt it was a sign of personal failure when she had to cast out one of her own flock, for when Esther Clear-Seer excommunicated someone, he or she remained excommunicated. There were about two dozen mounds of overturned earth baking in the Wyoming sun to attest to that fact.

No, maintaining faith was the real challenge, and no doubt about it: when choosing between either faith or heresy, faith was the far more lucrative.

All this Esther considered as she poured herself a tumbler of Scotch—a drink that was forbidden, as was all liquor, to her faithful acolytes—and slumped back into the tension-relieving vibrating recliner she had bought with proceeds donated by an unemployed auto mechanic from Duluth. She took a sip of the amber liquid from the heavy, hand-etched crystal and watched through drooping blue eyelids the activity outside her window.

There was some kind of problem out there.

It seemed that one of the new recruits was arguing with her acolytes.

She had noticed the funny little man, a Mediterranean type, when the rest of the group had descended from the rickety old bus that now sat in an overgrown patch of weeds near the gate.

He was older than the others, perhaps in his late forties, and he had a much younger girl with him who seemed to follow him, step by step, wherever he went. When Esther had first seen him, he was in his shirt-sleeves, having doffed his suit jacket, draping it over his forearms. But his clasped hands rested too far from his body, as if he was hiding something. Esther assumed that he was carrying something of personal value underneath the suit jacket. Whatever it was, her men would strip him of it when the time came.

Esther had dismissed the man from her thoughts. Now, watching with increasing concern, she hoped her Truth Church acolytes would resolve the situation peacefully. Unfortunately it seemed as though they were paralyzed with inaction.

The man barked something at them but Esther didn't catch it through the window.

The acolytes hesitated. This was not good. Why were they just standing there? Where was Truth Church discipline?

Quickly Esther Clear-Seer pressed the button that stopped the vibrating motion of her recliner.

The man snapped again. Even if Esther couldn't hear what he was saying, she could see her men backing off. The new recruits looked at the guards and at one another fearfully, faces confused.

"Damn!" Esther cursed. "This is my damn fault."

Almost a year before, her acolytes had administered ultimate chastisement against a young man who had refused to surrender his wallet upon arrival. As a result, the rest of the group he had arrived with, who were not yet fully indoctrinated into the ways of the Truth Church and capable of talking to the authorities, were stricken from church rolls, as well.

No one ever asked about them.

Since then, there had been a standing order, issued by the Prophetess herself, that no one was to be shot in the presence of any recruit still in the six-month initiation program.

That order came back to haunt her as she watched the small wiry man shove his way through the group of armed guards and gesture boldly toward the sprawling split-log ranch house. His hand snaked back under his rumpled jacket tail. His young companion followed, zombie like, in his wake.

The guards almost drew down on him, but the man was talking reasonably now. He gestured crisply toward the ranch. He had a definite way about him. Commanding.

The guards looked to one another in confusion.

The little man took this indecision as an opening and marched boldly past the guards, the girl following dutifully behind.

"Shit," spake Her Beatific Oneness.

She got up and went to the door.

The guards were behind him when she opened the door on the strange little man and his hidden package. Their confusion had already given way to alarm at his disturbing their divine leader. Their weapons were trained directly at the man's back.

He spoke without preamble. "A small biotechnical firm in Massachusetts has gone public as of 9:00 a.m. today," he said. "I have placed an order in your name. Your holdings have by now tripled in price. By closing today, you will have made a profit of 78,000 dollars on a ten-thousand-dollar initial investment, and by noon tomorrow it will pass the hundred-thousand-dollar mark. You may check with your broker to verify this information. Until then, I would recommend that you instruct your followers to refrain from shooting me.''

The man smiled a tight-lipped smile, told Esther the name of the company and took a seat on the small wooden bench beside her door. The girl stood dutifully beside him.

Esther was at a loss for words. The other recruits had seen all of what was going on and were watching for a reaction. The little man just calmly sat there. He tucked his coattails around the top of whatever he was holding in his lap. His eyes were black and unblinking, and his unwavering gaze reminded Esther of a dead-eyed reptile.

That decided Esther Clear-Seer.

She called her broker.

Yes, the information was true. Yes, if she had invested ten thousand when the exchange opened, she would have tripled her investment by this time. And did Esther want to sink some money into Biotechnics, Inc.?

Esther hung up the phone and went out to her porch. The man was wearing his jacket now, and there was something on the bench beside him.

''What's your game?'' she asked the strange little man.

''You are rich?'' he asked, standing.

Esther glanced at her acolytes. ''I am rich in the things that matter,'' she pronounced boldly. She dismissed the guards, ordering them to deal with the other recruits. When the guards were gone, she leaned over to the little man, whispering, ''What's your game? Insider trading?''

The man's smile broadened. Somehow the expression made his face appear even more reptilian. "In a sense," he admitted. He straightened himself up to his full height, but even so, Esther guessed that he could not be more than five foot five. "My name is Mark Kaspar," he said, "and we are destined, you and I, to become partners in the greatest enterprise in modern history." The smile flickered and faded, in an almost too-practiced manner, to be replaced by a more serious expression.

"We should go inside and talk." He collected his package from the bench and headed for the door. The dead-eyed girl followed, mute.

For the first time Esther clearly saw the item he hefted from the tiny wooden bench. It was a large carved stone urn with a heavy cracked lid. On the sides were intricate raised images of intertwined snakes that had been worn smooth with age.

As the strange man passed into her home, Esther Clear-Seer caught the pungent odor of rotten eggs.

2

His name was Remo, and he was tired of repeating it.

"Remo!" he shouted for the third time to the ump-teenth set of nerve-deafened eardrums.

"Zemo?" asked the elderly woman. She checked a clipboard on her desk. The clipboard was upside down. "Oh, dear," she clucked.

"I'm looking for Dr. Coffin," Remo explained as she made a vain attempt to search for the name Zemo Welby on the upside-down visitor's list.

The woman seemed lost somewhere on the page before her. When she finally looked up, it was as if she saw Remo for the first time. "Oh, hello," she said with a quavering smile. "Name?"

"Lawrence Welk," sighed Remo, walking past her and up the hall.

That was at the fourth-floor duty station. Things had gone pretty much the same at the third-floor duty station, the second-floor duty station, the information booth in the lobby and the guard's shack at the main gate of Sunnyville Retirement Community in Tampa, Florida.

No one Remo encountered was a day under eighty.

He wasn't surprised. Upstairs had told him that this would probably be the case. There were only six members of the Sunnyville staff drawing a regular salary and, Remo was told, the half-dozen individuals he was after were fairly young and not likely to be doing anything more strenuous than overseeing the real Sunnyville workers.

It was no secret that Sunnyville thought the problem with most retirement homes was that the residents felt used up; they were of no account, their days as contributing members of society behind them.

It was with this mind-set that the upper echelon at Sunnyville reinvented the entire nursing-home concept from the ground up. The result was a pioneering retirement community boasting a totally new method of dealing with the elderly and infirm.

They worked them like slaves.

Some of the aged were put to work in the kitchen preparing the daily gruel. Those who were still lucid were put to work in administration, answering phones, filing or typing. The balance toiled as groundskeepers, cleaning women, carpenters and janitors.

In recent months, Sunnyville had made national news when an eighty-five-year-old retiree, tasked to cut down orange trees in the Sunnyville grove, was stricken simultaneously with a stroke, partial paralysis and a hemorrhaging occipital lobe. A cheery Sunnyville spokesperson, trying to happy-spin the ''unfortunate, unavoidable incident,'' theorized the man's brain was probably already uncontrollably bleeding when he dropped the chain saw on his leg.

Once the story died down, Sunnyville lawyers opted for an out-of-court settlement, with a strict gag order.

And so the matter faded from public view. But not in all quarters.

Remo had been told about a rumor that Sunnyville had recently refined its lucrative business. Word going around was that whoever was too tired or old to work any longer, would suddenly succumb to death due to "natural causes." Just like that. And the vacant bed and job would go to the person next on Sunnyville's phone-book-sized waiting list.

Remo didn't bother to ask how the word got out. A private memo, some loose talk in a bar—it didn't matter to him. An assignment was an assignment.

Remo strolled down the antiseptic-smelling hallway, his thick-wristed hands swinging casually at his sides. Today his T-shirt was crisply white, his chinos black.

The building almost looked abandoned. The doors to the private rooms were closed. Remo could hear the faint rasp of asthmatic breathing coming from several of them.

The hallway itself was the opposite of his image of a nursing home. There were no laundry baskets, chairs, stools or medicine carts parked haphazardly about. Nor were there any elderly people bent over walkers or slowly pushing their blue-veined hands over the rubber tires of wheelchairs. It was as if the residents were under lockdown.

And there was something else. Something that lingered beneath the thick, combined odors of a thousand different prescription drugs.

It was fear.

There was no mistaking it. The smell was almost palpable.

It clung to the corridor walls, and no matter how many gallons of antiseptic cleansers were applied daily by overworked retirees, the odor couldn't be washed away.

Remo sensed the fear, though he didn't feel it himself, and he thought it odd that he could look back dispassionately on so strong an emotion.

When he was young, he had felt fear; but that was a million lifetimes ago, and at this point in his life he was able to remember the emotion as if it had been nothing more than a case of mild teenage acne.

The Sunnyville residents, however, didn't seem to have that option. The daily fear they lived with clung to them like garlic.

Perhaps, Remo thought, fear could be distilled like musk or sold in concentrated form like a can of frozen orange juice. Instant fear. Just add water. He decided that the market for prepackaged fear probably wasn't profitable enough. Why would people buy something they found in their everyday lives?

This in mind, he rounded a corner and nearly tripped over an elderly woman on her hands and knees on the floor.

A low, baleful moan escaped between the woman's parched and cracking lips. Her swollen, arthritic hands were extended before her. The flaking, bloated fingers of her right hand seemed to be clutching something as she painfully inched forward.

Remo gently took hold of the woman's birdlike shoulders and lifted her to her feet.

She wobbled unsteadily and leaned one gnarled hand against the wall for support, the other dangling by her side in a loose fist.

"Are you all right?" asked Remo softly.

"I'm not finished," the woman said. She panted as

she forced the words out. "Please, I can finish." She struggled to make a fist. "There," she said triumphantly. "See? I can still *do* it. It's not so hard. Really."

She tried to get back to her knees, but Remo's seemingly gentle touch on her upper arms held her firmly in place.

"Let me take you to your room," he said softly.

Sudden concern showed in her eyes. "Are you with Dr. Coffin?"

"No," Remo admitted.

"Oh, dear," the woman said. What little color she had drained from her face, and her exhausted frame tipped against the wall. "You mustn't tell them I spoke with you," she said desperately. "Please. They can't find out." Her watery eyes darted up and down the empty hallway in fear.

"Relax," said Remo quietly. With great delicacy he pulled the woman upright. "Everything's going to be just fine. Is there a nurse around here somewhere?"

"No!" she shrieked. She pulled away from Remo's grip with surprising agility. "Not the nurses! Please," she begged, her voice now muted. "Please, just leave. Leave me alone."

"Can I help you with something?" a voice behind Remo asked icily.

Remo turned to see a severe-looking woman standing near the empty nurses' station down the hallway. The knuckles of her plump hands rested on her boxy hips, and her eyes shot daggers at him. Her plain hair was pulled back in a bun so tight her eyes bugged out. She sashayed over to Remo, the coarse fabric of her heavy tweed skirt swinging like Quasimodo's bell.

"Oh, no," groaned the old woman. "I'm fine, Dr. Coffin. Honestly. See? I'm working." Using the wall as a brace, she slid slowly to the floor and unfolded a moistened ball of rag clutched in her hand. Remo watched in amazement as the woman—she looked ninety if she was a day—began scrubbing the floor wildly.

"See? I'm still working. And happy," she added. "That's what I was telling this young man here. I couldn't be happier." Straining her neck, she looked up and forced a smile.

"This is ridiculous," Remo said, shaking his head. He drew the woman back to her feet.

"Stop that!" the old woman cried. "I'm not too old to work!" Her arms flailed as she tried to pull away from Remo.

"It's all right, Josephine," said Dr. Coffin. "You may go now."

"But I haven't finished scrubbing the floor yet. Please let me work!" The old woman was in tears. "I *want* to work!"

"I said you may go," snapped Dr. Coffin.

Josephine turned her pitiful, red-rimmed eyes toward Remo and without another word shuffled painfully down the hall and out of sight.

"'So that our guests might enjoy their later years in quiet dignity and grace,'" said Remo, quoting from the Sunnyville brochure.

"Stuff it, Lean and Mean," snapped the woman. "What do you want?"

Remo shrugged. "Local reporter," he said. "Doing a piece for the Sunday supplement. Dr. Coffin, I presume?"

The nursing-home staffer suppressed a brief, mirthless smile. "Which local paper?" she sneered.

"Beats me," Remo admitted. "Daily something-or-other. Who pays attention to the masthead these days? I'm too busy racking up column inches. You up to an interview, Mrs. Coffin?"

"Doctor," she corrected. "Dr. Augusta Coffin." Her meaty face puckered painfully. Remo realized that this was what passed for Dr. Coffin's smile of triumph. "And you are no reporter," she added. With that, she whirled and, with a flash of thick calves, clomped over to the bare desk near the elevator foyer. With a stubby finger she dialed a security code on the old-fashioned rotary telephone.

"That's what my editor keeps saying," Remo said, "which is why I'm stuck doing Sunday fluff pieces." As he followed Dr. Coffin, he fumbled in the pockets of his new chinos for some paper but the best he could come up with was an Inspected By ##7 label. He held the tiny scrap of paper in the palm of his hand, ready to jot down notes when he suddenly remembered he had no pen or pencil.

Dr. Coffin didn't seem to care. She merely stood, bouncer-like, in front of the elevator doors, her arms folded across her crisply starched blouse.

"You've got other people here, don't you?" Remo asked. "Younger guys on the payroll? Where are they?"

Dr. Coffin ignored him.

"Is it true you recently unplugged an eighty-year-old woman from dialysis because her Medicare check was a day late?"

"I'm running a business here—not a charity." Dr.

Coffin's pug nose crinkled as she cast a sideways glance at Remo.

"Can I quote you on that?" Remo asked. He pretended to make a few scratch marks with his nonexistent pencil.

Dr. Coffin's gaze seemed to be hardening. "Who are you really?" she asked, looking him up and down. The edge in her voice softened. She rubbed a shoulder against Remo's chest. Or tried to.

Remo dodged the meaty shoulder. "The woman died," he said.

"We all have to go sometime."

"I'm glad you feel that way," said Remo, deflecting a clumsy paw from the front of his trousers. "There have been nine other similar incidents here in the past month."

"A girl's got to keep busy," Dr. Coffin purred. "What's that cologne you're wearing?"

"Bee pheromones."

"Yowza, yowza." Padded fingers sought Remo's short dark hair.

"Oh, get real," said Remo. He smacked her thick fingers away. "I haven't got all night. My editor's a stickler for deadlines. Where are your accomplices?"

"Accomplices?" asked Augusta Coffin innocently. "We have nurses on staff at Sunnyville, but refer to them as associates, not accomplices. You make things sound so sinister." She ran her tongue across her thick red lips. "There's a vacant room just up the hall, sugar," she said suggestively.

Suddenly the elevator chimed, and the doors slid open.

Five burly men lumbered out as if joined at the hip.

The seams of their white cotton shorts were stretched to the bursting point as muscle fought fabric in a contest Remo was certain the fabric would lose.

The man at the fore of the group appraised Remo's lean frame. "Another Fed?" he asked Dr. Coffin. A pin over his breast pocket identified him as Roy Harkness, R.N.

Dr. Coffin's face was flushed. She smoothed her dress as if she and Remo had been discovered in flagrante delicto. "He says he's a *reporter*," she said to Roy, crossing her arms and plumping her ample bosom.

"He don't look like no reporter to me," one of the meat-piles said from the back. "Looks kind of faggy, in fact."

"That's not quite the look I was shooting for," said Remo. "I thought of going for the grizzled-news-vet approach, but opted for the cub-reporter persona instead. Now, how many of you are guilty of murder? Can I have a show of hands?" His invisible pencil hovered over his tiny notepaper.

Dr. Augusta Coffin sighed. "I suppose you have to take care of him now," she said to Roy.

"We can't let him escape," Roy suggested. He seemed puzzled that she even asked the question. "You want a piece of him?"

"In the worst way."

They looked at her.

"I affect some women this way," offered Remo.

"Just do it," Augusta Coffin said, a hint of regret in her voice.

Roy and his male-nurse brigade escorted Remo onto the waiting elevator, piling in around the edge of the tiny car like a solid, living wall. The elevator groaned under the weight as Roy stabbed at the Down button.

"Isn't there a weight limit on these things?" asked Remo. "'Cause if there is, you're it." He pointed at a nearby pectoral muscle that looked like a beef flank.

"What agency are you with?" Roy demanded.

"Agency?" said Remo, feigning surprise. "I told you. I'm cub reporter Remo Welby, hot on a story that's going to win me the big prize that all reporters dream of."

"Da Pulitzer?" suggested one of them.

"That's the one. I'm gonna win it hands down. Now, first nosy question—how many old people have you guys snuffed so far?"

"Apparently, one too few," said Roy.

The other nurses snorted.

The elevator stopped downstairs at a basement laundry room. The five nurses escorted Remo out into the room and fanned out in a circle, surrounding him.

Roy cracked his knuckles against his open palm. "Sorry about this, buddy," he said to Remo. "But business is business."

"I wouldn't know anything about business," Remo said. "I went to journalism school. They taught us to be suspicious of anyone who worked for a living. But if you want, I can put something special in your obituaries."

All five rushed him at once. Rippling arms and tree-trunk legs swung and flew in wild arcs around Remo's head. Remo yawned.

A meaty paw flashed at his face, and Remo leaned back. The fist swooped past his head and landed with a thump on the temple of a male nurse closing in on

Remo. The man let out an "Oof" and sank to the floor.

"Oh, now that isn't fair," said Remo.

Roy shot out a right hook that flattened the face of one of his comrades, tumbling him into a laundry basket. Soiled linen flew everywhere.

"Hey," said Remo. "You're not supposed to do it yourselves. Leave me something."

"Something this, buddy," growled Roy. He wrapped his arms around Remo's chest and squeezed. This was how he had finished the first government investigators who had come to nose around Sunnyville Retirement Community. Roy had snapped their spines like dry noodles.

The other men—even those injured—pulled themselves up to gather around their leader. They liked to watch Roy in action. Roy could bench-press a transmission. One of his favorite moves was to stretch his fingers all the way around the ankles of selected elderly patients and break both legs with one squeeze. He called it "making a wish."

But something wasn't right with this latest government snoop. The skinny guy hadn't even turned red yet. He seemed to be breathing, too. At least it didn't look as if he wasn't breathing. And he was whistling. The tune sounded like "Everything's Coming up Roses."

"Spiffy trick, Roy," Remo chirped. He slid from the huge man's grip like liquid margarine and trotted across the room. He scooped something up from the floor. "See if you recognize this one."

The men lunged all at once, Roy leading the charge.

"Hey, I didn't get my turn!" said Remo. He mixed

with the charging behemoths, joining their attack. "Naughty, naughty," he admonished, dancing between them and clanging a silver bedpan from head to head. "Must play fair."

Five sets of sounds echoed through the room.

Bong! Crack! Four left.

Bong! Crack! Three left.

Bong! Crack! Two left.

Bong! Crack! Roy left.

"Bye, Roy," said Remo. "I guess you won't be playing with old folks or government agents anymore."

Roy seemed genuinely disappointed. "No more old folks?"

Bong! Crack! No more Roy.

"I TRUST YOU INCINERATED the body?" asked Dr. Augusta Coffin without looking up from her desk.

"Which one?" asked Remo.

Dr. Coffin's head snapped up. "Sweet thing, you're back!" She rose from her seat as Remo clicked her office door shut. "Where's Roy?"

"He took something for his head," said Remo. He glided across the plush green carpet to the gleaming mahogany desk. "You're next."

"I don't know what you mean," said Augusta Coffin.

Remo glanced to his right. An enormous Plexiglas window overlooked a well-equipped gymnasium.

Basketball court, weights, parallel bars—Remo assumed all of this stuff had been used only by Roy and the other nurses. To one side of the gym was an unused shuffleboard court. He imagined that the residents of Sunnyville—the people for whom all of this was intended—only saw the inside of the gym when they were forced to clean it.

"I'm glad you're all right," said Dr. Coffin. She circled the desk and pulled up beside Remo. "We can be good together, baby," she breathed.

"Did you have raw onions for dinner?" Remo tried to block the fumes with his hands.

"What's that?" asked Dr. Coffin, pointing to the shiny, dented metal object that Remo had been hiding behind his back.

"It's a bedpan," said Remo. "Don't see too many of these, do you?"

"Ick, of course not," said Augusta Coffin. "If they have to crap in a bucket, we don't want them around here. I didn't even think we had any more left. Where did you get that one?"

"Downstairs." Remo tapped it and smiled.

"It's not supposed to look like that, is it?"

"Nope. It should look like this." Remo flipped his wrist, and the bedpan, which had been dented by the skulls of the dead in the basement, popped back open like a folding top hat.

"Hey, that's neat."

"It gets better."

Dr. Coffin pushed in closer. "If you took care of Roy, you're somebody I can use." She rubbed her hands on his chest. "And you can use me, too," she added breathily.

"Keep it up," warned Remo. "It's only going to make it easier for me to kill you."

Augusta Coffin was startled back to attention. "Kill me?" she said.

"Thought you'd never ask," said Remo. He reached over and unplugged her life-support system, medically known as her cerebral cortex.

Whistling, Remo stuffed as much of her head as possible into the bedpan and flung her at the Plexiglas. The partition shattered, and Dr. Augusta Coffin skidded across the floor of the gymnastics area before landing on the "10" triangle at the top of the shuffleboard court.

"That's what you get when you mess with a member of the Fourth Estate," he pronounced solemnly.

REMO PARKED his rental car at a pay phone by a busy highway a block away from the nursing home.

He didn't have any change so he shattered the coin box with his forefinger and inserted one of the quarters that poured out back into the slot. He hummed to himself as he jabbed the "1" button a half-dozen times.

There was a series of clicks over the line as the call was rerouted halfway up the East Coast and back down again. Finally a parched, lemony voice came on the line.

"Report."

"The sun has set on Sunnyville," intoned Remo.

"Very poetic," the voice of Dr. Harold W. Smith responded dryly.

"And you might want to get someone over there to take care of the residents."

"I am making arrangements for the patients."

Remo sighed. "Knowing you, you're trying to sell the terminal cases on squandering their last days and life savings on the Folcroft three-meal-a-day plan."

Smith said nothing. The organization for which they

both worked operated under the cover of Folcroft Sanitarium. Although he had a virtually unlimited budget for clandestine operations, Smith insisted on running Folcroft as a business.

"I knew it!" Remo said.

"If there is nothing else to report, I suggest we sever this connection," Smith said tightly.

"There is just one more thing," Remo said. "About a hundred TV reporters saw me off that Coffin woman. I suggested they shoot me from the left. I think that's my better side. So if you tune in at about six-thirty tonight, you should see me on the news. And just so you don't think I hogged all the limelight for myself, I mentioned your name at least three dozen times."

Remo slammed the phone down, not even waiting for a response. Placing his hands on either side of the squat upright phone stand, he ripped the entire booth from the pavement and sent it skipping down the street like a flat rock on a placid pond.

"Connection severed," he announced to the empty night.

3

Esther Clear-Seer couldn't believe her luck.

She had been in the religion business for nearly twenty years and in all that time she had never experienced a genuine miracle until the day late last summer when Mark Kaspar showed up on her doorstep.

The Biotechnics stock deal had pulled in nearly five hundred thousand dollars in three days before the little man had instructed her that it was time to pull out. She had wanted to let the money ride, but Kaspar had been firmly insistent and, reluctantly, she had acquiesced.

The next day the bioengineering company had gone down in flames after a patent dispute with a larger pharmaceutical conglomerate. By then Kaspar had dumped half the cash in a five-hundred-acre parcel of land abutting the Ranch Ragnarok property, thus doubling the Truth Church's real-estate holdings, and invested the balance in a relatively safe soft-drink company. The money didn't explode like the initial investment had, but its value continued to grow steadily.

Which was just fine with her. If there was one thing Esther Clear-Seer could appreciate, it was the enrichment of Esther Clear-Seer. Especially if she didn't have to do anything to earn it. The land, however, was another deal entirely.

When she first learned about the property purchase, she had marched angrily over to confront Kaspar and to explain to him, in no uncertain terms, the Ranch Ragnarok pecking order.

The Truth Church ranch had been established by Esther on the grounds of a former industrial complex, and Kaspar and his silent female friend had moved into one of the many vacant cinder-block buildings that was set apart from the communal buildings where the rest of the faithful worked and lived.

As Esther approached the large building, she noticed a strange cloud of yellow smoke rising from the central chimney.

She sniffed the air like a hound on the scent of a fox. A smell like rotten eggs wafted through the afternoon breeze.

What was he cooking?

Esther stormed over to the building.

She had barely raised her hand to knock before Kaspar called out for her to enter. It was as if he anticipated everything. Shrugging, she pushed the door inward.

There was a communal fire area in the center of all Truth Church disciple buildings, and in this one, Kaspar had started a modest blaze out of sagebrush and broken fir twigs.

Over the flames he had set up some kind of staggered scaffolding system out of heavy barbecue cooking grates. A long pan of water shivered on the lowest rack. The water boiled relentlessly, bubbling up against the heavy stone bottom of Kaspar's mysterious urn, which he had placed on a thick steel grate above the pan.

The lid was off the urn now. Esther caught a glimpse of a granular yellow substance just below the rim.

Kaspar's female companion sat on a simple wooden stool next to the fire, her frail arms stretching a blanket up over her head. The woolen blanket caught the noxious yellow fumes that poured freely from the ancient urn, and the girl inhaled greedily as if it were steam from a vaporizer.

The rotten-egg smell was stronger in here. As Esther studied the glazed look on the girl's face, she assumed that the yellow smoke was some kind of narcotic.

Kaspar was seated in a plain wooden chair, stoking the fire with a simple metal rod. He looked up wordlessly at Esther Clear-Seer, fixing her with his dead-serpentine regard.

Esther's smoldering anger was quenched by the unexpected strangeness of the scene within the building. She pointedly ignored the girl, who was gulping ecstatically at the smoke issuing from the pot, and focused her attention on Kaspar.

"Why did you buy that damn land?" Esther asked.

"There are hot springs on the property," Kaspar explained.

"I already knew that," Esther told him. "That's why I didn't want it."

"The springs are crucial to our venture."

Esther hesitated. "How crucial?"

"They will make the difference between success and riches, and abysmal failure."

"Well, okay," Esther said grudgingly. "Just check with me next time."

Kaspar nodded agreeably. "Of course," he said.

And that was that.

What could Esther say? The strange little man deferred to her nearly every time she challenged him, and even when he didn't—as in the real-estate matter—he didn't strike up a bold or defensive posture. He merely stated his position quietly, almost subserviently, and half the time Esther walked away thinking she had come to the same conclusion herself.

Besides, the money Kaspar brought in was nothing to sneeze at. To Esther Clear-Seer, any business partner who swelled the coffers of the Church of the Absolute and Incontrovertible Truth and asked for next to nothing in return was the business partner for her.

The property Kaspar purchased had once housed a modest crop-dusting and stunt-flying business back during the 1930s. Today the only visible sign of that long abandoned enterprise was a rusting corrugated tin hangar squatting at the far end of a sage-covered, crumbling concrete runway. Kaspar had gone to work, refurbishing the structure and altering the basic design of the vacant building into a sanctuary for special worship.

At first Esther resisted the idea of using Truth Church funds on such an outlandish project. But after Kaspar had made her an additional four hundred thousand investing in a Texas cable company, Yogi Mom found her resolve weakened. The man did have a way with money.

"Besides," Kaspar assured her, "fabulous wealth

will begin rolling in just as soon as the temple is completed.''

"How soon?"

"Very soon."

Esther was shocked at how soon.

It was the day after construction was completed, nearly two months after Kaspar's arrival. The night was hazy, and thanks to the nearby hot springs, humid for Wyoming in autumn. Esther fell sound asleep the moment her head touched her pillow. She dreamed of gold and greenbacks. A soft yet persistent tapping at her front door awakened her after midnight.

Esther was half-asleep when she answered. One of the female acolytes who was part of the compound's nightly patrol stood nervously on her front porch. She remembered the woman's name was Buffy something. An airhead, though she looked deceptively intelligent with her crystal blue eyes behind horn-rimmed glasses and her raven hair.

"What is it?" Esther asked. It was obvious by her tone that she didn't like being disturbed at such an ungodly hour.

"Zen and Gary are here!" Buffy Braindead whispered urgently.

Esther blinked sleep from her eyes. Beyond the young woman she could see a rickety old Volkswagen van parked in the washed-out light of the Ranch Ragnarok compound. It was stenciled with daisies.

"What are you talking about?" Esther demanded groggily.

"You know, the ice-cream moguls," Buffy whispered. She shot a dreamy glance at the van.

Only then did Esther notice the two men standing near the rear of the vehicle.

One was thin and reedy, with a mottled gray beard, thick glasses and a green snap-brimmed golfer's cap. The other was about five feet tall, 250 pounds, with a balding pate fringed by about a yard's worth of stringy graying black hair. The sheen of sweat on his scalp twinkled in the moonlight.

She realized, with no small amount of surprise, that she had seen the pair of them an hour before. Their picture stared back at her from the side of a quart of almond-swirl ice cream in her kitchen freezer.

Wide-awake now, Esther pulled the acolyte aside. "So what do they want?" she hissed.

"They want to see *him*," Buffy answered, nodding toward the buildings where Kaspar had constructed his temple.

So it was that at 2:00 a.m. that October night, Esther Clear-Seer had found herself—in khaki pants, Army boots and silk pajama top—trudging through the fields between the Ragnarok compound and Kaspar's new rusted-tin-and-concrete eyesore, trailed by the nation's leading producers of specialty ice cream.

Neither man was in very good shape, and Esther found herself stopping every few yards to allow the wheezing, stumbling ice-cream gurus to catch up.

"What are you two dinosaurs doing here?" she asked after Gary—the fat one—caught his foot in a gopher hole and fell nose-first into a thorn bush.

"He told us it'd be finished today," the thin Zen answered.

In spite of the warm night, Esther felt a chill run down the gully of her back.

"*What* would be finished?"

"The temple, man, the temple," Gary intoned from his reclining position in the Wyoming scrub. He plucked a thorn from his lowermost chin.

Esther furrowed her brow. No phones were allowed on ranch property except for the one locked away in her private ranch house. As far as she knew, Kaspar hadn't left the grounds since his arrival more than a month and a half before. How could he have known his temple would be completed today?

With a shrug she led the pair the rest of the way across the field, through the gap in the hurricane fence and onto the newly purchased Truth Church annex.

The partially collapsed hangar had been scraped and repainted by Esther's obedient acolytes. After the rubble had been cleared away, Kaspar had instructed the workers to create a new addition to the sixty-plus-year-old building. A two-story rounded cinder-block room bubbled from one end of the building and engulfed an area of the new property where jets of natural steam rose from fissures in the craggy black rock.

Sections of the new ceiling were designed to roll away, and Esther noticed as they approached the building that the skylights were wide-open. Bursts of phosphorescent yellow smoke puffed from the roof holes and hung ominously in the hazy black sky.

Kaspar met them at the main entrance.

"What the hell are you wearing?" Esther whispered to him.

Kaspar's outfit was ceremonial in the extreme. A long white robe, heavily pleated at the bottom, trailed the ground behind him. A yellow shawl was drawn over his narrow shoulders, and its ends were tucked behind a wide lavender sash belted around his waist. A black skullcap, embroidered with the same intertwined-serpent motif that adorned the urn he'd brought with him to Ranch Ragnarok, fitted perfectly over his thin hair.

In his hand he carried a walking stick, no longer than a drum majorette's baton, but carved in the shape of a hissing snake. There was something in the strange image on the pole that reflected the reptile within the body of Mark Kaspar.

The most startling thing was Kaspar's attitude. He not only ignored her question, but he also seemed to ignore her very presence.

Without so much as acknowledging the Truth Church leader, he aimed his snake-staff at Zen and Gary and issued a single command.

"Follow. The future awaits."

Without another word, Kaspar spun on his heel and vanished into the smoky interior of the converted warehouse.

INSIDE, construction had already begun to link the temple with the underground network of tunnels on the Ragnarok property. A concrete flight of stairs in the foyer led deep into the earth but stopped short of the original Truth Church perimeter fence. That phase of the project had yet to be completed.

At Kaspar's insistence there was no generator for electricity. Along the walls, hundreds of flickering candles burned dimly among the clouds of yellow smoke.

Esther had never been here this late at night and never with the strange yellow smoke swirling everywhere. Kaspar's bizarre costume and mysterious attitude, plus the way the little man seemed to fade and reappear with the flickering of the candlelight, made for an unnerving experience.

"This place is creepy," she hissed.

Zen and Gary didn't seem to mind. The two of them babbled incessantly about ice cream, the evils of capitalism and their previous brief encounter with Mark Kaspar.

"It was in New England," Zen confided to Esther.

"That's where we got started," Gary explained.

"And how did you come to meet Kaspar?" Esther had asked.

Silent since they had entered the building, Kaspar spoke now with a quiet solemnity—like a priest in the confessional.

"I once offered them a small glimpse of the future," Kaspar admitted.

"The dude told us to go into frozen yogurt," Zen enthused.

"We made a bundle," Gary agreed.

Both of the men seemed suddenly ashamed.

"Filthy bourgeois capitalist system," Zen spit.

"Capitalism sucks," Gary agreed enthusiastically.

They made it through the labyrinth of hallways, crossed an expansive interior chamber and moved back into a series of dank chambers on the far side of the building.

It was easy to become disoriented. Esther wasn't quite certain where they were in the old building until she recognized the grey white smoothness of the recently constructed wall.

They had reached Kaspar's special chamber.

A heavy woven tapestry blocked the doorway to the inner hall, but it wasn't so thick that the jaundiced smoke did not seep from beneath it.

Esther's eyes watered. She wiped the tears on her pajama sleeve and tried to blink away the sharp, stinging sensation.

In the spooky gloom something brushed against her leg.

Esther nearly jumped out of her skin. "What the hell!" she shouted, spinning around wildly.

Some kind of animal was behind her. It stood quietly in the weirdly elongated shadows, the tiny bursts of candlelight reflecting in its frightened eyes.

It was a goat. Even in the darkness she could make out the rope that tethered the animal to a bronze ring in the cinder-block wall.

"What's with that?" Esther asked Kaspar.

Kaspar did not respond. Instead, he addressed Zen and Gary. "You will give the woman two hundred dollars, cash, for the sacrifice," he instructed.

Esther accepted the money sullenly, thinking she would eventually get Kaspar alone. What she was going to do to the insolent little turd when she finally did would be something.

Kaspar pulled the rope from the wall and handed the goat's leash to Zen. With no further comment, he swept the tapestry aside and ushered the others into the chamber beyond.

Esther Clear-Seer had watched the inner chamber take shape over the past month. On numerous occasions she had complained to Kaspar that it looked more like a bad Hollywood movie set than a legitimate place of worship. But in the eerie, scattered light of a dozen torches, with the skylights opened on the moonless black sky and with a vaporous cloud of burning yellow smoke floating like mist through the lifeless air, the huge vault took on a paganistic aura.

As the visitors entered, the pile of stone around which the room had been built spit irregular bursts of steam. The rock suggested the summit of a trapped and nearly buried mountain and made the room look like some kind of animal habitat, as if the surrounding walls formed a cage through which visitors could glimpse zoo animals in their natural environment.

And high atop this pile of rock, on a small three-legged stool balanced above the uppermost sulphur vent, sat the mysterious young girl who had arrived at Ranch Ragnarok with Kaspar. Her vacant eyes stared through the veil of yellow smoke and into the mists of time.

"Welcome to the magnificence of the Temple of Apollo Reborn," Kaspar said.

"Far out," Zen said.

"Karma-licious," Gary agreed.

"Apollo?" Esther muttered. "What is this crap?"

Kaspar mounted the stone steps that had been carved into the side of the rocky hill. When he reached the top, he turned and regarded those below.

"Sacrifice, and you will hear the wisdom of the Pythia," he intoned.

Zen and Gary looked at one another. They shrugged.

"Sacrifice?" Zen asked.

Kaspar reached beneath his brightly colored shawl and removed a long, curving dagger from a hidden scabbard. He threw the knife down to the waiting ice-cream merchants.

"Sacrifice," Kaspar repeated. He gestured toward the terrified goat.

It took some arguing and a lot of threatening and a great deal more work than they had expected, but in the end it was Zen who got to hold the wriggling goat while Gary stood ready to slit the throat of the hapless animal.

The girl on the stool writhed in ecstasy as the knife was drawn across the throat of the pitiful creature, and when the body was still she let out a cry that was distinctly sexual.

At Kaspar's instructions the bloody carcass was set at the foot of the stone staircase.

Afterward, when she sat back on her stool, her glassy eyes seemed somehow more fierce in the eerie torchlight. Esther noticed a flicker, almost a nervous tic, at the corner of the girl's mouth.

"You may ask your question of my master," Kaspar called down.

Nervously Zen and Gary stepped forward and addressed the girl who seemed not to be aware of their presence.

"What we need to know is should we open up a chain of Zen and Gary's Ice Cream Shops in Moscow?" Zen asked. "I mean, the political situation with the collapse of communism is awful from an anticapitalistic viewpoint, obviously. But..." Zen let his words trail away, looking for all the world as if he was ashamed of what he was thinking. He glanced at his partner.

"But can we make a buck at it?" Gary asked hurriedly.

Kaspar whispered into the ear of the young girl.

There was no considering the question. Seemingly no thought at all.

"The gods will smile on your venture," the girl called down, in a thick, rasping voice.

Zen and Gary high-fived one another.

At Kaspar's instructions, they paid Esther Clear-Seer a quarter million dollars with a Zen and Gary's corporate check—showing the Grateful Dead gorging themselves on Gary Garcia ice cream—and Esther didn't even notice that the check was made out to something called the Truth Church Foundation.

She was too busy watching the girl. It was the first time Esther had heard the girl speak, and the voice filled her with terror.

OF COURSE Zen and Gary told their friends about Ranch Ragnarok.

In a country where new trends in spirituality were eagerly embraced and salvation was the nearest zirconian crystal away, the idea of paying top dollar for the prophecies of a seemingly strung-out teenage girl was accepted with an alarming readiness.

Over the following winter a trickle of curious high rollers arrived at the Truth Church gates, all referred to Ranch Ragnarok by the ice-cream gurus. Several other New Agey business leaders, who were as ashamed of their success as Zen and Gary but who had nonetheless made small fortunes selling everything from preworn jeans to computers, posed questions to the oracle at Ragnarok. Esther once thought she recognized a United States congressman, but Kaspar had shooed her from the temple and conducted the man's session with the Pythia—as Kaspar now called the girl—in private.

Nearly eight months had passed since Kaspar first arrived at the ranch, and as the money in the Truth Church Foundation swelled from hundreds of thousands to millions, Esther Clear-Seer found her desire to confront him about his occasional lapses of insolence subsiding.

Esther even dismissed her original fear at hearing the voice of Kaspar's young female friend. She convinced herself that the girl's strange, guttural rasp could have been the result of a decade of cigarette smoking. It could even have been bronchial pneumonia. Lord knew, the girl wasn't looking very healthy of late.

Esther mentioned this to Kaspar as dawn broke one morning after a particularly grueling session with a sports announcer from one of the major television networks.

"Maybe you should have a doctor look at her," Esther muttered.

Kaspar was sorting through a stack of papers piled on a bench at the base of the central rock column. He seemed to have gathered a lot of paperwork since the start of this enterprise and he was becoming increasingly engrossed in whatever it was he was collecting.

With an effort he tore his eyes away from the papers before him. He looked up at the girl, still perched on the tripod, though the smoke from the rock fissure had subsided somewhat.

"Why?" Kaspar asked indifferently.

As if on cue, the girl on the stool swooned and

toppled over. The stool went one way, flipping out of sight down the back of the hill, and the girl did an unintentional somersault before tumbling roughly down the hard rock surface toward them.

Her bloodied, emaciated body landed in a crumpled heap at the feet of Esther Clear-Seer and Mark Kaspar.

Esther recoiled in horror. As the girl's breath became more and more ragged, she saw her increasingly opulent life-style slip away.

All at once the breathing stopped.

Esther crouched over the body. "She's dead," she announced anxiously.

Kaspar couldn't have shown less emotion if Esther had reported swatting a common housefly. He adjusted his bifocals.

"Then you'll just have to find me a fresh virgin," he said blandly.

"Me?" Esther gulped.

"You," Kaspar said, as if that ended the matter.

And he went back to studying his paperwork.

4

Harold W. Smith, head of the supersecret government agency CURE, sat stiff-backed on the rickety wooden chair in the living room of Remo Williams's home in Quincy, Massachusetts.

The chair was old and creaked at his every movement but, Smith noted wryly, it wasn't nearly as old and rickety as he felt.

He had headed CURE—the agency set up outside constitutional limits, whose paradoxical mission it was to preserve the document CURE's very existence flouted—since its inception, and had watched himself grow older and older in the post. Some said the presidency aged a man, but the pressures a President had to bear were nothing compared to the daily strains placed upon the tired, overworked shoulders of Harold W. Smith.

Intermittent humming came from another room. It was a strange, singsong melody with an odd cadence that stopped abruptly, only to begin again. The Master of Sinanju.

Smith squirmed in his chair. He prided himself on his excellent posture, but lately his lower back had been giving him trouble. Altogether it seemed to him that with his congenital heart defect that should have been treated by a pacemaker, recurring ulcers, frequent headaches, his list of physical problems was growing by the day.

Smith tried to sit up straighter in his chair, hoping to alleviate the pressure on his lumbar region.

All at once the humming in the distant room stopped. A moment later Chiun, Reigning Master of Sinanju, head of the most lethal house of assassins ever to grace the face of the earth, padded silently into the room on black sandals.

He was a delicate bird of an elderly Korean attired in a flowing kimono. His wrinkled skin had the consistency of rice paper. His bones looked fragile where they poked out from various joints. Puffs of cloudy white hair decorated his balding head. A wisp of a beard clung to his chin. His fingernails were long and wickedly sharp.

"Remo has returned," Chiun said to Smith.

Chiun had deserted Smith the instant the CURE director had arrived, claiming the need to attend to "other pressing matters" elsewhere in the house. Smith had volunteered his assistance—after all, Remo was not due for some time—but Chiun had quickly declined the offer, claiming that his work, if done in solitude, would bring even greater glory to his kind and gracious emperor. In truth, in the four hours since Smith had arrived, Chiun had been sitting by a back window watching the spring grass grow.

Remo entered the room a minute later.

"I see the gang's all here," he said, glancing at Smith. "What's up, Smitty?"

Smith stood, grateful for the chance to relieve the pressure on his spine. Chiun interposed himself between the two men and drew Remo to the far corner of the room.

"Where have you been?" Chiun demanded in a whisper. "I have been forced to entertain this decrepit white thing for ages." His hazel eyes cast a quick glance at Smith. "Look how he stands. Like a woman in her last, swelling days of pregnancy. Get rid of him soon, Remo, so that we might eat our dinner in peace." With that the Master of Sinanju sent a gracious nod in Smith's direction and moved back closer to settle to a lotus position in the center of the floor.

"Er, is there a problem?" Smith asked uncertainly.

Chiun waved his hand dismissively. "I was rebuking Remo for a previous wrong," he sniffed.

"I see," Smith said. He retook his seat, and Chiun cast him an impatient glance from narrowed hazel eyes.

Remo rolled his eyes. "I saw your rental car in the side lot, Smitty. What's up?"

"Remo, do you recall the incident with the Branch Davidians in Waco, Texas, a few years back?"

Remo grabbed a chair and sat across from Smith. "I remember the headlines at the time," he said. "Feds Fry Wackos In Waco. You should have sent me and Chiun in to take care of business before it got started."

"It was a consideration. Unfortunately you were on another assignment at the time."

"Yeah, it was a real mess," Remo said. "A bunch of peaceniks descending on women and children with tanks. Who would've thought the attorney general would have found time to play general in between lifting weights and initiating cover-ups?"

"Remo, please," Smith said. His back was sore, his ulcer was acting up and it seemed that he had completely lost the attention of the Master of Sinanju. He wanted nothing more than to return to his office in Rye, New York.

"Okay, Smitty," Remo said, waving a thick-wristed hand. "What's the deal this time?"

"A situation has developed in Wyoming, similar to the Branch Davidian problem. A woman claiming to be a prophetess of some new doomsday religion has isolated herself in a rural area of the state. She expects absolute obedience from her followers, as well all their worldly goods. In return she promises to protect them from the tribulations to come at the millennium's conclusion."

"This one cannot protect herself from Sinanju, O Emperor Smith," Chiun piped up. "Though she may surround herself with countless armies of fighting men, she cannot stay the shadowy hand of Sinanju."

"Thank you, Master of Sinanju," Smith said with a polite bow of the head. "Until recently the authorities were willing to look the other way on this obvious cult of personality. They were even willing, it seemed, to disregard reports of large weapons storehouses on the property. But I have recently learned that the FBI had someone under deep cover at the camp and that this operative has failed to report for several months. If they decide to send in more agents, the situation could escalate. It is my belief that this cult is becoming far too powerful. I want you and Chiun to take care of it before federal foot-dragging allows the FBI to initiate another Waco."

"Since when is it our business to bail out the FBI?" Remo asked.

Smith straightened his rimless glasses on his patrician nose. "It is not a question of bailing out anyone, Remo," he said. "Waco was a disaster, not merely because of FBI-ATF bungling, but because of the lack of leadership up the chain of command."

"Shouldn't we blame the voters for that?"

Smith sighed. "During the Waco incident there was a general misunderstanding among those in power of the proper use of force. In the end it was the posturing before and the denial after the fact that transformed Waco into a public-relations debacle. The Justice Department and the Federal Bureau of Investigation received largely undeserved media attention because of their lawful actions against the Branch Davidians."

"Basically you're sending us in this time so the Justice Department can get better PR? No way, Smitty. It's not my job to make sure somebody else doesn't get a black eye from the press."

"Remo, this is important," Smith insisted.

"Well, I don't see the FBI getting *us* any positive ink."

"Hear, hear," Chiun piped up.

Smith removed his glasses and rubbed the bridge of his nose. He suddenly felt weary beyond belief. With a sigh that sounded like it could have wheezed from the rusted belly of an asthmatic furnace, Smith replaced the glasses and addressed Remo.

"You both know that for our overall mission to succeed, the organization must remain anonymous," he said slowly. "Our charter absolutely precludes us from continuing to exist if the organization becomes compromised. We do not court popular opinion and we must absolutely not actively seek approval in a public forum.''

"Duh, Smitty," Remo said. "Tell me something I don't know."

"A little positive press never hurts, Emperor," Chiun said slyly. "If your enemies were to discover that Sinanju was guarding your throne, your regal head would rest easier. And the exposure would not necessarily be adverse for the House, either."

"Remo, please," Smith said, urgently.

"Okay, okay, we'll do the hit, Smith," Remo said. "But if Sinanju can get a few column inches out of it, ace reporter Remo Williams will be there with a byline and a ruler. What's this prophetess's name?"

Smith furrowed his brow in confusion at the obscure reference, but did not question Remo further. More and more the ex-Marine and former beat cop was becoming as intractable as his Korean teacher.

"Her name," Smith said, "is Esther Clear-Seer."

5

Bonnie Sweetwater was the oldest child of an upper-middle-class family in Thermopolis, Wyoming.

Bonnie was eighteen years old, bright, outgoing and, much to the chagrin of her contemporaries—both male and female—had neither "done it" nor intended to "do it" until her wedding night.

Bonnie didn't consider herself particularly religious, but she was a girl with old-fashioned moral values and she had no problem sharing this view with others. She belonged to the local chapter of Marriage First, a national grassroots organization for morally like-minded young people. They met every Friday night in the old city-hall basement from 7:30 to 11:00 p.m., rain or shine. It was an opportunity for Bonnie and the other Marriage Firsters to socialize without the worries and pitfalls of a typical teenage night out.

For most of the club's membership, the lack of pressure was a relief.

On this, as on most Fridays, Bonnie had volunteered to clean up the hall with her friend Kathy Kirtley after the meeting, but as usual Kathy had come up with a lame excuse to take off early, leaving Bonnie holding the bag. Literally.

Bonnie circled the hall methodically, scooping up

Pepsi-stained napkins and crumpled Dixie cups and dropping them into the large trash bag she lugged around behind her.

Somebody mustn't have liked the carrot cake she had made, for there was a half-eaten piece on a paper plate sitting smack dab in the middle of one of the seats at the rear of the hall.

Oh, well, she thought to herself, I'll try another recipe next week.

At the door Bonnie paused to survey the hall.

The place didn't look too bad. She'd come back in the morning to fold up the chairs and sweep the floor.

She snapped off the lights as she left.

Outside she deposited the trash bag in one of the large dented barrels that were lined up like tin soldiers at the rear of the former city-hall building and hiked up the small grassy embankment to the street.

Kathy had driven Bonnie, as well as two other friends, to the meeting that night. Kathy being Kathy, it was not unusual for Bonnie to be hiking home at 11:45 p.m. She didn't really mind. The streets were quiet, the April night air was warm and she liked to have a little think time to herself.

She had barely stepped out on the sidewalk when she heard a car engine start.

For a minute Bonnie thought Kathy had waited for her after all. She turned to look, but the car that pulled away from the curb was boxy and blue—not the fiery red Camaro Kathy's father bought her as a reward for passing her senior year at Custer High. Oh, well.

Bonnie continued down the sidewalk.

She walked a few more steps, but the car never passed by. The engine continued to rumble, and Bonnie slowly became aware that it had moved up directly behind her, keeping pace like a stalking animal.

Bonnie felt her heart quicken. Could someone really be following her?

Her feet suddenly felt like lead, and she forced them to move faster down the sidewalk.

The car kept moving behind her. It was running with its lights dim.

Bonnie's ears were ringing as she broke into a run, and the blood pounded faster in her head.

Out of the corner of her eye, she glanced left. She could just make out the hood of the car. One headlight stared at her like an angry yellow eye. Bonnie sucked in a nervous gulp of air, and turned her eyes straight ahead.

It was like a dream. Her head swam.

She couldn't look.

She *had* to look.

Bonnie stopped all at once and spun on the stalking car.

She recognized the woman behind the wheel. It was the nutcase who ran that religious camp on the outskirts of town. Esther something.

When Bonnie turned, the woman hunched down farther in her seat and slammed on the gas. The car lunged ahead—and Bonnie felt a wave of sheer relief as she watched the car take the next right turn and race off into the night.

Bonnie stood on the sidewalk for a few long seconds after the car had gone. As her body relaxed, she felt an uncontrollable shudder, as if someone had just dropped an ice cube down her bare back.

It was probably all perfectly innocent, she thought

hopefully. The woman had likely mistaken her for one of her followers, out for a night stroll. They had strict curfews up there, Bonnie had heard.

By the time she reached the next intersection, she had convinced herself that it was all just a case of mistaken identity. She was about to cross the street when a figure stepped out from behind a high row of hedges at the corner lot and touched her arm.

Bonnie all but jumped out of her freckled skin.

It was that woman. Esther Clear-Seer. That was her name. The blue car sat silently a few house-lengths up the side street, its lights off.

Bonnie's heart pumped wildly.

"I'm sorry," Esther Clear-Seer said. She tapped her forehead with the palm of her hand and rolled her eyes heavenward as if she was the flakiest thing ever to come down the boulevard. "I think I probably scared you back there, and I'm really, really sorry. I just need directions, and usually I like to ask a man this late at night, but there's no one out around here for miles and, well, I saw you coming out of your little meeting..." She shrugged like a helpless sitcom housewife.

To Bonnie, the woman, who had been alternately laughed at and demonized by the local press, suddenly seemed more human.

She was friendly and scatterbrained and she continued apologizing profusely as she asked for directions to the police station.

Any concern Bonnie had immediately abated. After all, how dangerous could someone be if she was asking the way to the police station?

Bonnie pointed down Maiden Lane into the washed-out light cast by thirty-year old streetlamps...

A hand snaked out, unseen, from under Esther Clear-Seer's jacket.

Bonnie's was just explaining the sharp left on West Street when the metal tire iron collided with the barrette at the back of her head. She crumpled like an aluminum can. Strong hands reached under her armpits.

A moment later the blue car was gone and there was no sign of Bonnie Sweetwater.

Virgin number one.

6

Remo and Chiun rented a car at the airport in Worland, Wyoming, and headed south along Route 789 in the direction of Hot Springs State Park.

According to Smith, the ranch belonging to the Church of the Absolute and Incontrovertible Truth was located in the northwest corner of Wyoming, on the southern edge of the Hot Springs State Park, near the town called Thermopolis. The church owned several hundred acres of real estate in the area west of town.

Chiun had remained silent for most of the plane trip, stirring from his strange quiescence only long enough to shoo away the bevy of buxom stewardesses that had flocked around. They were ignoring Remo and fussing over the Master of Sinanju, who sometimes brought out the maternal instincts in women who generally looked as maternal as Anna Nicole Smith in crotchless panties.

It looked as though the car trip wasn't going to be any better.

There were times when Remo would have invited Chiun to clam up, but that was when the Master of Sinanju was haranguing him about some niggling little peeve. As far as Remo knew, this time he hadn't done anything whatsoever to tick off Chiun.

"You didn't have to come, Little Father," Remo said when he could no longer bear the silence. He glanced at the Master of Sinanju, who was watching the aspens and cottonwood trees zip by in blurs of brilliant green.

"I did not have to sit at home, either," Chiun replied.

"You got me there," Remo admitted.

They rode on in silence for a few minutes longer before the Master of Sinanju spoke again.

"Remo?"

"I'm still here."

"Perhaps it is time we sought another client for our services."

Remo arched an eyebrow. "What, did you and Smith have a fight?"

Chiun's hazel eyes leveled on Remo. "If we did, he would not have breath to order you hither and yon."

"Then what gives? I thought you were happy with the current contract—all the gold you can carry and all the fish you can eat."

Chiun glanced thinly out the window. "Riches are not always the sole consideration of a Master of Sinanju," he said softly.

Remo nearly drove the car off the road. Almost before Chiun had started training him in the earliest Sinanju breathing techniques, long before Remo had mastered the subtle feats of dodging bullets and scaling sheer rock faces, Chiun had instilled in him the one eternal, transcendent tenet of all previous Sinanju Masters: cash only, always up front. And although a lot of haggling went on between Smith and Chiun, in the end Chiun was always secretly satisfied when their contract was renewed.

For Chiun to say that gold didn't matter was akin to O. J. Simpson pleading guilty, George Washington apologizing for the Revolutionary War and Santa Claus saying Christmas was a commercial scam—all rolled into one.

"Why would you want to just up and quit?" Remo asked.

Chiun's parchment features grew impatient. "I do not 'up and' anything. This is not a decision to be reached lightly. Smith always paid on time and therefore will be remembered as a great and wise ruler in the scrolls of Sinanju, though the glossary will doubtless define him as a raving lunatic with pounded rice paste between his fat white ears."

"All historical inaccuracies aside, why now?"

"Have you not noticed how his entire body creaks and groans? It is an effort for the man to stand straight. The vitality of Smith as emperor of America ebbs with each passing day." Chiun nodded at the wisdom of his own words. "It might not be long, Remo, ere we find ourselves without employment."

"We can cross that bridge when it falls," Remo said.

"We could send out feelers," Chiun suggested slyly, using a word he had picked up from television the previous day. "Smith need not know of our discreet, private inquiries."

"Look, I'm not ready to leave Smith in a lurch," Remo said. "Case closed." He gripped the steering wheel more tightly. "Why don't you check the map?"

he added, eager to change the subject. "See if we're anywhere near Thermopolis."

"I am an assassin, not a cartographer," Chiun announced haughtily. "And as the designated and sanctified chauffeur to the Master of Sinanju, it is your responsibility to find it for yourself." And with that he returned his gaze to the passing trees.

They rode the rest of the way to Thermopolis in silence.

THE FIRST THING Remo and Chiun discovered when they arrived in town was that there was a campaign going on.

Of course, there had been indications of political activity along the highway—a road sign here, a bumper sticker there—but downtown Thermopolis looked like the epicenter of a political earthquake.

Bumper stickers were slathered haphazardly on cars, windows and telephone poles, colored flags flapped gaily between buildings and giant billboards squatted like primordial birds atop seemingly abandoned flatbed trailers.

"Remo, did not this unstable land just have a time for this buffoonery?" Chiun clucked disapprovingly as they drove past lawn after lawn decorated with red, white and blue placards announcing the political leanings of the home owners. Most seemed to favor the reelection of Senator Jackson Cole.

"If you mean did we just have an election, yes," said Remo. "But that was for President. This guy Cole is running for the senate."

Chiun was confused. "Were not the senators elected at the same time as the President? I remember talk of his garment hems failing to sweep others into office in his wake.''

''You mean coattails,'' said Remo. ''Some of the Senate was up for reelection during the presidential campaign. And all of the House, I think. But the Senate races are staggered so that everyone isn't up for reelection at the same time.''

''Why is this so?'' Chiun asked, puzzled.

And lest Remo find himself explaining a process he didn't fully understand himself, he parked their rental car on a side street and got out to ask for directions.

The main thoroughfares of Thermopolis were lined with hundreds of cars, all abandoned. In fact, the entire town looked abandoned.

''Where the hell is everybody?'' Remo wondered aloud.

Chiun thrust his button nose in the air and sniffed delicately, like a foxhound on the trail of his elusive prey. His face immediately scrunched up in disgust.

''Pah! Is every corner of this land befouled by vile odors?''

Remo, too, caught the scent on the wafting breeze. ''Popcorn,'' he said. All at once they heard a loud cheer from somewhere beyond the highest buildings, toward the center of town. ''Must be some kind of rally, judging from all the signs,'' Remo guessed. ''They start earlier and earlier every campaign season.'' He sniffed again, this time detecting the distinct odors of warming pretzels and syrupy soft drinks.

Chiun was waving his kimono sleeve before his face. ''What this nation needs is one of those devices that is affixed to the sides of commodes to dull the effect of your foul white smells. And it should be built in this state." Chiun gathered up the hems of his brilliant canary yellow kimono. "I will investigate the source of these noxious fumes, Remo, while you attempt to find someone who can make sense of your country's incomprehensible electoral process."

And with that the Master of Sinanju padded off in the direction of the commotion.

Remo headed off in the opposite direction, looking for someone who knew the way to Ranch Ragnarok, and didn't want his vote.

On the sidewalk in front of a hardware store, Remo cornered a man in a plastic foam hat and a bright blue blazer festooned with all manner of pins and buttons and insignia declaring his commitment to Jackson Cole. Even the T-shirt he wore sported a likeness of the popular senator, but Cole's silkscreened face was drawn so tightly across the man's protruding belly it made the senator's gaunt features look broad and vaguely piggish.

"Hey, Lester," Remo said, reading a name off a square of masking tape over the man's breast pocket. When the man looked his way, Remo figured he'd gotten the name right. "Which way is Ranch Ragnarok?"

Bloodshot eyes rolled in sockets that were rimmed by yellow fatty deposits. "What do you want to go out there for?" Lester asked.

Remo shrugged. He wasn't used to having his motives questioned when he asked simple directions. "Enlightenment?"

"You'll get more enlightenment out of a fortune cookie," Lester said. "Those Truth Church nuts are dangerous." He sized up Remo's lean frame. "You don't look like you could handle the kind of trouble they dish out.''

Remo was suddenly interested. ''What sort of trouble?''

''Talk is they murdered a guy recently,'' Lester confided in a whisper louder than most people's normal speaking voices. ''Some kids were out snooping by the ranch one night a couple of months ago—you know how kids are. Anyway, they saw some of them Truth Church psychos gun this guy down in cold blood. At least that's what *I* heard.''

Remo thought of the missing FBI agent.

''Why didn't the police check it out?''

''You've obviously never seen the place,'' the man snorted. ''They've got guns up the wazoo. That Clear-Seer battle-ax runs a tighter ship than the U.S. Navy. No one leaves unless there's at least three of them together, and that's just to buy supplies. Ask old Harvey in here—'' he jerked a dimpled thumb toward the hardware store window behind him ''—those nuts have bought enough concrete to build a hundred Moscow tenements. They've got bunkers filled with ammo and explosives. Is that what you want to get yourself into?''

Remo said, ''I'm full-grown now. Just point me in the right direction....''

''If I don't tell you, I'd be doing you a favor,'' Lester cautioned. ''Why don't you come along to the rally with me? The whole town's already there. We got a lot more serious stuff going on than those Truth Churchers.'' He tapped his largest lapel pin, which declared The GOP Does It On Its Platform.

''Look—''

"Senator Cole himself is going to be there," Lester interrupted. "This is his hometown, you know. He and me went to school together. You know, I remember one time…"

And with that Lester launched into a well-worn tale of how he had once backed up Jackson Cole in a junior-high-school fight.

Remo rolled his eyes heavenward and hoped that Esther Clear-Seer didn't die of old age before he had a chance to pay her a visit.

SENATOR COLE'S advance people had coordinated with the local police to ensure the senator would have a clear path from his limousine to the bandstand.

The townspeople of Thermopolis were cordoned off in a wide circle around the speaker's area, leaving enough room for the senator's family and staff, local politicians and business leaders, as well as their families, and whatever media were covering the relatively minor photo op.

As it was, there were only a few print reporters from nearby towns and a couple of camera crews. The first crew videotaping the speech was from a small local cable station, so it was naturally shuffled off to the back. The second was the more professional of the pair. It was from WONK, a larger station in Cheyenne that already had a deal with one of the major networks to run on the national nightly news any newsworthy footage they collected.

The WONK camera had the sweetest location for filming, directly in front of the bandstand, and when it was announced that Senator Cole's limo was a block away, the cameraman checked his small black-and-white receiver to make certain the picture was in perfect focus.

He saw an egg.

The cameraman squinted his eyes in confusion.

An egg?

He looked through the camera viewfinder. There it was, a little fuzzy, but it was definitely egg-shaped. He brought the camera into focus, and the edges of the egg grew more defined. It was tan and unevenly colored, with puffs of angel's hair on either side. And it had ears.

The cameraman stuck his face around the camera.

A bald head that looked like it had escaped from an ostrich nest was positioned directly between the camera and the bandstand. Beneath the head the back of a golden kimono with brilliant red piping cascaded down to the well-trampled grass.

"Hey, Gramps, you're in the way," the cameraman complained.

The sounds of cheers suddenly erupted from the edge of the crowd and swept inward, toward the stand. The senator had arrived.

The cameraman looked around desperately. He could turn the camera to catch the senator as he climbed from his limo, but the wizened figure before him was casting a shadow across the equipment.

"Hey, you're standing in my light."

The old man didn't turn.

Maybe the old guy was hard of hearing, the reporter thought, so he spoke up again, louder this time.

There was an ever-so-slight movement of the gossamer webs above the ancient Asian's ears.

"The radiance of the Master of Sinanju is light

enough for a thousand of your recording devices," the old man intoned without turning.

"Wha—?" The cameraman looked around. The police were occupied with crowd control. The senator had climbed out of the car and was waving to the crowd. Graciously he helped his wife and daughter from the limo.

The wife was an attractive, sixtyish woman. Her hair color was right out of a bottle and her hair seemed lacquered so tightly into place that if one follicle broke free the entire cliff would explode in a spray of hairpins and dried Lady Clairol flakes. She smiled at the crowd with perfect capped teeth.

The senator was tall and gawky. His hairline had long ago scurried to the back of his head, and his awkward height had given him a slight hunch. Good humor danced in his beady eyes.

Their combined effort, however, was far greater than the sum of both their parts. The daughter, Lori Cole, was beautiful. Fifteen years old and already a heartbreaker. Her wave to the crowd was almost regal.

No sense thinking it, the cameraman thought. Fifteen'll get you twenty, and besides she was said to be even more conservative than her old man. And anyway, he had a job to do.

A job!

He had forgotten about the old man.

The Asian still stood rooted before him, seemingly as immobile as an ancient, slender elm.

The arrival footage was completely ruined. Maybe he could make up for it with coverage of the speech itself.

The thick black cable that connected his mountain

of remote equipment to the WONK news van snaked directly beneath the robes of the tiny Asian.

The cameraman glanced around. The cops were still busy with the senator. No one was looking his way.

He grabbed the cable in both hands and yanked.

Later, when he awoke in the hospital, the cameraman was assured that he need never worry about adequate lighting again. The small battery-operated light meter that he usually affixed to his camera had somehow found itself embedded between his ribs. The far end had been lodged in his heart in such a way that any attempt to remove it would prove fatal.

One of the doctors suggested that until the batteries ran down, he might have a hard time sleeping, but he'd have no trouble reading in bed.

LESTER'S CHILDHOOD story had gone on way too long, and appeared to have no point whatsoever—at least none that Remo could discern. Remo was ready to sever Lester's spinal column and go off in search of Ranch Ragnarok by himself, when the large man's attention drifted to somewhere across Remo's right shoulder.

"Lordy, Lou, will you look at that," said Lester.

Remo glanced over his shoulder and saw a long black stretch limousine turn onto Thermopolis's main drag.

He looked back at Lester. "So what?" he said.

"So we don't get too many of them stretch jobbies in Thermopolis," whispered Lester. "It must be Senator Cole himself."

The limousine drew to a stop in front of Remo and Lester. For one horror-filled moment Lester thought that it was indeed Jackson Cole, come to confront him about the bogus childhood story he had been boring people with for the past forty years. But when the tinted rear window powered silently down, a familiar head that didn't belong to Jackson Cole jutted into view.

Remo recognized the giant ears and nose, as well as the close-cropped stubble of steely gray hair. The forehead seemed to go on forever, and the spindly neck vanished below the edge of the car window. On TV, Moss Monroe looked like Mr. Potato Head, but in real life he looked like Mr. Potato Head on steroids, thought Remo.

Lester was beside himself with shock. "Dang!" he gasped. "Moss Monroe in the flesh!"

"Could you boys just tell me where I could find that Ragnarok Ranch I keep hearin' so gol-darned much about?" a familiar nasal twang asked. His sharp Adam's apple bobbed enthusiastically.

"Um, it's..." Lester began, "you, well, you follow this road to the edge of town and then take a right— no, a left. A left to a blinking amber light. Then just follow the road through the woods." He looked to Remo for agreement.

"How the hell should I know?" Remo returned sharply.

Lester shrugged feebly.

"Well, that's just wonderful, that's just great," came the excited drawl of Moss Monroe from the back of the limo. "I'm much obliged, son. I'm more grateful than a live turkey on the day after Thanksgivin'."

The darkened window rolled back up, and the limo sped off.

Remo pointed after it. "You'd tell him, but you wouldn't tell me?" he said, peeved.

"Hey, I still remember the '92 campaign," Lester explained nervously. "If he asked for directions to the inside of a lion cage I would have driven him there myself."

CHIUN WAS WAITING in the car when Remo returned.

"Things have just gotten more complicated," Remo informed him as he slipped back in behind the wheel.

"I saw the funny little man with the big ears," Chiun said. "Was his friend with him?"

Remo raised an eyebrow. "What friend?"

"The one who did not know his name or where he was. You remember, Remo, he starred in the television program where the president of vice won an argument, but was declared the loser, the next president of vice lost, but was declared the winner and the old man with the hearing aid did not listen to the questions at all."

After the most recent presidential race, which had practically put the nation to sleep, the previous contest seemed like ancient history.

"General Stocking?" Remo said finally. He remembered the geriatric general Moss Monroe had dragged out of mothballs to be his running mate, thus proving to the vast majority of American voters that he was about as serious a presidential contender as Pat Paulsen. "No, Stocking wasn't with him."

Chiun considered. "It is a shame that program was canceled," he said pensively. "It was very funny."

Remo nodded. "At least America would have had a good laugh while it was being mugged," he agreed, starting the engine. "Find out anything, Little Father?"

"Do you know those little lights on the sides of television cameras?"

Remo arched an eyebrow. "Yeah?" he said leadingly.

"They are detachable."

And by the look of serenity on the Master of Sinanju's face, Remo knew enough not to ask.

7

Moss Monroe had become a multibillionaire by accepting a huge number of lucrative business contracts from the federal government, before making himself a household name by publicly railing against the same government policies that had launched him from the ham-and-beans income-tax bracket to the stratosphere of the caviar and private Learjets.

Of course, Moss didn't start complaining until the last of the government checks had cleared.

Monroe first exploded onto the political scene as a guest on the "Barry Duke Live" cable-TV program. On that show Moss Monroe fielded phone calls from average Americans as if he were just another John Q. Public. And when those typical citizens asked what could be done to fix what ailed their country, Monroe was blunt: absolutely nothing could be done. America was finished. He said this, however, with a down-home folksiness that made him sound like a cross between Will Rogers and Jed Clampett, and won over people who couldn't tell down-home from dumbed-down.

From the beginning, people were so captivated by the way Moss Monroe spoke, no one paid much attention to what he was actually saying.

His legislative agenda had the intellectual complexity of a Road Runner cartoon, and his entire political philosophy—though discussed with a reverence that made one think it had been carved of Mount Sinai granite—had been written by a five-hundred-dollar-per-hour PR agent.

The pithiest of these "Mossy Musings" were laminated on a set of giant glossy placards that Monroe carted around wherever he went to sell himself. Because that was exactly what his entire game was: selling Moss Monroe, political savior.

He had once stormed out of a live network-news broadcast because the anchorman conducting the interview insisted that Moss Monroe answer a direct question without referring to the large shiny charts that had been set up on an easel next to the anchor's desk. Without his charts Moss Monroe was as helpless as a baby. A crybaby.

That this man, whose main asset was a well-stocked cupboard of aw-shucks platitudes, had risen to national prominence by declaring the nation was completely bereft of ideas was, perhaps, the most ringing endorsement of his own premise.

In spite of his best attempts at blowing smoke, Moss Monroe hadn't been much of a player in the most recent presidential race. It had been an unspirited snore in which he had been relegated to the role of yapping Chihuahua.

And while to his supporters Moss would always be the ultimate political outsider, to Moss himself it was getting pretty cold outside.

Since the time nearly two years before the 1992 campaign when Moss had begun carefully orchestrating his "surprise" announcement to run, to the point in 1996 when his hopes had been dashed almost before they had gotten off the ground, Monroe had been forced to postpone the year he expected to finally take possession of the Oval Office. He was now looking at the year 2000, and if past experience had taught him anything, it was that he couldn't win now without a truckload of luck.

What to do. What to do.

He heard through the grapevine that, for the right price, luck could be purchased inside the hurricane-fenced perimeter of a small ranch somewhere in northwest Wyoming. And if there was one thing Moss Monroe had, it was purchasing power.

The shiny black limousine with the Stand Tall, America vanity license plate ground to a halt before the high metal fence of the Truth Church ranch.

The place looked like a Second World War prisoner-of-war camp. Through the tinted rear windows, Moss Monroe could see a pair of concrete towers on either side of the main gate. High above, beneath slanting corrugated-steel roofs, snipers peered down suspiciously at the new arrival, sunlight reflecting brilliantly off matching black sunglasses.

About a hundred yards away in either direction, another pair of sentry posts squatted amid the Wyoming brush.

Moss Monroe understood that some denigrated the Truth Church as a cult, but those were probably the same individuals who labled him a crackpot, and so when the gates creaked open to swallow him, he didn't hesitate to order his chauffeur to drive on in.

There was a perfectly ordinary-looking ranch house

about a half mile up the packed dirt drive within the Ragnarok compound. Behind the ranch, Monroe could see a series of low-lying, interconnected concrete structures obviously built for function rather than style. On these, fatigue-clad men strolled back and forth with high-powered rifles hanging in the crooks of their arms.

Monroe's limo circled around, ghosting to a stop alongside the long, rough-hewn porch running the length of the split-log ranch house.

A robust woman with long coal black hair stood at the top of the rickety wooden staircase, waiting to greet the perennial odd man out of U.S. politics.

"You have come to acquire spiritual enlightenment," Esther Clear-Seer announced as Moss Monroe's slight, four-foot-six-inch frame climbed down out of the limo.

"Now, hold on there, missy," Moss Monroe said. His nasal twang sounded peeved as the red Wyoming dust settled atop his hand-tooled ostrich-skin cowboy boots. "I got one thing to say to you and one thing only—where's the feller what can tell me the future?"

Her face sunk. "You want to see Kaspar," she said glumly.

"Yeah. Kaspar. That's the jasper's name. I hear he can tell a feller when he's next gonna get paid, laid or made," Monroe whanged. "Trot him on out."

Esther Clear-Seer composed her crestfallen face. Lately fewer and fewer supplicants came to the ranch willing to cede their wills to her. The money from Kaspar's venture was good, but Esther felt she was losing control over the crucial aspect of the Truth

Church ranch—the need to manipulate the drones. The acolyte pool was stagnating.

Esther nodded to Moss Monroe. "Very well," she said resignedly. "I'll take you around back."

A new voice cut the air.

"Don't bother."

Esther turned. Stepping out of the door behind her was Mark Kaspar. He must have taken the newly completed tunnel that connected the Pythia Pit to her ranch, she knew. Esther was surprised. Rarely these days did Kaspar venture from the Pythia Pit.

"Are you the feller I came here to see?" Moss Monroe demanded, clomping up on four-inch heels.

"The question is irrelevant," Kaspar replied calmly. "There will be no oracles for you. Please leave."

"What are you doing?" Esther asked out of the side of her mouth. "Do you know who this little martinet is?"

"Now, looky here, son," Moss Monroe protested. "I don't think you unnerstand who you're talkin' to."

Kaspar smiled. "On the contrary. I know all too well."

He clapped his hands twice, sharply. Instantly squads of Truth Church disciples appeared from coigns of vantage around and atop the surrounding buildings, all training high-powered weapons on the diminutive but unmissable target that was Moss Monroe.

"Are you out of your mind?" Esther hissed. "This is Moss Monroe. The guy blows his nose on thousand-dollar bills. Take his damn money."

Moss Monroe tilted back a ten-gallon hat that sat

atop his head like a pelican about to lay eggs on a rock. His eyes got beadier, if possible.

"Son, I am prepared to offer you one hundred million out of my own personal savings account if you'll get your little future teller to do some predictin' for me."

Kaspar ignored Monroe. He gestured to the poised snipers above.

"Granted, they are not the feared Black Panthers, who I'm told are fond of performing calisthenics on your front lawn, but they are still quite effective."

"This is crazy." Cupping her beringed hands before her mouth, Esther Clear-Seer barked, "Everyone, back off!"

The Truth Church squads didn't move.

Esther's eyes flew wide.

"Back off!" she shouted once more. Still nothing. "This is Yogi Mom speaking. As the Beatific Head and Prophetess of your church, I command you to return to normal sentry stations."

But her acolytes refused to budge. When Esther turned to face Mark Kaspar, her pale face was a marble mask of pure hate.

"The power of the Pythia's prophecies is great," Kaspar intoned with a broad, knowing smile.

Despite public impressions to the contrary, Moss Monroe was a man who knew which way the wind blew. When he saw that the woman had failed to order back the throng of armed zealots, he beat a hasty retreat to the rear his limousine and hightailed it from Ranch Ragnarok. Pronto.

He watched out the rear window as the twin watchtowers of Ragnarok's front gates slipped below a hill in the road behind him, and silently vowed to make it his mission on earth to destroy everyone who promised that pack of crazies could tell him at all about his future. From now on, for Moss Monroe, it would be nothing but tea leaves, tarot cards and an occasional seance.

"WHAT DID YOU DO to my acolytes?" Esther Clear-Seer demanded. They were in her ranch house, away from prying ears. Kaspar had dismissed his troops, and they had obeyed.

Now he dismissed Esther Clear-Seer's concerns.

"It is irrelevant. There are more pressing matters at hand."

"Pressing, my ass. You've corrupted them. You've turned them against me. Do you have any idea how long it takes to break their will? Some of them have been here for years."

"They will still obey you," Kaspar intoned.

"But they obey you first."

"Irrelevant," Kaspar repeated with a wave of his hand. "We must prepare."

"For what?"

"The force the Pythia spoke of. This Sinanju. It is an ancient power that can destroy everything we've worked for."

"So what is it?" Esther asked testily.

Mark Kaspar closed his eyes. His face assumed a wary cast. His voice grew doleful and full of portents.

"It is here."

8

Remo had contacted Harold Smith before leaving Thermopolis, and the CURE director's orders had been explicit: they were not, under any circumstances, to enter Ranch Ragnarok while Moss Monroe remained on the premises.

"What if he stays there a week?" Remo complained.

"You will wait."

"Great," Remo said sarcastically. "Smitty, the local paper is reporting there was a kid kidnapped in town last night. Maybe Chiun and I could take a look into that while we're waiting."

"That is not our business."

"You're all heart, Smitty," Remo groused.

"You will proceed to the ranch," Smith instructed, "where you will await Monroe's departure."

As it turned out, they didn't have to wait long.

Remo had barely turned off the rural asphalt route onto the wide dirt path that wound through the woods to Ranch Ragnarok when Moss Monroe's limousine burst into view over a rise in the rutted, dusty path.

The limo became airborne for a split second before it bounced roughly back to earth. The driver momentarily lost control and nearly broadsided Remo's rented

Jeep before he skidded out onto the mangy strip of state tar in a cloud of dust that obscured the entire vehicle.

But only for a second.

As if yanked by a giant rubber band, Moss Monroe's limo launched from beneath the cloud cover and rocketed back toward Thermopolis. Smoking rubber strips burned up the road nearly a quarter mile behind America's premier political outsider.

"That man departs in haste," Chiun intoned, the sides of his mouth a network of wrinkles.

"He probably remembered the deadline for filing papers to run for king of Rwanda," Remo suggested.

They ditched their Jeep and ducked into the dense woods that closed in on either side of the narrow dirt access road. There were various cameras and motion-detection devices hidden in the trees and along the forest floor, but the two men avoided the electronic devices with ease, sensing their vibrations and magnetic fields instinctively. Sinanju made them at one with the universe and honed their awareness of all its combined forces.

It was not long before they found a path. Nearly imperceptible indentations marked it.

"Foot patrols?" Remo asked Chiun.

The Master of Sinanju nodded. "They have passed five times so far today," he said, noting barely visible heel marks and freshly snapped twigs.

Remo cocked an ear. "Sounds like they're going for six."

His sensitive ears had picked up the sounds of heavy breathing and of awkward, stumbling men progressing from the direction of the ranch.

Chiun nodded and slipped wordlessly into the woods beside the path.

There were still times when his teacher's skills amazed Remo. Here was Chiun, a century old and dressed in a kimono—the garish yellowness of which made him resemble a ripe, ambulatory banana—vanishing in an evergreen forest with the utterness of a scrap of ignited magician's flash paper.

Remo had little time to appreciate the artfulness of the move. As the patrol closed in, he also faded into the patchy shadow of the forest, his black T-shirt and chinos becoming part of their warp and woof.

He met up with Chiun a few feet off the beaten path.

"Why did you hesitate?" Chiun demanded in a squeaky whisper.

"I was just thinking...." Remo said, smiling knowingly at Chiun.

When Chiun detected the softness in Remo's voice, his features became less harsh. "Please, Remo, refrain from thought when we are on a mission. I would not want the smoke issuing from out your ears to give away our position of vantage."

He raised a bony finger to his lips to stifle Remo's inevitable retort. "Silence. They come."

There were four of them—all dressed in Army-surplus cammies. They carried AR-15 rifles balanced across their shoulders like yokes for carrying water buckets. According to Remo's highly trained senses, an unusual and difficult posture.

Every man on the path—and especially the leader—seemed anxious to brandish the weapons before him. And although he didn't completely understand why, Remo was certain that was exactly what they ordinarily did.

These men were used to carrying their weapons in their hands. So why weren't they?

It was clear that none of them ever had any serious military training, and it became more clear with every stumbling misstep that they were as out of place in the woods as lost Rockettes. They lumbered up the path, wheezing with every uncertain footfall.

From the way they were peering into the overgrown brush as they moved along, it was apparent they were in search mode.

Whatever it was they were after didn't matter. If they were disciples of Esther Clear-Seer, they were expendable.

"I'll take the right," Remo whispered. He shot a glance to Chiun, but the Master of Sinanju was already gone. Remo caught a glimpse of yellow silk as Chiun glided between a pair of giant, pitted evergreen trunks.

"And why don't you take the left?" he suggested to the unhearing wind.

Remo slipped silently right.

The patrol was clumsy. They had probably made this same circuit through the woods hundreds of times, but not one of them seemed comfortable in the forest environment. Remo noticed a tree root that had been worn smooth from countless stubbed toes. He pictured booted feet tripping over that same root a dozen times in the same week, surprised that it was still there.

Amateurs.

As the group advanced, Remo circled around before them, at times keeping pace, other times moving a few steps ahead. He knew Chiun would be mirroring his own moves on the soldiers' opposite flank. There was no hurry.

All at once the group came to a halt.

Remo froze. What were they up to?

The men **fell** to discussing something among themselves.

"This is the spot?" the leader asked. "You sure?"

"I counted it off," offered one of the others with a nod. "It's 334 paces."

The leader stepped away from the other three and stared into the depths of the forest, nearly at the spot where Remo stood.

The leader shot a glance back at his men. "You're positive?"

The other soldier nodded.

Enough was enough. Remo's curiosity was piqued, but not so much so that he'd stand in the middle of the woods until moss sprouted out his north side. He moved an inch.

The lead soldier spoke up. "Hello?" His voice echoed uncertainly in the forest.

Remo remained frozen, his breathing keying down to minimal cycles of respiration.

The Ragnarok soldiers searched the silent evergreens with nervous eyes.

"This *is* the foretold spot?" the leader said, turning to his men once again.

"*And* the right time," stressed the second man.

"Maybe they're not here," someone else suggested.

In the thicket Remo focused his senses beyond the soldiers. A few yards into the woods on the opposite side of the path, he could hear the sound of Chiun's breathing—inaudible to anyone's ears but his own.

The Master of Sinanju had stopped beneath the lazily swaying bows of an evergreen. Remo could tell by his shallow intake of air that Chiun was pondering the strangeness of their situation.

It looked like the soldiers were expecting someone. Intruders. Infiltrators. But other than he and Chiun, there was no one around. And there was no way they had been detected. Even something as impalpable as an infrared beam would have been felt by either Remo or the Master of Sinanju if they had interrupted the beam with their stealthy bodies.

Yet the leader was calling out to someone. Calling in their approximate direction.

"Hello? Excuse me, gentlemen."

He couldn't be talking to us, Remo thought. I didn't make a sound.

He thought of Chiun. Not only would the Master of Sinanju never make an unintentional sound, but he would also disown Remo at the merest suggestion of such an accusation.

That brought it back to Remo again.

Remo tried to recall if he'd stepped on a branch or dried leaf. One thing was certain: if Remo had made a noise, he'd never hear the end of it.

"They're not here," said another of the soldiers.

"He insisted they would be. He also said they'd be hiding." The lead soldier addressed the woods once more. "We've been instructed to meet the two of you and lead you back to Ranch Ragnarok," he called out.

How could they possibly know we'd be here? Remo thought.

And because Remo could think of nothing better to do, he stepped out onto the path.

Even though they were looking for someone, the soldiers were still surprised to see their quarry materialize before them. The three at the back started to reach for their weapons, but thought better of the move. Their hands returned to their sides.

"Looking for me?" Remo asked airily. He pointed a finger at his own chest.

"Yes, sir," said the lead Ragnarok soldier. "We're your escort."

"We didn't call ahead for an escort," Remo said reasonably.

"But you *are* expected."

Remo pitched his voice over their heads. "What do you think, Chiun?"

"It is rude to refuse an escort," a squeaky voice came from too close behind the soldiers.

They spun around, coming face-to-face with the Master of Sinanju. He perched on the path like some great yellow parrot, face inscrutable, hands tucked inside the sleeves of his billowing kimono. The elderly Korean had slipped up behind them without so much as a whisper of his sandal soles.

"That's it," said the second man to the patrol leader. "Two of them." He and the others glanced nervously up and down the path, obviously uncomfortable with the idea that the woods through which they had marched so frequently could have harbored unseen assailants all along.

"Will you gentlemen follow us?" the patrol leader invited.

And with that the patrol turned and headed back down the path.

Remo shot a glance at Chiun. The Master of Sinanju

wore a puzzled frown. What else could they do? They were obviously expected.

They fell in step behind the soldiers.

"Think Smith told them we were coming?" Remo whispered out of the corner of his mouth. A tree branch hung in his way. It became so much falling wood chips after Remo made busy motions with his hands.

Chiun's hazel eyes squeezed like a wary cat's. "Smith is a lunatic, but he is not stupid."

"Did you tell him you wanted to quit? Maybe this is his idea of an ambush. Dead assassins tell no tales."

"And live ones sometimes speak too much," Chiun replied. "I am not stupid, either. Of course I did not speak to Smith of our intentions."

"*Your* intentions," Remo corrected.

"Details," the Master of Sinanju said dismissively.

About a half mile along, the path opened up on a vast expanse of virtually barren fields. An eight-foot-high fence, woven at the top with tumbleweeds of gleaming razor wire, sprouted from the parched Wyoming plain—the only crop in this wide, alien vista.

The fence was broken up at regular intervals by concrete guard towers. Remo and Chiun were escorted between a pair of the three-story structures. A small gate, just large enough for one man to pass through, swung open at their approach.

"Side door?" Remo asked the soldiers.

The patrol leader grunted his assent.

Within the Ragnarok compound, Remo and Chiun found a cluster of ugly concrete salt-box structures squatting together about a hundred yards beyond the fence.

Another building was set apart from the others. It stood alone on a tract of land beyond a section of rolled-up fencing and looked for all the world like a giant, half-buried tin can. Remo could tell by the fresh scars in the earth that the hurricane fence had only recently been extended around this new area.

There was a smaller area corralled off by the isolated building, and Remo could see hundreds of tiny black heads speckled within the pen. Some were butting horns, others were running frantically for reasons that were entirely their own, but most were standing around, sullenly chewing whatever vegetation they could scrape up.

"You boys must be on that strict all-goat diet I keep hearing about," Remo commented, nodding across the field toward the pen.

The soldiers didn't respond.

Near the main grouping of structures, a young woman stood patiently waiting, an AR-15 slung across her shoulder as casually as a handbag.

"A reception committee?" Remo said quizzically. He shot a look at Chiun, but found the old Korean distracted.

The Master of Sinanju had raised his nose barely perceptibly and was pulling in delicate puffs of air. He seemed focused on the solitary building beyond the goat pen within the newly constructed fence.

"I'll take them from here," the woman announced when they reached the perimeter buildings.

The men nodded and headed in toward the largest communal building.

"Welcome to Ranch Ragnarok," the woman said

once the men had left. Her intelligent blue eyes swam behind horn-rimmed glasses.

"I've got to compliment you. This must be the most hospitable concentration camp I've ever been in," Remo said. "Don't you agree, Little Father?"

Chiun ignored him.

"Now, of course you don't really mean that," the girl admonished. But there was a twinkle in her eyes.

"Are you the Clearasil woman?" asked Chiun.

"Hardly," the girl said. "My name is Buffy Brand. I'm an acolyte in the Church of the Absolute and Incontrovertible Truth. Welcome again."

"Care to share this incontrovertible truth with a disbeliever?" prompted Remo.

"You're standing in it, Mr....?"

"Falwell," said Remo, adding, "and I find it hard to believe that a trainload of mortar mix dumped out in the middle of nowhere somehow holds the mystery of creation."

"It's not creation that's a concern to us here at the Truth Church," Buffy explained. "We're looking more toward the other end of the time line. We are preparing for the End Times."

"That anything like halftime?" asked Remo.

"Remo, why prolong this prattling?" Chiun squeaked. "This is not the one you seek. You," he commanded imperiously, pointing to Buffy Brand, "show us the way." His hazel eyes strayed back toward the distant building.

"Who put a knot in your bloomers?" Remo asked.

"This is not the time for insolence," Chiun warned, chopping the air with one long-nailed hand.

Remo accepted the rebuke in silence. "I guess he's

calling the shots,'' he said, turning to the girl. "Lay on, MacBuff.''

"YOU ARE father and son?'' Buffy asked once they were hurrying alongside the nearest buildings. Her squeal of excitement when Remo nodded made it sound as if until that moment, she had thought that such a family relationship was only possible in a fairy tale. "How wonderful for you.'' She searched their faces. "You don't really look much alike, do you?''

"He is adopted,'' Chiun confided.

"Actually, I adopted him,'' Remo said, peeved. He was sick of being passed off as some kind of charity case.

"I allow him his delusions,'' Chiun declared. "For if I did not, he would never listen to me. Not that he heeds well now,'' he added quickly.

"'A wise son heareth the doctrine of his father: but he that is a scorner heareth not when he is reproved.' Proverbs, chapter thirteen, verse one,'' Buffy said.

"Shut up,'' Remo suggested.

"Let the child speak, Remo,'' Chiun said. "This one is wise beyond her years.''

Buffy blushed. "I'm only quoting,'' Buffy said, embarrassed. "The Prophetess says anyone can quote. She comes up with wholly original doctrine. She insists that it's as good as gospel, though.''

"I'll bet she does,'' Remo muttered.

Buffy frowned intelligently. "She doesn't seem to know too much about the actual Bible, either.''

"That way she can make it up as she goes along,'' Remo suggested.

"That's not a very nice thing to say,'' Buffy chided.

There wasn't the venom one would expect from a religious fanatic, Remo noticed.

"And anyway, she sure as shootin' knew you were coming," Buffy added.

"How did she know that?" Remo wondered.

Buffy shrugged. "Beats me. Maybe Kaspar told her."

"And I'll bet Richie Rich gives her the weather forecast."

"Don't be, silly," Buffy said. "Mark Kaspar showed up a couple of months ago. The rest of the acolytes seem to gravitate more toward him lately, but my allegiance is still to Yogi Mom."

Remo nodded to himself. It sounded like there was some kind of power play going on in paradise. He'd have to check out this Mark Kaspar once he was finished with Esther Clear-Seer.

They rounded the last of the concrete buildings near the main gate of the complex, and Remo was startled to see a perfectly ordinary-looking ranch house jutting out from the cluster of converted warehouses.

It looked like the giant urban cinder-block nightmare that was the rest of the Ragnarok complex was in the act of gobbling up a defenseless western cabin, but upon closer examination Remo realized that the cabin had been constructed after most of the other buildings.

"'Behold the dwelling of God with men, and he will dwell with them,'" Buffy piped up. "That's in chapter twenty-one of Revelations. And this is it." She motioned to the small, rustic ranch home.

"I think the Almighty probably had something other than a six-room, split-entry ranch with attached garage in mind when he wrote that," Remo pointed out.

Buffy led them up to the porch and rapped carefully on the heavy oak door. It swung open at her touch.

"Prophetess?" Buffy called as she stepped through the doorway. Remo and Chiun followed.

There was no one in the house proper, but Remo detected the odor of freshly overturned earth and felt the rush of cool air that preceded the smell. Somewhere in the back of the house a tunnel had recently been dug.

There was movement from a rear room, and a beautiful raven-haired woman stepped out into the living room, looking like a cross between Liz Taylor and Imelda Marcos.

The earth smell was strong on her, so she had come up through the tunnel, Remo reasoned. But there was another, stranger odor. Remo sniffed the air. Beneath a thick layer of expensive bath soaps and perfumes, the woman smelled of rotten eggs.

"Your friends are here, Prophetess," Buffy announced respectfully.

Esther Clear-Seer smiled coolly.

"Ah, Mr. Williams. Mr. Chiun. Welcome to your unavoidable destiny."

9

"You seem surprised, Mr. Williams," Esther Clear-Seer said calmly. She dismissed Buffy Brand with a nod, and the girl backed out dutifully from the house.

Remo and Chiun exchanged narrow glances.

"An assassin doesn't make many friends," Esther speculated. "Would you feel better if I called you Remo?"

"Whatever you call me, it won't be for long," Remo replied flatly, but his eyes, usually as cold and unwavering as a midnight sea, could not mask a spark of confusion.

"Spoken like a true professional," Esther murmured. She turned her attention to Chiun. "But you, Korean, are the truest professional. Master Chiun. Elder of the House of Sinanju. I feel as if I've come face-to-face with history personified."

Chiun's wrinkled visage was impassive. He deigned not to look at Esther, but stared at the wall beyond.

Esther went on thoughtfully. "You truly are an assassin's assassin, aren't you, Master Chiun? How old were you when you killed your first man?" She passed a hand before her face, as if the movement would erase the words she had just uttered. "You were thirteen," she said. "A boy by any standards, but an infant according to your House. He was a Japanese soldier, scrounging for food in your village. He stole. You stumbled upon him. And you slaughtered him like a mongrel dog. Strange how his deathly face appeared in your dreams all those years afterward."

"Chiun?" Remo asked, bewildered. "This true?"

The Master of Sinanju made fists like thorns, his eyes frosty and still.

"It's encouraging that you two hooked up," Esther said to Remo. "You an orphan, Remo. Master Chiun, a maker of orphans. You were meant for each other."

"That's it, lady, you're dogmeat." Remo made a move toward her.

A pipe-stem arm lashed out before Remo like a crossing gate. "Halt, Remo," Chiun commanded.

"Huh?"

Esther laughed. "I'd heed him if I were you, Remo."

"You're not me, sister," he growled. But he didn't move.

"No, that's true," Esther said, drawing close. "But there have been times when you wished you weren't, either."

Remo whirled on the Master of Sinanju. He seemed to have some idea of what was going on. "Chiun, what the hell is this?"

"Examine her hands," Chiun commanded.

Remo did. A powder, the color and consistency of mustard flour, coated Esther Clear-Seer's slender fingers.

"She's as hygenic as one of those goats," Remo said. "So what?"

Chiun held up a restraining hand. He tilted his nose

into the air and sniffed once, all the while watching Esther Clear-Seer through steady, thin-lidded eyes.

"That scent, Remo..."

"I smell it," Remo snapped. "It stinks like an egg-salad-sandwich factory."

"It is sulphur," Chiun explained.

"It is rank," Remo retorted.

"The old man knows," Esther said, pleased at his deduction. "By the way, is it permissible to be seated in the presence of the Master of Sinanju?" Not waiting for a response, she gathered up the trail of her robes and dropped to a crushed velvet sofa.

Remo had had enough. He meant to flash over to the sofa. He intended to crack every one of Esther's vertebrae one at a time. He planned to crush her skull to powder, do a little jig on the woman's body and then run tear-ass back to Folcroft where Smith and his damn computers would be able to figure out what the hell was going on here.

All this Remo fully intended to do. But when he tried to move, a bony hand on his chest stopped him dead in his tracks and as unmovable as a redwood.

"Quit it, Little Father," Remo said. He tried to move his legs, but they had taken root in the highly polished hardwood floor. His arms, too, hung uselessly at his sides. Only then did Remo realize Chiun's free hand had drifted around to his lower spine. By manipulating the proper pressure points simultaneously, the Master of Sinanju had effectively paralyzed his pupil.

"Come, Remo," Chiun said softly. "We go."

"Go?" Remo said, dumbfounded. "We can't go."

"Oh, you will leave," Esther said with infuriating certainty.

Remo ignored her. "Now is not the time to give our notice, Chiun. She knows too much. She can blow the whole shooting match. We can't leave her."

Remo strained until beads of perspiration and frustration formed on his forehead, but he failed to move a single millimeter.

"We cannot help by destroying this one," Chiun said, sniffing the air once more. "She is a mere agent of her master."

Esther got back to her feet and strolled over to Remo, standing nose-to-nose with him. The noxious rotten-egg smell clung to her billowy garments.

"Listen to your father," Esther breathed. "The House of Sinanju has reached the end of its cycle in this millennium. It is time for one more powerful than the mortals of your pitiful village to rule the earth. Be frightened, Sinanju, for your every thought, your every action, your every reaction, is known. Your years of glory are near an end." She smiled gleefully. "East has met West, the prophecy is fulfilled."

Her smile rapidly changed to a look of horror as Esther found herself suddenly airborne and sailing backward into her living room.

She slammed full force into the wall over the couch. Her head snapped back, cracking soundly into a wide, gleaming window frame. She crashed painfully to the floor, upending cushions from the couch. Her nose gushed a fountain of bright, sticky blood.

In that flash of time Remo saw the blurry hand of

the Master of Sinanju—kimono sleeve flapping—as it settled back to Chiun's side.

"Know you this, agent of evil," Chiun intoned. "Sinanju will never be sport for your master's underlings. We acknowledge his presence in the world at this time and will lie in wait for the day when he once again walks among the gods. Until that hour, Sinanju yields."

With that, Chiun whirled the protesting Remo around like a mannequin and propelled him hastily from Ranch Ragnarok.

ONCE THEY WERE GONE, Esther pulled herself painfully to her feet. She ripped a handful of tissues from an end-table dispenser and tried to soak up the ceaseless flow of blood that ran from her rapidly swelling nose.

When she heard the footsteps coming down the hallway, she didn't even bother to look up. She knew that steady, confident tread.

"Aren't you worried they'll come back?" Esther honked.

"They are gone for now," Kaspar said. He eyed her appraisingly. "You performed well."

"Thanks," Esther said snidely. "That's the last time I take a crash course in your gobbledygook. I think that old fart broke my nose."

"The Master of Sinanju is a formidable opponent," Kaspar agreed. He sat in one of Esther's garish Louis Quatorze chairs.

"What is a Master of Sinanju?" Esther asked.

"And what was all that assassin crap you made me parrot for them?"

"It does not matter now," Kaspar said thinly.

"Bull—"

Kaspar shot her a controlling glance.

Esther let the matter drop. She tested her bloody nose with a clean tissue. The crimson flow had slowed.

Kaspar paused briefly, watching as Esther heaved the scattered cushions back on the sofa.

"The latest oracles appear to have drained the current mortal vessel."

Esther glared up at him through tearing, blurry eyes. "Don't even think it," she snarled.

"The appearance of the Sinanju masters was disturbing to Apollo's emissary. He vented his agitation through the Pythia."

"I am not doing a kidnapping a day for you, Kaspar!" Esther railed. "No matter how good the money is." Esther gathered up her bloody tissues in a damp wad and fell back onto the couch. "Tell him to count to ten before he vents next time." She massaged her temples gently with pale, tapering fingertips.

"It might not be immediately necessary," Kaspar said, knowing full well that the latest vessel would not last the week. He brushed the crease of his dress pants casually. "The Pythia has indicated that there might be a new investment opportunity for you," he added slyly.

Esther considered his words. She dropped the gory wad on the end table. At last she spoke. "I make no promises," she said dully.

Kaspar smiled. For her the money was everything.

She would gather more vessels for his master. The Pythia had foreseen it.

To Esther, he said, "You have done well so far. Our master is pleased."

"He ought to be." She pinched her nose gingerly and winced at the pain. "I've got to get some ice on this," she said morosely. Then she got up and headed for the kitchen.

"I have to go away on business in a few days," Kaspar called after her. "Will you be able to handle things in my absence?"

Esther came out holding a dish towel clinking with ice cubes to the injured bridge of her nose. "I was handling church affairs long before you showed up, Kaspar," she snapped.

"Of course," he demurred. "It was not my intention to insult. It is just that, in dealing with our master, there are matters with which you might not be wholly familiar."

"Wholly familiar, please," she mocked. "I've seen you do it a hundred times," she said. "Kill a goat, hatch a prophecy. How hard can it be?"

"How hard, indeed?" Kaspar smiled an infuriating, tight-lipped smile. He stood to go. "If we have guests, you will escort them to me?" he said unnecessarily.

"With bells on," Esther muttered. She screwed her eyes shut, trying to blot out the image of the annoying little Greek.

"In that case, good night." He headed for the door.

"Good night," Esther murmured.

After he had gone, she fumbled the makeshift ice bag back onto her nose, wincing at a flash of new pain.

As the soothing ice numbed the stinging, she wondered briefly who this Master of Sinanju was and why Kaspar had refused to meet with him himself. For Esther's part, she hoped she'd see him again. She'd see to it that the old man wouldn't land another cheap shot on her holy person.

In the meantime, she would have to secure Kaspar's continued investment advice by supplying virgin number two.

10

The last rays of the dying sun had burned away in streaks of orange brilliance across the gently undulating surface of Long Island Sound, and Harold W. Smith had completely failed to notice.

To some the setting sun was a grand testament to nature's awesome design, but to Smith it was nothing more than the inevitable rotation of the planet on its axis.

Harold Smith felt that it was foolish to be awed by something that happened 365 times a year—366 times during leap year, because whoever had come up with the twenty-four-hour day had produced a flawed model.

And so the sun had set, the shadows in Smith's office elongating slowly to envelop the sparsely furnished room, while Harold Smith continued to sit hunched over his desk oblivious to, what was for most, the completion of yet another life-affirming day.

Smith typed with swift, precise pecks at the touch-sensitive computer keyboard at the edge of his desk. The computer screen, buried beneath the glossy black surface of the desktop, as was the keyboard, shed a weird amber glow upon his pallid features.

He was repeating a procedure Smith thought he had

used for the final time only a few short days before. And while he monitored his progress on the angled computer screen, one nagging question continually tugged at the back of his mind.

What was Moss Monroe's business with the Truth Church?

As part of his preliminary research into suspected illegal activities on the part of Esther Clear-Seer, Smith had executed a background check on the Church of the Absolute and Incontrovertible Truth weeks ago. It was during this search that he learned of the purchasing and stockpiling of armaments on the grounds of the sprawling ranch complex, and of the lavish life-style the self-proclaimed Divine Prophetess enjoyed on the backs of her shorn flock.

Even with that evidence in hand, Smith remained leery of committing CURE's resources to the destruction of the Truth Church. The public memory of the Branch Davidian fiasco was too fresh, and at the time of that siege Smith was concerned the federal government was involving itself in a quagmire of sticky constitutional issues it had no business testing. To this day Smith felt America had sat in their living rooms and calmly watched the violation of the First and Second Amendments and, quite probably, the Fourth and Fifth, as the fires in Waco raged.

Smith believed to the very core of his rock-ribbed, patrician soul that the Davidian leader was delusional, and that those who followed him were doomed dupes. But there was no law against religious cupidity or blind, unswerving acceptance of a madman's ravings. In the end the Davidians had simply fallen victim to a different kind of zealotry.

It was this frame of mind that had Smith willing to shelve the potential problem near Thermopolis earlier in the year. Only recently, after learning of FBI interest in the ranch and of the disappearance of one of their operatives, had Smith reexamined the situation.

As Smith's knobby fingers tapped remorselessly along the desk's edge, the mute computer keyboard lit up like a patchy pale fireworks finale.

What was Moss Monroe's interest? he wondered.

A red alarm light in the upper left-hand corner of the screen began blinking.

Smith had hacked into the files of the Thermopolis First State Bank, and now the computer was demanding the proper access code.

At this, as at each subsequent level of the system, Smith repeated the codes that had gained him admittance once before.

It took but a moment to access the account files of the Church of the Absolute and Incontrovertible Truth and its head, Esther Clear-Seer.

Smith's brow furrowed as he scanned the information. Nominal changes since the previous check. In fact, there was too little change. Nothing had been taken out of either account in more than a week, and even then it was only a pittance. He reviewed the computerized records. Up until eight months before, there had been a constant cash flow in and out of both accounts. Understandable, considering the funds required to run a complex the size of Ranch Ragnarok.

Smith pursed his thin, bloodless lips.

If these accounts were now dormant...

Smith pecked rapidly at the keyboard, calling up a

listing of all accounts controlled by either Esther Clear-Seer or the Truth Church.

It took only three seconds for the computer to respond. There was only one other account, opened at the precise time the other two had been virtually abandoned.

It was an ancillary account in the name of the Truth Church Foundation. The account was wholly separate from the main church account, which was part of the reason Smith had missed it until now.

He cursed inwardly, remonstrating himself for allowing his advancing years to taint the methodical manner with which he approached a problem. Not too many years ago it would have been routine for him to examine the bank files thoroughly the second time through. As it was, he had settled for the two known accounts on his reexamination of the records, and then he was largely concerned with the earlier weapons and explosives purchases. Whatever the reason, it had simply never occurred to him to check for a new account.

For the man who virtually pioneered the discipline of forensic accounting, it was an unforgivable lapse. Age was taking its toll.

Smith read the first few lines detailing the Truth Church Foundation account transactions, then stopped before he came to the first withdrawal.

Smith removed his rimless glasses and blinked several times, as if his vision had suddenly become blurry.

Once he had replaced the glasses, he checked the screen again.

There was no mistaking the figure glowing in amber. The funds of the Truth Church had exploded into the millions of dollars in a matter of two short months.

Urgently Smith traced the numbered record of the first major deposit.

He had the answer in a matter of seconds. Zen and Gary, the ice-cream kings of New England, had dropped a quarter million dollars into the Truth Church coffers. Their bank kept digitized photocopies of all canceled checks. Smith called up the record of this particular transaction. He was presented with a color image of a garish check. In the lower left, on the memo line, someone had scrawled, "Prophecy."

Smith frowned like a lemon drying.

Was this a joke? Esther Clear-Seer *had* been calling herself Prophetess. But that was just her title. Or was it?

Smith dismissed the possibility. No one parted with a quarter of a million dollars to hear his fortune.

Smith returned to the Truth Church Foundation account and traced the next deposit. It was a woman's name that meant nothing to him, but when he cross-referenced the name with those listed in CURE's massive database, he discovered that she was a Hollywood actress, famous for her roles as a defunct prime-time soap-opera diva and subsequently as mistress to a New Age faith healer.

Smith felt a tightening in his throat.

He scanned the computer files rapidly.

Some of the checks were harder to trace than others, but the pattern formed by those that were more easily identified demonstrated that the Truth Church ranch had recently become a magnet for the crystals-and-caviar segment of American society.

At the beginning of the cycle, it seemed as if the church had touched only the fringes of wealthy soci-

ety. Transaction after transaction showed that numerous celebrities had made the Truth Church the payee
on dozens of checks. But the most alarming aspect was
the trend appeared to have begun moving into the
mainstream. The CURE computers traced checks to
various political figures and business leaders whose
names Smith recognized.

That's why Moss Monroe had gone out there. The
specific motivation was as yet unclear, but obviously
there was something to be had at the Truth Church
ranch for which these people were willing to pay
dearly.

Smith withdrew from the Truth Church Foundation
account and severed his computer connection with the
Thermopolis First State Bank.

Once he backed into the computer's main drive, he
leaned back in his cracked leather chair. The instant
his fingertips left the keyboard's capacitor field, the
letters winked out. The desktop became a pool of
blackish onyx, the computer screen a single, unblinking amber eye staring sullenly up at him from some
fearful nether region.

There was nothing more to go on.

Smith glanced at his Timex. It was 11:00 p.m.

Remo had yet to check in. But that wasn't unusual.
CURE's enforcement arm had never been as punctual
as Smith would have liked, and it was possible that
Moss Monroe was still at the ranch. Engaged in what,
Smith did not know.

There was no doubt that something strange was going on out in Wyoming. Something larger than Smith
had originally guessed. Perhaps it had something to do
with Zen and Gary's "prophecy," but until he had

something more concrete to go on, this part of the investigation was dead in the water.

Smith was shaken from his reverie by the ringing of a telephone. For an instant he thought it was Remo checking in, then he realized it wasn't the blue contact phone jangling. He pulled open a drawer desk and lifted the receiver of the clumsy red AT&T standard phone that was his direct line to the White House.

"Yes, Mr. President," Smith said crisply.

"Smith," the familiar hoarse voice said. "Sorry to call this late."

"Go ahead, sir," Smith prompted.

The President seemed to be at a loss for words. He cleared his throat a few times, uncertainly.

"Is there something I can do for you, Mr. President?" Smith queried. His clipped, lemony tones showed no underlying curiosity.

The President forced the words out. "It's been brought to my attention that out west there's an establishment of—let's say ill repute. Members of my party have been...frequenting this establishment."

The uncharacteristic trepidation in the man's voice led Smith to a safe conclusion. Circumstances had often brought the world's two oldest professions into conflict from time immemorial, and it appeared as if the President had a potentially embarrassing political situation on his hands.

Whatever else Smith was, he was not a pawn of any political party.

"Mr. President, you are aware that it is not part of our charter to get involved in domestic political situations."

"I know that," said the President. "Of course. But—"

"Then you agree it would be inadvisable for us to investigate a matter of a delicate political nature."

"Ordinarily, yes," the President agreed. "But there's more to this than that."

Smith pursed his razor-thin lips. "I am listening."

"Have you ever heard of a place called Ranch Ragnarok?"

Harold Smith listened to the President for barely five minutes.

The Chief Executive explained how he had been approached at a party fund-raising dinner earlier that evening by a congressman who had helped the President win a surprise victory for a piece of important legislation in the House. The man insisted that he had been told at a ranch in Wyoming the identity of those in the opposition who needed to be strong-armed and precisely what personal information would persuade the men to sway their votes. In private life this was considered blackmail, but in Washington it was business as usual.

The President was willing, at first, to dismiss the man and his claim as mildly eccentric, but twice during the same dinner—once by another congressman, once by a contributing business executive—it had been confided to the leader of the free world that all his questions about the future could be answered at the same small ranch.

The President cleared his throat noisily. "Do you—do you think there's anything to this?"

"To fortune-telling?" Smith retorted skeptically.

"When you put it that way, no. Of course not. But—"

"But what?"

"Well, my wife believes in this stuff. In fact, she spends a lot of time in the Red Room talking to Eleanor Roosevelt."

"Claiming to talk to Eleanor Roosevelt, you mean," Smith said.

"Er, sometimes I listen at the door," the President said guardedly. His voice dropped to a hoarse whisper. "Sometimes I hear *two* voices. What do you think of that, Smith?"

"Not much," Harold Smith said truthfully. "And I would steer your political allies away from Ranch Ragnarok, if I were you," he added.

Repeating CURE's directive to avoid political entanglement, Smith excused himself and hung up.

For a long time after he had replaced the receiver, Smith's hand continued to grasp the warm red plastic.

He had his answer. The cryptic scrawl in the corner of that first check had been no joke. Reputable people with something to lose were willing to risk public ridicule to travel to the Truth Church ranch.

For a glimpse into the future.

At long last Smith released the receiver and pushed the desk drawer silently back into place.

He spun his chair toward the window behind him and stared at the silent, black waters of Long Island Sound.

For the first time that evening, he noticed that night had fallen.

11

Michael "the Prince" Princippi had been out of politics for a decade, and although most Americans were relieved by this prolonged absence there were some—granted, a very small minority—who longed for the Prince of Massachusetts politics to return to the public spotlight. There was no one who held this view more strongly than Mike Princippi himself.

His rise to the head of the presidential pack a decade before had been both surprising and meteoric. He was far from flamboyant, but not deliberate enough in his demeanor to be considered reserved. He was, quite frankly, dull.

No one thought Princippi would get the nomination of his party during the 1988 presidential contest and, therefore, no one in his party campaigned much against him.

After the dust of the primary battles had settled, the other contenders were shocked to find out that their previous year of squabbling and backstabbing had effectively handed over the presumptive nomination to a man with the charm of a haddock and the charisma of a bucket of chopped ice. A broken space heater projected more warmth, the party chairman had lamented.

Princippi had staked his claim to the White House by touting the exploding economy he had presided over as governor of Massachusetts, and he was right in singling out his stellar achievement. What he failed to tell the nation was that the real miracle in his home state was the fact that the makers of red ink were able to produce enough of the stuff to keep up with Princippi's wild spending spree. This was the secret Michael Princippi effectively hid from the voters for so long: although he was an experienced technocrat with a penchant for knowing where all the paper clips in the governor's office were, his administration blew through money like a thresher through a field of autumn wheat.

For much of the race, it seemed that the voters would overlook Princippi's obvious shortcomings.

That was until the question.

It was at the second debate. He was up against the then vice president, and Barney Shea, the cable anchorman, had asked a personal question that the reporter hoped would help the governor dispel the silly notion that he lacked passion.

"Governor Princippi," the anchorman began, "Kiki Princippi is decapitated and her twitching body violated by four sweating stevedores. What do you do?"

Kiki. His wife. As the cameras whirred away, as the satellites beamed the small man's image to millions of homes across the country, Michael Princippi paused for dramatic effect, pondering the question.

At long last the man who would be president spoke.

"I'd identify the body, obviously, Barney—well, at least the head...."

The full text of the response, though telecast almost

daily up until election day, was irrelevant. The Prince had screwed the pooch.

Principi lost the race in a landslide.

When his party surged ahead four years later, retaking 1600 Pennsylvania Avenue for the first time in twelve years, Michael Principi had gone on the few talk shows that would have him and pontificated his opinion that the then president-elect's victory was a ratification of Principi's own abortive campaign. Four years after his dream had gone down in flames, Michael Principi was still claiming victory. Something deep about having lost the battle but won the war.

During the most recent presidential race, his party had treated him like a poor relation. His calls to offer assistance to the national committee headquarters in Washington had gone unreturned. He'd gone full cycle from being courted to becoming a pariah.

He swore for the absolute last time, as he had so many times in the past, that his career in the fickle world of politics was at a definite end.

And this time his resolution held, until he heard through his remaining political connections of a place out west where all questions could be answered...and all answers were guaranteed to come true.

IT WAS AFTER MIDNIGHT when Michael Principi arrived in Thermopolis, Wyoming. The battered Volkswagen Beetle he had driven since his days in law school coughed clouds of thick exhaust into the warm spring air.

The former governor's excessive personal frugality had been fodder for the stand-up comedians during the heady days of the '88 campaign, and the rickety old car had borne the brunt of many an attack. While the worst of the barbs were flying, Michael Princippi's only concern was that the ridicule would force him to go out and buy a new car. After all, this one only had 190,000 miles on it and forty-eight oil changes.

Ten years later, with the odometer a few miles shy of its fourth restart, Michael Princippi chugged past the sleepy Thermopolis houses with their Re-elect Senator Jackson Cole signs tapped arrow-straight in their neatly tended lawns.

He remembered with some bitterness that Jackson Cole had been a friend of his opponent during the presidential race and he briefly considered aiming the Volkswagen across a few of the tidier lawns that displayed the senator's owlish visage. But back in Ohio, he had been forced to bind the rusted-out muffler in place with his shoelaces, and he was afraid the jostling would snap them loose.

Princippi left the images of Cole behind him as he passed through the far side of town. A few miles out he came upon the flashing amber light that was suspended above the twisting paved road, and he turned left onto the well-marked dirt path that led to Ranch Ragnarok.

He drove several miles into the thickening woods before his washed-out headlights caught sight of armed patrols. At each twist in the path where he saw them, the Ragnarok guards would pause briefly—like deer mesmerized by the flash of light from the oncoming vehicle—before resuming their march through the cluster of trees.

Princippi passed through the gate without incident. Either no one recognized him after so many years out of the political spotlight, or the Ragnarok soldiers were trained not to be awed by celebrity—something Michael Princippi still considered himself to be. Whatever the reason, no one batted an eye as Mike "the Prince" Princippi pulled up to the ranch house at the end of the main path.

A full-figured woman in white-and-gold vestments waited for him on the wide hacienda-style porch. When Princippi climbed out of his car, she rose from a small wooden bench beside the door.

"You're here for Kaspar," she intoned.

It was a statement, not a question. Her eyes were dull and her voice flat. For a second he thought she was wearing a mask. On closer inspection, he realized both of her eyes had been blackened. Painful dark rings encircled both eyes, making her resemble a raven-haired raccoon. Her nose was bluish and slightly swollen.

Princippi cleared his throat. "I'm here to see my future."

The woman sighed. "You want Kaspar," she said, nodding to herself. "Everyone wants Kaspar."

She beckoned him inside the ranch.

There was an office in a former bedroom at the rear of the building and, between a pair of four-drawer filing cabinets, a concrete staircase descended into the earth below.

Princippi followed the woman down.

The tunnel was cool and musty. Lally support columns held up iron cross beams, and the side walls were stacked with cinder blocks as far into the distance as Michael Princippi could see.

The dirt floor was boxed in with open frames of

wood, which butted up against one another. Princippi
had to step over the four-inch-high cross sections of
wood every few feet.

"They start pouring the concrete tomorrow," the
woman called over her shoulder by way of explanation.

At several points along the way the new tunnel met
with sections that appeared to be older. Vast storehouses faded into the distant shadows both left and
right of the tunnel.

There were rooms packed to the ceiling with U.S.
Army surplus supplies. Boxes of K rations left over
from the Korean War were piled neatly on forged
metal shelves. One room held nothing but jug upon
jug of bottled water. Most of the rooms, however,
seemed stuffed to near overflowing with crates bearing
sinister-sounding names like White Phosphorus and
Thermite in bold black stenciled letters on the sides.
There were various cryptic warnings on all of the con-
tainers concerning the danger of exposure to fire or
extreme heat. Disconcertingly these were packed next
to huge galvanized steel drums that reeked of gasoline.

Other rooms were lined with rack upon rack of
guns. More weapons than Princippi had ever seen—
even during his famous photo-op tank ride during the
1988 presidential race. Ragnarok soldiers shuffled
sleeplessly through the underground chambers in a human parody of a paramilitary ant colony.

Judging from where they had entered the tunnel,
Princippi guessed that the rooms were all near or beneath the large, warehouse-type buildings he had seen
in the distance on his drive up, and he was relieved

when the woman led him beyond this area and into another long stretch of newly constructed tunnel.

This section seemed to go on forever, but at last he saw that the thread of insulated wire that was tacked to the cinder-block wall and hung at regular intervals with sickly yellow lights along the whole length of the tunnel finally turned upward.

He was escorted up another flight of concrete stairs and soon found himself in the torch-lit interior of the old airplane hangar.

Without a backward glance, Esther Clear-Seer led him through the building to the Pythia Pit.

Inside the newly constructed room, Principi saw an emaciated girl with stringy hair perched atop the rocky hillock in the center of the room. The girl stared, immobile, into space. Thin wisps of yellow smoke spluttered up from somewhere in the riven rock beneath her.

Resplendent in his priestly garb, Kaspar stood at the base of the small hill, a tethered goat staked to the dirt floor near him. He smiled when he spied Principi.

"I was expecting you," he said politely. "I am Kaspar. Present your offering to the priestess of the Ragnarok Oracle."

Principi blinked at the name, but said nothing. He nodded and fished in the jacket pocket of his suit, pulling out his checkbook.

"How much was it again?"

"The fee is twenty thousand."

Principi gulped. "Dollars?" he squeaked.

"You were aware of the fee before you came," Kaspar said flatly.

"I'm a former presidential candidate. Is there a discount?"

When he saw the stony expression on Kaspar's face, Princippi dragged a Bic pen from his pocket. Reluctantly he filled out the check, double-, then triple-checking the amount he had filled in before turning the scrap of paper over to Esther Clear-Seer.

"Give the woman two hundred dollars for the goat," Kaspar commanded.

Princippi balked. "I don't want a goat," he complained.

"The goat is for sacrifice. This you knew, as well."

Princippi was ready to put up a stink about the goat clause, but it seemed as if this Kaspar already knew everything Princippi himself knew. Suppressing a shuddery wave of personal anguish, he handed over the cash to Esther.

Kaspar next presented Princippi with a gem-encrusted knife.

"Slaughter the animal."

Princippi stared at the knife dully. He looked down into the wide, fear-filled eyes of the tiny creature before him.

"What if PETA hears about this?" he asked fearfully.

"Oh, for heaven's sake," Esther snapped. "Give me that." She grabbed the knife away from Michael Princippi and slit the throat of the terrified animal. At the top of the rock incline, the ecstatic twitching of the young girl became a bizarre parody of the spastic death movements of the bleeding goat.

The smoke from out of the fissure grew more dense.

Kaspar slowly mounted the hewed-rock steps and took his place beside the dazed girl.

"The Apollo Pythia awaits your question," Kaspar intoned.

The former governor of Massachusetts swallowed hard. "Can you make me President?" he blurted out. His glowering features brightened momentarily with a hopeful half grin. His fat black eyebrows bunched together like butting sheep.

The Pythia's reply was immediate. "I foretell events. I do not affect them." The girl bounced like a palsy victim on her tripod.

Princippi appeared crestfallen. "You've got to," he begged. "I've got to get back in the game. Please. I gave you twenty grand."

"It is as I have spoken."

Kaspar interceded. "That is not to say, Mr. Princippi, that foreknowledge of events does not allow you to alter your approach to those events, thus changing the presaged outcome."

"I can change the future?" Princippi asked. "Is that what you're saying?"

"Most assuredly."

Princippi faced the Pythia once more. "Tell me how to affect the future so that I can one day become President," he asked boldly.

The Pythia twitched on her tripod.

"Your future exists as one with him who stands before you. You are the past. My priest is the future. Together you will change tomorrow."

Princippi scrunched up his face.

"I don't understand."

The girl appeared to be tiring. Her body twitched

less spastically now, like the faint spasms of someone in her death throes.

"My priest," she wheezed. "He is your destiny."

And with that, she fell from the tripod.

"Shit!" snapped Esther Clear-Seer. She bounded up the stone staircase as Kaspar made his somber way back down to Principi's level.

"I still don't get it," Principi said, once Kaspar was beside him again. "What did she mean?"

"She's dead, Kaspar," Esther Clear-Seer shouted down. "You told me she'd last a while longer. It's been barely ten hours."

Kaspar ignored her.

"You have maintained your contacts with your state organizations?" he asked Principi.

"Some," Principi admitted with a shrug of his sagging shoulders. "But they're not mine anymore. They go with the flow."

"But there are people who are loyal to you exclusively. People who would obey your orders. People who, if asked, would help you mount another campaign?"

Principi felt an old thrill return to the pit of his stomach. "Absolutely," he replied quickly.

"Then the wish of my master will be realized," Kaspar said with certainty. "Together we will change the course of tomorrow."

Michael Principi could hardly contain his excitement. "Then that's it?" he said, awed. "Finally? After all these years in the wilderness I'm going to get another shot at being President?"

Kaspar allowed himself a small smile.

"Not you," the strange little man said. "Me."

12

It was early Sunday morning when Harold W. Smith pushed open the side stairwell door of Folcroft Sanitarium and stepped out into the light of a brand-new day.

His weary eyes winced at the brightness of the rising sun.

Smith had stayed at his desk throughout the night, awaiting Remo's report. When dawn broke without a call from his enforcement arm, Smith decided to allow himself the luxury of a brief trip home for a shower and a change of clothes. As he walked from the building, he fumbled in his pocket for his car keys.

Smith rarely used the building's main entrance, preferring instead to use the parking-lot door. This allowed him to come and go with relative anonymity, without alerting the civilian staff to his irregular work hours. But this early on a Sunday the sanitarium was operating on skeleton staff, with most staff spending time with their families. So there was no one to see the spare-framed old man as he crunched across the gravel driveway toward the staff parking area.

The parking lot was spotted with only a few cars. Smith's ancient station wagon sat unobtrusively in the space nearest the building.

As he approached, Smith noted with some concern the growing patch of rust that had formed the previous winter over the right rear tire well. He had been warned that if the spot wasn't properly attended to it would continue to eat like a cancer at the helpless fender.

Smith placed his battered leather briefcase on the ground before him and stooped to examine the scab of rotted metal. He pursed his lips disapprovingly as he squinted at the jagged, rusted edges.

While he contemplated having the rust patch taken care of, he noticed a blur of yellow in the dull surface of the pitted chrome strip along the side of the car.

Placing his left hand carefully beside the rust spot for support, he turned on creaking bones and noted with some curiosity the arrival of a Checker cab by Folcroft's main entrance.

There was a guard's shack near the closed gate, and the man on duty leaned out the door. Smith could hear him shout something to the cab and he assumed that the guard was informing the cab's occupants that visiting hours at the sanitarium did not begin until eleven o'clock.

The taxi didn't move. In fact, it sounded as if someone inside the vehicle was yelling.

Still crouched near his own car, Smith pitched an ear toward the gate, his face puckering unhappily as he attempted to discern the focus of the commotion.

A shrill voice began squabbling with the driver from the cab's rear, and it was with a sudden burning sensation in the pit of his acid-churned stomach that Smith realized he recognized the voice.

All at once the taxi's rear door burst open, and the

Master of Sinanju spilled from the back seat like an angry summer squall. Before Smith's horrified eyes, Chiun wrenched the driver's door from its hinges and hurled the offending chunk of metal and glass down the road as if flinging papier-mâché.

This accomplished, Chiun plucked the driver from behind the steering wheel and repeated the same maneuver, except the door had bounced less.

Ignoring the stabs of pain in his knees, Smith pushed himself quickly to his feet. Briefcase in hand, he hurried down the driveway to the gate.

The Master of Sinanju had ducked back inside the cab by the time Smith got there. The guard had abandoned his post and now stood on the Folcroft side of the gate, uncertain what to do, but obviously wishing he could do it somewhere else.

Through the iron bars of the gate, Smith spied the cab driver up the road and was relieved to see the man dragging himself up on wobbling legs.

"Is there a problem?" Smith asked crisply.

The guard spun around, surprised. "Oh, Dr. Smith." He relaxed slightly. He had unfastened the snap at the top of his hip holster, and his hand rested nervously on the butt of his revolver. "We've just had an assault on that man up there," he said, pointing at the taxi driver, who stood about twenty yards away from the cab and seemed unwilling to come any closer. "I was just going to call the police."

"Don't bother."

"Huh?"

"Have the driver treated for any abrasions he may have suffered. I will see to it that he is compensated for his trouble."

"But the cabbie," the guard said, pointing. "That old guy tossed him up the road like he was a rag doll."

Smith dismissed the guard's complaints. "He is on a special vitamin diet."

The guard looked toward the cab where the parchment-covered skeleton had vanished moments before. "Whatever he's on, better cut the dose down," he said.

Chiun chose that moment to exit the taxi a second time and, simultaneously, the opposite rear door sprang open and Remo popped from the cab like a tightly wound jack-in-the-box.

"It's about frigging time!" Remo yelled at Chiun.

Smith's eyes darted around the empty road, grateful that it was still early morning.

"There is no need to shout," the Master of Sinanju said calmly.

"There is every damn need to shout!" Remo shouted. "In fact, I don't think I'm shouting enough!"

"Perhaps we should discuss this matter inside," Smith suggested nervously through the metal bars. He ordered the guard to open the gate.

Remo wheeled on him. "Perhaps I don't want to discuss it inside. Maybe I want to discuss it out here, in front of the whole damn world."

The guard had unlocked the gates but held the bars open only one inch. "Shouldn't I check their ID or something?" he asked. He still wasn't sure this wasn't some kind of bizarre security drill.

"That's quite all right," Smith said quickly. "He is a former patient."

With a great deal of hesitation, the guard pushed the gate open and Chiun breezed through.

"Do not tip the driver, Emperor Smith," he instructed. "The lazy lout would not carry a lone inert, bundle."

"Stop talking about me like I'm some frigging hatbox," Remo snarled, storming through the gate behind Chiun.

Smith pulled the Folcroft checkbook from the pocket of his gray suit and reluctantly filled out a generous amount to ensure the driver's silence. He then hurriedly ushered Remo and Chiun up to his office.

Once he had closed and locked the office door and taken his seat behind his black-topped desk, Smith asked the pair what had happened in Wyoming.

"Nothing happened," Remo groused. "Chiun got a breeze up his skirt and dragged me from the ranch before I could make the hit."

"Would you have come voluntarily?" Chiun asked, calmly.

"Hell, no," Remo snapped.

"My actions, therefore, were justified." With the smug expression of a television commentator, Chiun sank to a lotus position in the center of the threadbare rug.

"Justified, my ass," Remo snapped. He whirled to Smith. "He froze my vocal cords over South Dakota."

"It was the most peaceful airplane ride I have taken in years," Chiun chimed in.

"Master of Sinanju, am I to understand you paralyzed Remo and carried him through a public air terminal?" Smith asked.

"Right onto the damn plane," Remo interjected.

Smith thought of all the people who had seen the tiny Asian transporting the much larger man through the airport parking lot, into the airport terminal, onto the plane, off the plane at LaGuardia, through the terminal and out to a waiting cab. His eyes darted longingly to the drawer where his antacids and aspirins were stored.

"The Clear-Seer woman is still, er, with us?"

"Could be," Remo said sarcastically. "Unless Chiun has her stashed in the taxi's glove compartment." He slumped into Smith's office sofa.

"This is important, Remo," Smith said. "I would like a straight answer."

Remo sighed. "Yeah, she's still alive. Chiun was too busy hauling me like a donkey from there to here to worry about her."

Smith forced his thoughts away from Remo and Chiun's trip to Folcroft and considered the problem at Ranch Ragnarok.

"Perhaps it is for the best at the moment," Smith said absently.

"Best?" Remo asked. "What the hell does that mean? Did you want her snuffed or didn't you?"

Smith winced at Remo's choice of words. "It may be that you were sent in before I learned all the facts," he said. "Was Moss Monroe at the ranch when you arrived?"

"Barely," Remo replied. "He almost ran us down on our way in."

"Did you notice any other celebrities on the grounds?"

"Yeah, Soupy Sales tried to get the jump on us, but Chiun creamed him," Remo said dryly. "What the hell kind of question is that?"

"I have just learned that in recent months Ranch

Ragnarok has become popular with a great many famous people.''

"Well, I didn't see any paparazzi there," Remo said. "Just a bunch of weekend warriors with guns. And that's another thing," he said suddenly. "Everyone knew we were coming."

Smith sat up even straighter in his chair. "Explain," he said.

"It was like they were expecting the freaking queen or something. They met me and Chiun in the woods and escorted us through the gates like we were royalty."

Smith considered the information for a moment. "Perhaps this is the way they treat all their guests," he said slowly.

"They meet them in the middle of the woods, Smitty?" Remo asked sarcastically. "Besides, they said they were looking for two guys. Me and Chiun. They even seemed to know where we were hiding in the bushes. They called out to us. I have to admit, they were pretty polite about the whole thing."

"Is it possible they saw the two of you with surveillance equipment?"

Remo shook his head. "There were cameras and motion detectors and a bunch of other stuff, but Chiun and I don't have a problem with gizmos. The only way these guys could have known we were there is if we made noise."

Smith's mouth had grown dry. "They were somehow alerted to your presence," he said, shaking his head. "Is it possible you made some noise you were unaware of?"

"Hey, I didn't make a sound," Remo said defensively.

"And I do not make sounds," Chiun said from the floor.

Smith shook his head. "It is a coincidence," he said. "It cannot be anything else. A sentry must have seen you enter the woods. His companions merely guessed your position."

"Brace yourself for an even bigger coincidence, Smitty. Esther Clear-Seer knew who we were."

Smith placed his palms flat on his desk. What little saliva remaining in his usually parched mouth dried to sand. "What do you mean?" he croaked.

"She knew it was us specifically," Remo explained slowly, as if to a particularly thick child. "She called me Remo and called Chiun the Master of Sinanju." A concerned frown crossed his face. "She even knew my real last name, Smitty."

Smith felt his larynx constrict like a knotted drinking straw. He gulped but could pull nothing down his cracking throat. "CURE," he ventured, his voice a grating rasp. "Did she know about CURE?"

"Relax," Remo said. "She never mentioned the organization. She just went on about me and Chiun and Sinanju."

Smith felt some of the pressure drain from his chest. He loosened the knot of his green Dartmouth tie and forced himself to swallow calmly.

"That is somewhat of a relief," Smith said. "But until we learn more, we cannot disregard out of hand her knowledge of Sinanju." He turned to Chiun. "Master Chiun, is it possible that you have, er, advertised your services?"

This had been a problem several times in the past. Chiun would sometimes take out a full-page ad or buy airtime on a local television station in order to scare up business or to rail against "amateur assassins." It was possible that one such advertisement had eluded Smith.

"I know of your desire for secrecy, Emperor Smith," Chiun informed him. "Inexplicable as it might be, this wish will remain inviolate evermore."

Smith raised a puzzled eyebrow. "I appreciate that, Master Chiun," he said.

"You might want to check up on a guy named Kaspar and his connection to all this," Remo suggested. "One of this Clear-Seer woman's cronies mentioned him. It sounds like there's some sort of schism going on at the Truth Church. Kaspar's the head of one of the factions."

"I will look into it," Smith assured Remo. With practiced fingers Smith booted up his computer. "I must sift through this new data before I decide our next course of action," he said, drumming his fingers atop the surface of the gleaming black desk. The faint glow of the buried keyboard responded to his touch. "In the meantime I want you to remain on alert. It may become necessary to send you back to Ranch Ragnarok on short notice."

"On alert?" Remo complained. "Geez, Smitty, what do you think we are—a couple of battleships?"

Chiun had slipped from the floor like a puff of steam rising from a teakettle. "Know you this, Emperor," he intoned. "That even in the darkest center of the coldest night, Sinanju is alert. Distance does not weaken the mighty bond of my House to one as great and worthy as you."

Smith shot a confused look to Remo. "Thank you, Master of Sinanju," he said in puzzlement.

Chiun bowed to Smith across the room. "The thanks are mine," he said. "Your name, Wise Emperor Harold, shall be recorded in the histories of Sinanju by my very hand. Rest assured, you will be remembered forever as the greatest and most benevolent of rulers. Great reverence for your limitless beneficence shall grace the lips of Masters of Sinanju long after your earthly form has taken glorious flight into the Void. All hail, Emperor Smith."

Smith seemed more embarrassed now than confused. "Again, thank you," he said, nodding awkwardly. The formality of Chiun's words made him feel as though he should stand or bow or something equally unseemly.

Remo recognized the big kiss-off when he heard it. "Um, Smitty," he said, casting a weary eye at Chiun. "He's telling you he's quitting."

Smith shot to his feet. "Quitting?"

Chiun wrinkled his nose distastefully. "A crude term," he said to Smith. "And inaccurate." He shot a withering glare at Remo. "I assure you that Sinanju does not quit. It moves on. But you need not be concerned, Wise Harold, for only a very small percentage of former emperors have met with foul play. Your safety is virtually assured, though vast oceans separate us."

"But—but we have a contract," Smith sputtered. "Remo?"

Remo held up his hands. "Don't look at me. I'm not getting into the middle of this again."

"The gold for the unfulfilled portion of the current contract will be returned to you," Chiun assured him.

"Whoa," Remo said, wheeling on Chiun. "You're giving rebates now?"

"Quiet, insolent one," Chiun shushed.

Smith was calculating quickly. "It will take several days to prepare the submarine for your return to Korea," he said. "I assume this is still the mode of transportation you prefer?"

"I do not wish that fat-faced son of Kim Il-Sung to greet me like a weepy maiden at the Pyongyang airport," Chiun sniffed.

"Then let your final days in my service end as they began. Here, at Folcroft. I will have your old rooms reopened and I will send for your things in Massachusetts."

Chiun considered. "You are gracious to the end, Emperor Smith," he said with a polite bow.

"And you honor me with your presence, Master of Sinanju," Smith replied. He returned the bow.

"Let's hold the frigging phone for a minute, shall we?" Remo countered, shocked by Smith's easy acceptance of Chiun's resignation. "You're just going to let him up and hi-de-ho out the door?"

"I don't seem to have a choice," Smith said.

"Wisdom flows like honey from your delicate lips," Chiun said, nodding serenely.

"Bulldookey," Remo snapped. "Each one of you thinks you're scamming the other, and whenever that happens I'm the one that always winds up holding the stinky end of the stick."

"Forgive him, Emperor," Chiun said. "He is crass and does not understand an agreement between his betters."

"Of course," Smith replied. He retook his seat. "I will make the preparations for your departure." And with the promise made, Smith once more began typing swiftly at his keyboard.

"Come, Remo," Chiun commanded. "We shall retire to our rooms." And with that the Master of Sinanju breezed from the office.

Remo watched Chiun go and then glanced back at Smith. The CURE director was hunched diligently over his hidden computer console.

"Right smack in the middle, every time," he muttered to himself. He slowly pulled the door closed.

Once Remo was gone, Smith peered up over the top of his rimless glasses.

His promise to Chiun of a submarine had been a delaying tactic.

While Smith ordinarily didn't like to proceed on instinct, at the moment his instincts were screaming that something big was happening in Wyoming. This was not the time for hardball contract negotiations.

Whatever Chiun's game was, Smith had to move fast. He had effectively stalled the Master of Sinanju for a few days. He hoped it would be enough.

Smith attacked the keyboard with renewed vigor. Time was of the essence.

13

Candy Clay was hiking through town on her way home from the movies.

It was late—much later than Candy was supposed to be out alone—but Heidi Lovell's father had gotten called away on an emergency job, so he wasn't able to give Candy a ride home like he'd promised. He left a note on the kitchen table telling Candy that she was welcome to stay overnight if she wanted and that he'd pick up the tab next time the two girls went to the movies together.

But Candy had swimming lessons early in the morning, so even though her father would kill her when he found out, she decided to walk the three miles home. Her father would have to learn that he couldn't treat her like a kid anymore. After all, she was starting fourth grade in the fall.

Arapahoe Street in Thermopolis was quieter than on most nights. Folks were worn-out after the big weekend rally. There was barely any traffic as Candy crossed the street. She saw a sign advertising the upcoming Hot Springs State Fair on the first weekend in May and she was a little embarrassed that she was as excited about the event as she had been when she was little. Passing the fair advertisement, she cut through the park toward the west side of town.

There were still signs and banners everywhere left over from the Jackson Cole rally, and when Candy saw his big owlish head staring at her from a poster in Pumpernick's restaurant window, she wondered what the big deal was. Everyone in town seemed to worship the senator. Heck, it was practically a public sin to say you were voting for T. Rex Calhoun.

She wondered what her father would say if she told him that Heidi's dad was voting for Calhoun.

Candy cut across the new construction site at Canyon Hills Road onto Shoshoni Street.

Shoshoni was still mostly wooded, though a few washed-out flecks of light in the distant blackness hinted that two or three new homes had been constructed at the far end of the street.

The city had recently sold this stretch of land to a private contractor, and development was supposed to begin in September.

Candy remembered hearing that there had been a big fight about the Thermopolis city council approving the sale, and now there was an even bigger fight about the lack of streetlights on this stretch of Shoshoni.

The city had a policy of not putting streetlights in wooded areas, and that was going to stand until the new houses were complete.

Candy knew her father had been upset about that decision. He railed about how dangerous Shoshoni Street was and how a lot of high-school kids used the area for a drag-racing strip weekend nights. Over and over he vowed that there was going to be hell to pay the day somebody got killed.

Her father could be such a drip sometimes.

Candy picked up a stick and dragged it in the powdery dirt at the edge of the road.

As she walked deeper into the enveloping darkness, she noticed for the first time a car parked in the shadows at the side of the road.

Candy heard the vehicle before she had really become aware of it, for, though its lights were off, the engine was running.

The car didn't move as she approached.

Candy couldn't see anyone inside, and when she was a few feet away from the vehicle, she stepped up onto the grassy embankment so she wouldn't get hit if the car drove off in a hurry. She was also a little curious to see what the car's occupants were doing hidden down behind the dashboard.

When she had gotten high enough up on the embankment and had drawn parallel to the car, she peered carefully down into the vehicle.

In spite of the darkness she could see the front and back seats of the big blue car clearly. But to Candy's great disappointment there was no one visible inside.

There was something spooky about the abandoned car.

Candy Clay was about to run home to tell her father about the parked car with its engine running, when something happened that would confirm the elder Clay's worst fears about the darkness on Shoshoni Street.

Someone suddenly raced out of the woods and grabbed Candy from behind.

Candy tried to fight as she felt a strong hand wrap around her neck. All at once she felt herself lifted into the air and she realized with horror that she was being carried bodily to the phantom car.

She thrashed and twisted frantically in the air. A hand covered her mouth, its thumb and forefinger clamped firmly over her nose. Candy tried, but couldn't pull in a breath.

The young girl twisted her head hard to the side one last time, desperately trying to catch a glimpse of her attacker, but her kidnapper jerked the head back. A little too hard.

There was a hideous snap, and Candy Clay's head lolled lifelessly to one side.

Candy's attacker propped the girl—now dead-weight—against the side of the quietly purring car and spun her around. A pair of small, dead eyes stared blankly back at her.

"Shit," said Esther Clear-Seer. She shook Candy Clay a few times. The little girl's head flopped from side to side like a rag doll that had lost all the stuffing in its neck.

She dropped Candy Clay into the litter-strewed gutter and climbed quickly behind the wheel of her car, muttering all the way.

"Spit, shit and double shit," Esther Clear-Seer hissed angrily. She drove away, leaving the body of Candy Clay at the roadside. Esther needed another virgin. Fast. She hoped the nine-o'clock show at the local movie theater hadn't gotten out yet.

Ten-year-old Candy Clay lay in the filth of the gutter for almost six hours until she was spotted by a police cruiser. They would have found her sooner, a police spokesman said the next day, but they were already busy, what with the abduction of the eleven-year-old Forrester girl near the Wishy-Washy Wash-ateria.

Also, the sheriff's office complained, Shoshoni Street was way too dark. Somebody ought to see about putting up some lights.

When they read the report in the papers the next day, the residents agreed that the sensible thing would be to get some streetlights put up on Shoshoni.

Apollo had claimed numbers three and four.

14

The Pythia writhed on the tripod as the yellow smoke swirled around her head. Curls of chestnut brown hair rippled across her porcelain skin as she tossed her head back and forth in ecstasy.

"Your life will be changed in the near future," the Pythia intoned.

Beside her, Kaspar smiled. "The meaning of that is obvious," he called down to the well-dressed man at the base of the hill.

"Can she be more specific?" the man called up hopefully. He glanced around the torchlit chamber but saw only the woman who had led him through the tunnel to this place.

"You have made your future your own," the Pythia rasped.

The man's face became a puzzled frown. He wore a political button on his expensive gray flannel jacket. It said Vote Calhoun.

"The result of the campaign," Kaspar explained. "My master has proclaimed it a foregone conclusion."

A flicker of a smile toyed nervously with the corners of the man's broad lips. "You're telling me I'm going to win?" he asked.

"All will be as I have foreseen," the Pythia announced with finality.

With that the smoke from the crevice puffed to a near stop—as if someone had doused a fire—and the Pythia's writhing slowed to a jumble of tiny, spastic nervous tics. The young girl's chin dropped lazily to her chest.

Kaspar tapped the blunt end of his wooden staff ceremoniously against the metal grate beneath the tripod twice before descending the rocky steps to the earthen floor.

This was T. Rex Calhoun's second visit to the Pythia Pit. He had been advised to stop here by his party's bigwigs in Washington before Senator Cole availed himself of the infallible predictions of the Ragnarok Oracle. If he was the first in the water at Ragnarok, it was suggested by the higher-ups, perhaps the enigmatic Kaspar would see to it that Jackson Cole was excluded from the Pythia's oracles altogether.

"The future is secure," Kaspar said as he approached Calhoun.

"That's great. That's really, really great." He sounded more like an excited teenager than a serious senatorial candidate. "By the way, it's very kind of you to waive the fee," Calhoun added with a nervous smile.

Kaspar waved the staff in a dismissive arc. "My only interest is that the right man represent our fine state."

Calhoun was still apologetic. "The campaign has limited funds," he said with an awkward shrug.

"Of course."

Kaspar knew full well that Calhoun had married a

young woman with a trust fund in excess of three million dollars. Not included in this amount were her family's vast real-estate holdings and a burgeoning stock portfolio that she stood to inherit when her father passed away. The only thing the old man insisted on was that T. Rex Calhoun make something of himself. It was this that had motivated his father-in-law to manipulate the opposition party's political apparatus in order to ensure that his son-in-law became the candidate that would face off against Jackson Cole in the fall. Compared to the huge chunk of change the old man had already pumped into Calhoun's campaign coffers, the fifty-thousand-dollar fee for the services of the Ragnarok Oracle had been a mere trifle.

T. Rex Calhoun, however, had learned from the brightest stars in his party that it was best to talk poor, even if by comparison your personal wealth made the income of your opponent look like that of an unsuccessful paperboy.

"I'm glad I could do you a little favor," Calhoun said with the idiotic giggle his handlers had been unable to quash. "It sort of makes me feel like I'm pulling my weight."

"Quite," Kaspar said flatly. He glanced over at Esther Clear-Seer, who stood silently in the shadows near the door tapestry. "You have spoken to your friend on my behalf?" he said quietly to Calhoun.

"Absotively," T. Rex said in a feeble attempt at jocularity.

Kaspar's features remained bland.

Calhoun sobered slightly. "He'll be expecting you in Washington a week from Wednesday," he said, clearing his throat. "They start at nine, but they'll want you there at least an hour before."

"Excellent."

The Pythia let out a sudden yelp, flinging her head up and staring wildly around the chamber, then her chin settled back down to her chest. It was a movement that Kaspar had witnessed in all of the Pythias at one time or another—a not uncommon aftereffect of the sulphur smoke's power.

Calhoun watched the girl shudder a few times, as if chilled. All at once the tension seemed to drain from her body and she was still, save the occasional labored intake of air. Her rhythmic breathing sounded like a softly squeaking door.

"Is she okay?" Calhoun asked Kaspar.

"She is too young," Kaspar said loudly.

He seemed to direct that last comment at the woman over by the door. There was an edge to his voice, and T. Rex Calhoun realized that he must have stumbled into a private argument.

Calhoun squinted up at the tiny figure on the tripod. "That's not the same girl that was here the other day," he said.

"The Pythia periodically demands a new vessel," Kaspar explained.

"Ah," Calhoun said, nodding even though he did not understand what the strange little man was saying. "She looks kind of familiar," he added.

"Doubtless you read about her in the papers," Kaspar said with a tiny smile.

And T. Rex Calhoun realized with a sudden flash of horror that he did indeed recognize the girl. She and three others had had their pictures plastered across the front pages of papers from Cody to Cheyenne. He knew with a feeling of dread that the girl who had prophesied for him a few short days before had been another of Thermopolis's kidnapping victims. This girl—who looked drugged out of her mind and sounded like an eighty-year-old emphysema sufferer—was the latest victim. He even remembered her name. Allison Forrester. It was her disappearance, as well as the death of another girl named Clay, that had brought the kidnapping spree to the attention of the national media.

When he was finally able to tear his eyes away from the girl, Calhoun was unable to mask his look of abject fear from Kaspar.

"In case you were considering contacting the authorities for some reason," Kaspar said smugly, waving his staff in Allison Forrester's direction, "I would find it difficult to remain silent about your unusual...appetites."

Calhoun puffed up his chest. "What do you mean?" he bluffed.

Kaspar drew his tongue lazily across his teeth, making a peculiar sucking noise. "I have heard from an unimpeachable source that you have certain animal cravings," he said with an evil smile. "Tell me, how young must the boys be? Twelve? Thirteen? Younger? Your father-in-law is a powerful man indeed, to hide something so explosive from the public."

In the most pragmatic part of his near dormant brain, T. Rex Calhoun did some rapid calculations.

Kaspar, through the Pythia, knew everything and was threatening to spill the beans if Calhoun opened his mouth.

If the news got out, his father-in-law would go ape-shit; his wife would divorce him; he probably couldn't, if his life depended on it, get his partnership back at the law firm where he'd met the soon-to-be-former Mrs. Calhoun; and he'd be flat, dead busted broke.

On the other hand, he could screw his lips up tighter than a Mafia clam and land in Washington come January.

So what if this man was responsible for the disappearance or death of at least four young girls? So what if T. Rex Calhoun could blow the case wide open? And so what if T. Rex Calhoun was responsible for brokering a deal that was going to get this vile kidnapper national attention?

In a matter of seconds T. Rex Calhoun reached a decision that was more firmly set in stone than any in the history of politics. And that decision was: different strokes for different folks.

"So you kidnap a little," Calhoun said with a magnanimous shrug. "It's not like you're killing anyone." He thought of Candy Clay. "It's not like you're killing all of them," he added with oily smoothness.

"I knew you'd see it my way."

Calhoun glanced up at the Pythia. The dead eyes of the girl were aimed down at him, boring into the blackest depths of his soul. He felt an icy frisson race up his spine.

"I bet you did," T. Rex Calhoun said. And he meant it.

"If it eases your conscience, you will be pleased to know that they are serving a much higher purpose," Kaspar said.

"Doesn't interest me," Calhoun said. "Look, I've

got to go." He started for the tapestry door but stopped suddenly. "Oh, I forgot to give you this." He dug deep in his pants pocket and removed a sweaty scrap of paper, handing it over to Kaspar. "That's the private Washington number. They want you to call this week for the preinterview."

"Thank you," Kaspar said with a graciousness that was all condescension. "You are most kind."

"Don't mention it," Calhoun said. *"Please."* He headed for the door.

Esther Clear-Seer hefted aside the tapestry at his approach.

"I'll see my own way out," Calhoun growled.

The candidate passed beneath the tapestry, and Esther let it slip from her fingers. The heavy cloth flapped dully against the cinder block door frame.

With a blank glance at Esther Clear-Seer, Kaspar proceeded to follow Calhoun. She barred his way.

"What's your game, Kaspar?" Esther asked.

He paused impatiently. "Do not concern yourself with the affairs of gods you do not acknowledge," he said to her.

Kaspar started to move around her, but she slipped her hand beneath the tapestry and planted it against the door frame, blocking his path with her forearm. "Three kidnappings and a murder make me concerned," she said. "Not to mention your accomplice."

Slowly Kaspar trained his penetrating reptilian eyes on her. "Pangs of conscience do not suit you," he said.

"It's not conscience, Kaspar, just simple business sense. This ranch is already the center of all evil as far as those hicks in Thermopolis are concerned. I'm surprised nobody's accused me of any kidnappings yet.''

"Don't blame me for your incompetence," Kaspar said sharply. "I am not the one who limited your search to Thermopolis. You could have driven a hundred miles in any direction to collect worthy vessels. You chose the route of least resistance available to you. And the ones you have brought me are nearly useless." He indicated the shell of the Forrester girl seated up on the tripod. "The Pythia has predicted that I will not get a week out of this one."

"A week?" Esther said disappointedly. She thought of how nearly she came to being caught when she picked up Allison Forrester near the coin laundry. A police cruiser had followed her a few blocks, and she was terrified that they'd pull her over and find the unconscious girl slumped on the floorboards. It was a false alarm. But the prospect of being arrested and imprisoned for kidnapping was terrifying. And now she was going to have to go through it all over again in another week.

"Apollo's emissary needs stronger vessels," Kaspar said. "These you have collected thus far are so weak they are not worthy of the Pythia's essence."

"What about the one you brought here with you? Why did she last so long?"

"That vessel was athletic. She had been a gymnast in her previous existence. As such, she was stronger than the ones you are bringing me. Now, if you please..."

Esther relented. She removed her hand from the door frame, and it dropped leadenly to her side. Once it was free, the tapestry rocked almost imperceptibly back and forth in the dancing torchlight.

Kaspar lifted the heavy tapestry and started to exit the room, but he paused momentarily. He turned to Esther.

"You no doubt heard that I am going to Washington next week," he said. "That night, so the Pythia has instructed me, another vessel will be ready for harvesting. She is in Thermopolis, but the Pythia has indicated that she will not be difficult to obtain. I will give you detailed instructions before my departure." He squared his slim shoulders. "Perhaps we will make your job a little easier for you this one time," he said. And with that he vanished behind the tapestry.

"Don't do me any favors," Esther muttered bitterly.

Before she, too, left the room, Esther cast one last look up at the girl on the tripod. None of them had been easy to collect, and it only promised to get harder. With a self-pitying sigh, she followed Kaspar out the door.

On the lips of the Pythia, behind the curling wisps of yellow phosphorescent smoke, something that almost appeared to be a smile followed Esther's retreating form.

15

It had been ten days since Remo Williams had been dragged back to Folcroft Sanitarium, and he had been suffering from cabin fever nearly as long.

Smith would have had a fit if Remo strayed into the patient wing of the sanitarium, and so Remo had taken to prowling the empty, antiseptic hallways of the isolation wards of the building where they were staying like a tormented, lost soul.

There had been long stretches of time in the past when he and Chiun had lived at Folcroft, but Remo had never been comfortable here. He figured it had something to do with the fact that this was the place where he had awakened after he had been tried and executed for a crime he didn't commit and railroaded into working for the secret organization, his previous existence erased from the public record. A little detail like that tended to take the shine off a new environment.

Remo found the door to his suite of rooms and shoved open the gunmetal gray panel.

A low, singsongy voice assaulted his ears as soon as he entered. It was the same off-key melody Remo had been forced to listen to for the past ten days.

"I'm back," Remo announced glumly.

Chiun didn't stop humming. If anything, the noises emanating from his mouth and nose had become even louder. He was puttering around his collection of steamer trunks in the far corner of the room, and the silver dragons on the back of his fiery red kimono appeared to leap and cavort with each cheerful toss of his bony shoulders.

"Glad you missed me," Remo muttered to himself. He had walked to a convenience store in town to pick up a clutch of newspapers. He pulled them out from under his arm, and set them on the bland, hospital-green carpeting.

He then sank down to the floor and proceeded to spread the papers across the rug in front of him, like a child reading the Sunday funnies. Remo scanned the headlines.

There were no stories of further kidnappings in Thermopolis.

When he had first heard about the attempted abduction and murder of Candy Clay, as well as the kidnapping of the Forrester girl, Remo had wanted to hop the first flight back to Wyoming. He was annoyed with himself for not looking into the original abductions when he had the chance. But Smith had insisted that Remo stay at Folcroft until the CURE director was able to piece together accounts of the Truth Church Ranch.

Smith wanted to sift through the bank records of everyone who had visited the ranch, and the computer searches were taking longer than he had anticipated.

Smith had also argued, quite logically, that with all the press attention Thermopolis had been getting for the kidnappings in addition to the already choking media coverage of the senatorial race, Remo would not be able to perform his job with anonymity. With much regret Remo had relented.

So all he could do now was sit and wait.

And the form the waiting had taken was a daily study of the national papers to see if the media swarm in Thermopolis had diminished.

Remo was leafing through the entertainment section of one of the New York papers when Chiun's humming abruptly ceased. The Master of Sinanju snapped the bronze latches on a gleaming blue trunk and shuffled happily into the center of the room.

"Welcome back to the land of the living," Remo commented.

"I had to be certain nothing was stolen," Chiun said matter-of-factly. "Who knows what manner of thieving imbecile Smith employed to carry my precious trunks from that backward state-that-is-not-a-state. They could have lined their pockets with my most cherished possessions."

"You've been taking inventory for more than a week," Remo growled. "Every stolen hotel towel and packet of stale oyster crackers accounted for?"

"If you are asking if the meager possessions of a poor old man, which will bring him joy in the twilight years of his life, have been left undisturbed, the answer is yes," Chiun replied coldly.

"I'm sorry," Remo said with a sigh. Chiun had barely spoken to him in a week, and Remo hadn't meant to pick a fight with him right now.

Chiun appeared to accept the apology. He had carefully spread his woven tatami mat on the carpet when their things had first arrived, and Chiun now alighted on it, settling to the floor as gently as a downy feather in a windless room.

"Is there news from Smith?" he asked.

"News?" Remo asked, puzzled.

"On the vessel that will return us to Sinanju."

Inwardly Remo rolled his eyes. He doubted Smith had even bothered to begin making arrangements with the Navy for their transport back to North Korea. There was going to be hell to pay when that bill finally came due.

Remo shrugged nonchalantly. "I haven't asked him," he said noncommittally, and turned his eyes back to the newspaper's Ann Landers column.

Chiun's face grew puzzled. "That is strange," he said. "In the past, he has arranged transport for us on much shorter notice."

Remo only grunted.

Chiun's hazel eyes narrowed suspiciously at Remo, but his pupil remained captivated by a male correspondent who was having trouble coping with his female supervisor's amorous advances. Finally Chiun produced a small black remote control device from the folds of his kimono and snapped on the television set in the corner of the room.

The vacuous heads of two anchorpeople appeared on the screen, and Chiun settled in to watch the videotaped highlights of the day's degeneration of Western civilization.

Remo pulled his nose out of the paper. It seemed as if Chiun's interest in the tardy submarine had passed for now. Remo was determined not to get in the middle of anything between their employer and the Master of Sinanju. But there was still a question that begged an answer. Something that Chiun had brushed impatiently aside as immaterial while he had been inspecting the contents of his steamer trunks.

"Little Father," Remo said, "you never did tell me why we were quitting."

"Shh, Remo," Chiun urged. "I am busy." Chiun's bright eyes were staring at the bubble-brained anchorwoman on the screen as she traded overwritten ad-libs with her blow-dried coanchor.

"You've been busy all week," Remo complained. "This decision of yours affects me, too. I think I have a right to know why we're leaving."

Chiun sighed. He carefully pressed the Mute button—something he wished all whites were fitted with—and turned to face his pupil. Behind him the coanchors silently giggled and quipped their way through terrible stories of flood and famine.

"You have surmised that our departure is connected in some way to our hasty withdrawal from the military encampment," Chiun said.

"The thought had crossed my mind," Remo admitted.

Chiun considered. He stroked his wispy beard thoughtfully. At last he spoke. "Remo, I have never told you the story of the braggart Master Tang."

Remo was suddenly sorry he had asked for an explanation, realizing that he had inadvertently opened himself up to another Sinanju legend. He had heard these stories countless times in the past. More accurately, he had heard *most* of the stories. He usually tended to nod off about two minutes into each. If Sinanju legends were nothing else, they were great tranquilizers. Now he would have to sit through an hour's worth of the braggart Master Tang's brush with history.

"Didn't Tang discover Japan?" Remo asked, wearily.

"I said he was a braggart, Remo, not an idiot," said Chiun. "Please do not interrupt."

"I'm all ears," Remo said, resignedly.

"That is hereditary, Remo. There is nothing I can do about them." He folded his hands in his lap, settling into his role as storyteller. "Before he became known as a braggart, Master Tang suffered a far more ignoble distinction," Chiun began. "Remember, this was well after the time of the previous Master Tang, who was trained by the Master Ti-Sung."

"Of course," said Remo.

"Just so you do not confuse the two," Chiun explained. "I know it is difficult sometimes for your mind to focus on more than one thing at a time. Sometimes it has difficulty even with the one thing."

"Yeah, Chiun," sighed Remo, "We all know how dense I am."

Chiun continued. "You remember the rotten egg odor that surrounded the woman in that encampment of idiots?"

"How could I miss it," said Remo. "It smelled like her breakfast was repeating."

"Master Tang encountered that same odor in the past. It has been so recorded in the Sinanju histories."

"How do you record a smell?" Remo asked, frowning.

"The tunic of the braggart Tang has been preserved so that all future Masters will recognize the odor and beware. And it is a most deadly future that we are now trying to avoid.''

Because he could sense the deep concern in Chiun's demeanor, and out of respect for his teacher, Remo decided to listen to every last word of the braggart Master Tang legend.

That determination lasted all of four seconds.

"Hey, Chiun, look," Remo said, pointing to the television.

A hunching, intense figure with a pair of giant, thick, black-framed glasses glared out from the screen. An ugly print tie was framed on either side by a pair of bright red suspenders. He wore no suit jacket, and his blue-striped dress shirt, though newly ironed, somehow still appeared wrinkled. His long, avian nose and black eyes gave him the appearance of a rumpled buzzard.

Remo stood and took a few steps toward the TV.

He recognized the man as Barry Duke, the cable-TV talk-show host who had inexplicably become a kingmaker two presidential races before, even though he had yet to make anybody king of anything. Duke's star, as well as his ratings, tended to rise dramatically during campaign seasons.

Beside him sat a slight man in a neatly tailored blue suit. Duke ignored the man at his side and blathered pointlessly at the camera, his mouth snapping open and closed like a gulping fish. The oddness of the spectacle was heightened by the continuation of the television's mute mode.

Chiun was losing patience with Remo's interruptions.

"Remo, your appetite for distraction never ceases to annoy me." He tilted his head to look at the screen.

A caption glowed beneath the tiny man who sat beside Barry Duke.

Remo read the name aloud. "Mark Kaspar," he said. "Chiun, isn't that the name Esther Clear-Seer mentioned?"

He was just turning back to Chiun when he saw something black and shiny fly from the tips of the old man's fingers.

The thrown remote control impacted the television screen in an explosion of blue-and-orange sparks. Jagged chunks of picture tube crashed to the rug and tiny glass shards from a dozen shattered tubes sprayed from the interior of the set amid a plume of black smoke.

"Are you nuts!" Remo yelled. He hopped through the mine field of sparks and broken glass and pulled the plug on the television. It continued to spill a cloud of thick, acrid smoke into the room.

"You were not listening," Chiun said placidly.

"Dammit, Chiun, what's gotten into you lately?" Remo griped. "I think that was one of the guys we're after."

"We are not after anyone," Chiun corrected sternly. "We are currently between clients. Now, sit down, Remo, so that I might continue the story of Tang in peace."

"Master Tang can wait," Remo said, stepping carefully through the shattered glass toward the door. "I've got to find a broom and clean this mess up."

After Remo had gone, Chiun cast a sorrowful eye over the remnants of the television. It was a shame he had been forced to destroy the wonderfully entertaining device, but if he hadn't Remo would have been off on some fool's errand before he had learned all of the facts.

That this Kaspar on the television was the same one the Clear-Seer woman had spoken of, Chiun had no doubt. Even on the small picture screen Chiun had seen the faint trace of yellow on his fingertips.

The man was obviously Greek. How fitting. All was as it had been foretold.

Alone in his basement room at Folcroft, Chiun's face was grim. When Remo heard the tale of Master Tang, he would understand.

"WOW, THAT'S just amazing," Barry Duke garbled excitedly to his television audience. "You say you're not affiliated in any way with either of the two major parties?"

"I'm totally independent, Barry," Mark Kaspar said proudly. "But that doesn't mean there isn't common ground between the parties. I think everyone can agree on that point." He paused only a second. "Except, of course, the Republicans and Democrats."

The next five seconds were filled with a frightening sound which emanated from Barry Duke's throat. It sounded like someone had filled a blender with rocks and hit the Puree switch. This was Barry Duke's trademark laugh.

"You sound like a man running for political office," Duke announced once he had flipped the switch of his jocularity mode to the standby position.

Mark Kaspar's features grew concerned. "That isn't up to me," he said somberly. "I've got no political aspirations. I don't do things for selfish reasons, which, Barry, I think you'll agree seems to be the motivation behind everyone who gets into the game of politics these days. No, I long for a simpler time. A time when people did things out of love for their country or for their god. I think that can happen again in America, but not without a lot of hard work and many, many sacrifices.''

At this, Kaspar seemed to smile at his own private joke, and for an instant the reptile beneath almost overtook him. Then his smile broadened and he announced, ''To address your comment, Barry, if the American people decided today that I should run for something, obviously I would have to give it serious consideration.''

Barry Duke shuddered visibly at the words. ''Oooo,'' he announced to his audience. ''This man sounds serious.''

Kaspar appeared to take the talk-show host's quirky mannerisms in stride. He was a different man from the one who had shown up in the Truth Church compound eight months before. On television, Kaspar was uncharacteristically jovial and charismatic. He smiled and joked with Barry Duke and grew serious only when the questions demanded a level of stoicism.

Eventually the conversation turned to national politics, and Kaspar confided his own view that the leader of the free world should be someone who was able to find qualified individuals to run even the most mundane positions in the federal government. To fail in this, Kaspar felt, was a sure sign of weakness that America couldn't afford to demonstrate in these perilous times.

"And you think this is the case now?"

"Far be it from me to throw stones," Kaspar began, "but we can take our current president as a prime example. He's nominated Guthrie Mudge of MUT as assistant secretary of state. Talk around Capitol Hill is Mudge is a shoe-in for the job." Kaspar leaned forward conspiratorially. "I am guaranteeing you, Barry, that Mudge is not going to get that post. And if the President can't work any magic with the boys on Cap for something as simple as a junior State Department appointment, I worry about the next time he has to sit down and talk tough with the Japanese or Germans, or even the Russians."

Barry Duke said, "Wow! This man is going out on a limb."

Even Duke, who understood politics about as well as a brick understands quantum physics, knew that Congress wasn't going to fight the President over a nothing appointment like Mudge's. Duke immediately changed the subject. "You're from Wyoming," he informed Kaspar.

"The Equality State," Kaspar returned proudly, as if he were instrumental in Wyoming's decision the previous century that allowed women the right to vote.

"There's a hot Senate race going on out there now," Barry Duke said. "Care to make any prognostications?"

Kaspar laughed. "Just that the race isn't as hot as everyone thinks," he said. "Jackson Cole isn't polling very high, and I have it on good authority that his opponent, T. Rex Calhoun, is about to drop out of the race because of some troubling personal problems."

For the first time in his on-camera career, Barry

Duke seemed at a loss for words. His office had endured call after call from T. Rex Calhoun on Kaspar's behalf. Calhoun had even managed to get the chairman of his party to put in a call in favor of Kaspar. Duke had been hesitant to put a national nonentity like Kaspar on the air—no matter how influential his friends—until Calhoun's father-in-law had agreed to foot the legal bills for Duke's latest divorce. Now Kaspar was using this forum to turn on the man who had been responsible for helping him step into the national arena.

"What kind of problems is Calhoun facing?" Duke asked after swallowing his bewilderment.

"Let me just say that I hope the charges aren't true and leave it at that, okay, Barry?" It was a nod and a wink to the host.

"Wow!" said Barry Duke, reiterating the interjection he fell back on whenever he couldn't think of anything else to say. "Let's open the phone lines up to callers now. Orvis from Bourbon, Kentucky, you have a question for Mark Kaspar?"

"Yeah, hi, Barry," the caller began nervously. "I just want to know how soon Mark is going to run for office and where I can sign up to help!"

"Wowee!" Barry Duke exclaimed, in the hyperexcited manner that looked out of place on his sagging features. "I guess there's one vote for you out there already!"

Kaspar shook his head. "I only want what the people of America want," he said.

Apparently the people of America wanted Mark Kaspar.

Several more callers phoned in their support for a

Kaspar candidacy during the show's first segment. While the number of calls coming in to the "Barry Duke Live" switchboard could never be deemed a flood, they were still a good fifty percent higher than most Wednesday nights.

Barry Duke got the good news through the radio earpiece concealed under a side bulge of his jet black hair. An awkward smile rose up beneath his hawk-like nose.

"One more call before the break. Gus from Houston, Texas, you're next on the line with Mark Kaspar."

Although he was trying to disguise it, the voice on the line was distinctly Southern, with clipped, nasal tones. The man launched into an attack even before Barry Duke finished speaking.

"That Kaspar feller is the cheatenist low-down dog that ever crawled on his belly in a flea-filled wagon rut. He is stealin' another man's life right out from under the noses of everyone in the country out there, and you, Barry Duke, are helpin' and aidin' right along in his goldurn act of thievery. Me and my world-class family are shocked, I say, shocked at the shamelessness of this cheap display."

Barry Duke's eyes squinted in suspicion under his enormous glasses. "Is this by any chance Moss Monroe?" he asked.

The caller immediately hung up.

"Wow!" said Barry Duke. "I think it's time we took a little break. We'll be back to political prognosticator Mark Kaspar right after this."

REMO SNAPPED OFF the television in Smith's office.

The image of Barry Duke collapsed into a single

white dot in the center of the tiny black-and-white screen.

"I guess we know their game plan," he told Smith.

Leaving Chiun, Remo had made a beeline for Smith's office. He and the CURE director had watched the "Barry Duke Live" program with growing concern.

"I am not certain we do," Smith said somberly.

"The guy is setting himself up to run for President," Remo said, jerking a thumb toward the TV. "I think he made it pretty clear."

Smith didn't wholly agree. The older man knew that on the Barry Duke talk show, as on most shows of its type, there were very few real surprises. The questions, as well as a sketchy version of the responses, were thrashed out well before airtime. What made Smith sit up and take notice were Kaspar's comments about the Wyoming Senate race. Obviously Kaspar felt he had something pretty damning on senatorial candidate T. Rex Calhoun if he was willing to take the risk of mentioning it on national television. Wordlessly Smith began typing rapidly at his computer keyboard.

"What was that stuff about the state department?" Remo asked.

Smith pursed his lips as he continued to type. "I honestly have no idea," he admitted. "Sadly, Kaspar is correct. The assistant-secretary-of-state position is not something most politicians are willing to weigh in on. According to my information, the President has ample votes to place his nominee."

"Then the guy is just plain schizo," Remo said with a shrug.

Smith's sudden intake of air brought Remo to his feet. The old man was peering at his computer, a look of dread on his lemony features.

"Calhoun was arrested on child-molestation charges three times in the past five years," Smith announced.

Remo bounded around the desk and quickly scanned the information on the computer screen buried beneath the gleaming black surface. It was a police file from Cheyenne, listing Calhoun's infractions alongside the dates the various charges had been filed. A picture of the candidate himself stared glumly up from the screen.

"This is a pretty big thing for the press to miss, isn't it?" Remo asked angrily.

Smith's hands became a blur as his slender fingers dug deeper into the Cheyenne police records.

"The charges in all three instances were dropped," he announced momentarily. "Calhoun was never brought to trial."

"I smell a payoff," said Remo.

Smith nodded as he considered Remo's words. "Calhoun's father-in-law is quite wealthy," he admitted. "It is a plausible scenario."

"You bet your ass it's plausible," Remo griped. "First the skunk buys his way out of the state penitentiary, and then Daddy runs out and buys him a Senate seat. If Kaspar's got the goods on him, I say we let the chips fall where they land."

"Remo," Smith interjected, "we mustn't become sidetracked. Our primary concern remains the Truth Church itself. From what I've been able to determine, Kaspar has been directly benefiting from the subsidiary Truth Church account."

"It can't possibly help the guy's political aspirations to be hooked up with some nutty doomsday cult," Remo said.

"There is nothing that directly links Kaspar to the Truth Church," Smith explained. "If it came to it, he could always claim ignorance, saying that his organization accepted payment from individual church members only. But there is no doubt that he is in partnership with Esther Clear-Seer. Perhaps she is engineering this entire political movement of Kaspar's to create an ally in the federal government."

"Then let me take her out, Smitty," Remo begged. "I'm going out of my mind cooped up here."

Smith nodded in agreement as he tapped out a few brief commands on his computer. "If it is as I suspect…" he muttered as he awaited the results. "Yes," he said, momentarily. "I've checked with Washington National, and Kaspar is not scheduled to return to Wyoming until the day after tomorrow. We have a window of opportunity with negative press attention in Thermopolis. If you fly into Worland tonight, you can be gone before he returns."

"What if he's one of the bad guys?" Remo said. "Shouldn't I wait and zap him, too?"

"We will deal with that when it becomes necessary." Smith paused. He seemed filled with dread by what he was about to ask. "Where is Master Chiun?" he asked finally.

"He's downstairs sitting on his steamer trunks waiting to catch the next sub to Korea."

"Er, yes. The submarine."

Remo raised his hands, palm up. "Don't tell me,

Smitty," he warned. "I don't want to know. It's between you and him."

"Fine," Smith said, relaxing somewhat. "You will fly to Wyoming alone."

Remo was quietly relieved. Chiun had been acting strangely ever since he had conjured up a thousand-year-old Sinanju legend from the malodorous cloud that surrounded Esther Clear-Seer. The old Korean would never have allowed Remo to return to the Truth Church ranch.

Another part of his mind hoped that the inevitable blowup over the no-show submarine would happen while he was out of town.

In any event Remo was no longer stuck on the sidelines. And that made him very glad indeed.

"I'll be back tomorrow with the false Prophetess's noggin on a platter," Remo announced as he left the office.

Smith started to push himself to his feet, ready to go after Remo, but he stopped in midmovement. If he objected now, it might prompt Remo to follow through on his threat. Reluctantly Smith settled back in his seat, hoping to himself that Remo was only joking about the final resting place of Esther Clear-Seer's head.

If not, an old coal furnace in the Folcroft basement would become the crematorium for the Prophetess's cranial remains.

16

"I just talked to Barry Duke's producer, and he says your positive-phone-reaction ratio was eighty-five percent. They're telling me that Moss Monroe's the only one who ever came close to touching those numbers." Michael Princippi was more excited than he had been the first time he and Kiki had gone "all the way" in the tiny back seat of his Volkswagen Beetle, circa 1963. "They want to have you on again next week," he added happily.

Kaspar was seated in the green room of the "Barry Duke Live" cable program, reading a copy of the *Washington Post*. He gazed blandly over the masthead at Princippi. "Tell them no," he said thinly.

Princippi was crestfallen. "You've got to do it, Mark," he said. "It's the only way to keep yourself in the public eye. The 2000 presidential race is a good ways off."

"A child must walk before he can run," Kaspar said by way of explanation.

"Huh?"

"Advice given me by the Pythia," Kaspar said.

Princippi glanced around nervously. "Ixnay on the ithiapay," he whispered once certain there was no one within earshot. "Believe me, any whiff of psychic sulphur can torpedo your nomination before you're even out of drydock.'' He folded his hands in supplication. ''Please do the show. It'll cement your image in the public's mind. Trust me, the American people have the attention spans of white mice.''

Kaspar folded the paper into neat quarters and placed it on the ugly plaid sofa cushion beside him. ''We will do Barry Duke's program again,'' he said. ''But we will do it on my terms. There are certain housekeeping chores that I must first attend to. Think of this as a relay race, not a hundred-yard dash.''

With a disappointed sigh, Princippi nodded. ''Okay, I'll tell them,'' he said reluctantly. ''But they're not going to be happy about it.'' He paused at the door. ''By the way.'' His thick eyebrows gathered together worriedly. ''I was just on the phone with the chairman of my party—''

''Your *former* party,'' Kaspar interjected.

''Right,'' Princippi said, with a nod that dismissed his lifelong political affiliation as irrelevant. ''Anyway, he called up screaming to find out what kind of dirt you have on Calhoun. He almost plotzed when they handed *me* the phone. Guess he figured I was gone for good.'' Princippi sounded pleased at the prospect of rattling cages in the organization that had shut him out for over a decade.

A slight smile crossed Kaspar's lips, and Princippi half expected to see the tip of a forked tongue dart out from between his near absent lips.

''I am not surprised that he would be displeased,'' Kaspar allowed.

''Displeased?'' Princippi scoffed. ''He's screaming for your blood, along with Calhoun's for putting him in the middle of this Barry Duke thing. And then—get this—he asks me to see if you'll come over and join the party.''

Princippi nodded. ''A pragmatic man,'' he said.

At that moment a stagehand stuck his head around the door. ''Sorry to interrupt, Mr. Kaspar,'' he said. ''But there's a call for you on line three.'' He indicated the simple black phone on the end table near Kaspar's elbow, then slipped away.

''I've got to make a few calls myself,'' Princippi said, excusing himself. ''I've set up an informal breakfast meeting with some friendly press for tomorrow.''

He left Kaspar alone in the green room.

Kaspar hefted the bulky receiver and depressed the flashing button.

''Yes?''

Esther Clear-Seer's shrill voice practically leapt through the phone like an escaped wildcat. ''Kaspar, what the hell is going on?'' she demanded.

''It would be helpful if you could be more specific,'' he said, examining his fingernails. He noticed a chip on his right index finger and wondered if there was someplace nearby where he could get a good manicure this late at night.

''How specific do you want me to be over an open line?'' she asked through tightly clenched teeth.

Kaspar looked toward the open green-room door and hoped no one was eavesdropping around the corner. ''Is there a problem?'' he asked calmly.

''Only that I was stupid enough to get hooked up with you,'' she said sarcastically.

He let the remark pass. ''Did you procure the latest vessel, as instructed?''

"I followed your directions, Kaspar," Esther said tartly. "Your new 'vessel,'" she said, her tone dripping malice, "is going completely psycho."

His voice remained calm, but he felt his stomach clench like a hollow fist.

"What do you mean?" he asked.

"Psycho. Bonkers. Stark raving bananas, Kaspar," Esther hissed. "I put the vessel up on the stool and she immediately started jerking around like she was on angel dust or something."

Kaspar relaxed. "That is not unusual for a new Pythia," he said.

"Yeah, well is it unusual for a new Pythia to be screaming about Sinanju being on the way?"

Kaspar felt his already cold blood turn to ice. "Sinanju? *Now?*"

"She's keeps yelling about the first hour."

Kaspar knew that that meant sometime between midnight and 1:00 a.m., mountain time. With the time difference, if he got a flight out of Washington National within the next hour, he could make it back. But it would be close.

"Brief the acolytes," Kaspar instructed briskly. "Make it clear to them that this is not a drill situation. I will return as quickly as possible, but if I do not arrive in time, you must be ready."

"Oh, I'll be ready," said Esther. "I owe that old chink a shot in the nose."

"Just be prepared."

"What about your new vessel?" Esther asked. "She's going to kill herself the way she's thrashing around up there."

"That would be problematic," Kaspar said.

"Yeah," Esther said indifferently. "Why?"

"Just take special care of this one," Kaspar advised.

"All right already," Esther said. "Just hurry back here. I don't know why this new one is so special," she added, severing the connection.

Kaspar listened to the humming dial tone momentarily. In spite of the grave prospect of another Sinanju visit, he allowed himself a tight smile. "You will find out soon enough," he said, quietly hanging up the phone.

KASPAR HAD BEEN very specific about when and where Esther Clear-Seer would find his latest vessel: 9:30 p.m., Wednesday. The precise time he would be on the "Barry Duke Live" talk show.

Esther thought it was strange that this late in the game Kaspar would help out with the procurement of a new Pythia, and she found it odder still that he would send her back into Thermopolis after having scolded her for collecting the first several virgins from the nearby town. But at this point she was grateful for anything that made this aspect of the job a little easier. Some of these little bitches put up one heck of a struggle.

The residence Kaspar had indicated was on Sagebrush Street in the expensive side of town. Esther first drove slowly past the girl's house, checking for cars or movement on the grounds or in any of the windows. As Kaspar had promised, the house was as lifeless as a crypt.

There was only one small light on inside the house itself—in a side rear window. A kitchen night-light left on by the girl's parents, Esther guessed. The only other illumination wasn't even inside the house itself, but rather was arranged carefully around the large Colonial structure. Spotlights were trained on the exterior of the house, brightening the whitewashed clapboard walls like new paint.

There were several halogen bulbs, set into the front lawn, which shone on the front of the house as dazzlingly white as a thousand angels of the Second Coming. One of these was trained on the raised black numbers above the front door, which announced the street address to all passersby. A line of conical lights, low to the ground and spaced at perfectly measured intervals, illuminated the paths up to the front and side doors. Twin spotlights were aimed carefully at the empty driveway.

The house was expensive looking—especially by Thermopolis's middle-class standards—but seemed worth so much attention. Esther wondered why anyone would feel compelled to light up their home brighter than the Washington Monument at midnight.

She shut her own headlights off and coasted quietly down to Sagebrush Street's dead end.

True to Kaspar's word, there was a dirt access road that connected Sagebrush Street to Cheyenne Drive and was blocked by a heavy concrete barrier at this time of year. Esther backed her car up to the barrier and crept on foot back along the woodsy path to the street.

Although Kaspar had repeatedly assured her that the Pythia was not wrong about the ease with which this vessel would be procured, Esther remained nervous as she snuck through the strip of woods that ran along the side of the house.

She held her breath as she listened for approaching cars. When she heard none, she screwed up her courage and darted across the brightly lit driveway, ducking into the shadows behind the main house.

She threw herself roughly against the rear wall beside the broad back deck and listened. Somewhere far away a dog howled into the moonless night.

Esther's heart trip-hammered. Safely hidden from the road, she took a few deep, cleansing breaths. She felt the odd, late-night coolness of the clapboards through her black cotton blouse. Esther shuddered.

This was it. She had come far enough in this business without having to tear around on someone else's ghoulish errands in the dead of night.

It ended with this one. If Kaspar wanted more girls, then let him go out and get them.

The money was good—that much was certain—but every time she'd had to go out on one of these damn missions, she found herself digging in the Ranch Ragnarok survivalist rations for painkillers just to relieve the stress-induced migraines that invariably followed. She had taken almost a dozen ibuprofens since the afternoon just to get through this night's ordeal.

Enough was enough.

She'd get this one, but then Esther Clear-Seer was cashing out of the virgin-procurement business for good.

As for Kaspar—well, he would just have to worry about the next one on his own.

That decided, Esther mounted the wooden steps of the deck double-time and slid stealthily across the green plastic outdoor matting that had been designed to look like grass by someone who had apparently never seen a square inch of genuine lawn.

As foretold, she found the back door key in the clay saucer of a potted plant beside the rear steps. She let herself into the large house.

By the harsh floodlight glow pouring in through every window, Esther made her way easily through the rear mud room, along the central hallway and to the main stairwell at the front of the house.

The stairs were carpeted, and she made no sound as she climbed carefully to the second floor.

Kaspar had told her that the fourth step from the top squeaked loudly, and so she avoided it, stepping gingerly from the fifth to the third.

When she reached the second story, Esther moved quietly left. She counted down two doors. With more calm than she felt, she removed a small plastic sandwich bag from her pants pocket. Inside lay an ether-soaked square of surgical cotton. She pulled the moist wad free, stuffing the bag back into her pocket.

She took one last deep breath, careful not to inhale any of the ether herself, and placed the palm of her free hand against the smooth painted surface of the heavy oaken door.

The door swung inward on silent hinges.

It took a moment for Esther's eyes to adjust to the room's interior.

The shades on the two large windows had been drawn down to the sills, but stabs of light from outside sneaked around the sides of the shades and into the room.

Stripes of light, like fire in the dead heart of night,

burned across the ceiling, the round braided rug and the plain white walls.

A single beam crossed the peaceful, sleeping features of a young girl, no older than her late teens, stretched carelessly in an oversize T-shirt across the rumpled bedcovers.

Even in the nearly complete darkness, Esther could see that the girl was beautiful. She had that wholesome, middle-American quality that Hollywood could never quite get right no matter how artfully the makeup technicians tried.

There was also something strangely familiar about her. No big deal. Esther assumed she had seen the young girl in town.

On tiptoe, Esther crossed over to the bed.

She could hear the girl's breathing. A tiny, hissing intake of air, nearly inaudible.

Esther looked down at the youthful, innocent features and, without hesitation, slapped the wad of treated cotton over the girl's mouth and nose.

Green eyes snapped open; the head thrashed. Hands came up, first in shock, then in desperation, trying to ward off the terrifying attack.

Esther immediately dropped onto the girl, using her imposing weight to pin the younger woman to the bed. It worked.

In a second all resistance faded. The girl's arms dropped to her sides, but her fingers continued to move lazily, as if motioning for help to some unseen guardian.

Soon her eyes rolled back in her head, and the lids gently fluttered closed.

Testing, Esther pulled the cotton slowly away. She

couldn't chance the girl playing possum. She stood ready to slap the ether-soaked wad back into place. But a minute passed and the young girl didn't move. Satisfied, Esther stuffed the cotton back in the sandwich bag and shoved the package into the zippered pocket of her baggy khaki trousers.

She got up from the bed and looked down upon the once more peaceful figure.

Now came the hard part.

Esther grabbed the girl by the arms and pulled her as gently as possible to the room's thick braided carpet.

As she dragged the limp body out into the hallway, she vowed once more that this was the absolute last one she was going to get for Kaspar. From now on the damn Greek was on his own.

With great difficulty, and many rest periods, Esther used a modified fireman's carry to get the girl outside.

The lights were on timers, set to go on and off at preset hours, and some had already snapped off by the time Esther reached the driveway. Most, however, still burned brightly; silent accusers in the chilly spring night.

With her heart pounding, she dragged the unconscious girl as quickly as possible into the relative cover of the nearby strip of woods.

It took Esther ten minutes to reach her car. Ten minutes. An eternity during which she could have been discovered by a nosy neighbor, a police patrol or anyone out for a late-evening drive.

Fortunately the furor over the early abductions was keeping folks indoors, and she made it to her car without encountering a solitary soul.

Once she had heaved the girl's limp body into the trunk and slammed the lid tightly closed, she allowed herself a second of relief.

Esther was sweating profusely and panting like a woman in labor. She wiped the sweat from her brow with her now grimy, bare forearm and, with a final glance around the desolate access road, she climbed behind the steering wheel.

As she drove back down Sagebrush Street, past the innocent-looking house and out onto the main drag, Esther, as she had coming in from the opposite direction, again failed to notice the mailbox at the end of the large home's driveway. It sat hidden between a well-tended rhododendron shrub and a hedge of budding forsythia bushes.

Kaspar wouldn't have been surprised by her lack of perception. The Pythia had foreseen it.

The mailbox sat atop a sturdy oaken pole and was designed to look like a scale-model barn. There was a tiny door for the hayloft, windows along the side, and the main barn door rested on a well-oiled hinge to allow for daily insertion of mail. The mailbox even had a freshly painted, bright red exterior, and a rooster weather vane perched atop the roof, shifting in whatever direction the breeze happened to blow it.

There was, however, one small concession to the box's practical purpose. A street address and a name had been stencilled on the tiny barn's side to identify the occupants of the large home beyond.

The street address was irrelevant to Esther, since she had gotten the number from the well-lit front door of the house itself, but the name, had she seen it, might have held some interest to her.

It read J. Cole.

Virgin number five.

17

The midnight sky over Wyoming was a limitless black canvas peppered with the white-hot specks of a million scattered stars as Remo Williams drove through the desolate stretch of country between the airport at Worland and Thermopolis.

Houses—indeed, any sign of civilization—were few and far between for vast reaches along this lonely route, and Remo found it oddly disconcerting to be traveling through the darkened fields and forests with barely a road sign or streetlight to mark the presence of man in this nearly unspoiled wilderness. The highway itself ran like a flat black desecration through it. Driving along, Remo felt like he had taken a turn into the Twilight Zone—especially when he neared the hot-springs area and the air became humid and thick.

He was relieved when he at last arrived in Thermopolis.

Due to the lateness of the hour, the town was understandably quieter. The crowds were gone from downtown, but the place still held an old-fashioned charm about it. It was almost as if this tiny rural hamlet was a throwback to an earlier, simpler America.

A minute later Remo realized that life in Thermopolis was not as simple as he had thought.

State police cars patrolled the streets, backed by a handful of local police cruisers. Remo assumed this was connected to the spate of kidnappings two weeks earlier.

He avoided two cruisers that flew angrily past in rapid succession, their blue-and-red lights cutting fierce wedges into the otherwise silent night. Another patrol car was parked near the edge of town, forcing Remo to detour around it, carefully threading his way through a maze of shadowy back streets. He eventually managed to slip out the far side of town undetected.

The blinking amber light that signaled the turnoff to Ranch Ragnarok sprang up over the horizon like a gaunt, one-eyed sentry, and Remo eased onto the bumpy path, kicking up a cloud of dust in his wake. Gravel bounced back atop the asphalt road like excited popcorn kernels.

Remo didn't slow the car until he was several hundred yards along the access road, in the secure darkness of a ponderosa pine forest. He killed the ignition.

Before the engine fully died, Remo was out of the vehicle and moving along the narrow dirt road like a fitful shadow.

As he moved, his heightened senses detected a pack of four large animals—most likely wolves—tramping among the trees to his left. Their stealthy movements would have been undetectable by ordinary human ears, but to Remo they might as well have been baying and howling with every clumsy footfall.

They had heard his car and were coming to investigate.

The wolves wouldn't find anything. Remo left the car and the wolves behind as he ghosted into the blackened pines toward Truth Church ranch, leaving neither scent nor spoor.

AT THE PRECISE MOMENT Remo disappeared into the woods, Buffy Brand was wondering what the devil was going on at Ranch Ragnarok.

The blare of Klaxons had awakened all true acolytes from their bunkers only hours before. Buffy had followed her squad to the main compound, where they met up with the rest of the two hundred or so permanent ranch residents.

It wasn't unusual for residents of the Truth Church ranch to be roused in the middle of the night. At times Esther Clear-Seer called Armageddon alerts at least twice a month—most notably four years ago when she had insisted that all Truth Church followers worldwide quit their jobs and move to the ranch in preparation for the final nuclear holocaust that would wipe out Western civilization. The warheads had, of course, never landed. Esther had brushed aside the false alarm as a "reality-derived readiness drill."

She had also come away from that panicky period several million dollars richer.

There had been other, more subdued drills since then—smaller in scope, mostly owing to the diminished church membership since the failed Apocalypses of previous years—and so no one blinked when they were suddenly put on final alert. What was unusual this time, they soon learned, was that the acolytes, after being issued antiheathen arms, had been instructed to stay topside. Up where Yogi Mom had always insisted the deadly firestorms and radioactive fallout would obliterate the planet's less blessed inhabitants.

Only a handful of Esther's followers remained underground. Buffy Brand was one of them. She had been placed in front of a bank of monitor screens in the situation room and told to remain on alert. When she asked the acolyte master sergeant what she should be looking for, he had snapped that she'd know it when she saw it. Truth be told, Buffy doubted that the man knew himself what terror they were awaiting.

And so, like the others, Buffy was kept in the dark as her weary eyes shifted from screen to screen across the high-tech board.

The area the exterior cameras monitored was vast. It included the exteriors of the Ragnarok buildings, as well as the plains and forests surrounding the ranch. Mounted on poles and trees, on the high guard towers or on the desolate stretches of fence that cut across the lonely prairie, the cameras kept vigilant eye on the unsuspecting night.

Occasionally a camera would swirl around, and Buffy would catch a glimpse of a Truth Church foot patrol stomping its way through the brush, their black-clad shapes bathed in the washed-out green of night-vision filters.

As her eyes wandered across the vast Wyoming frontier—made alien by the eerie green glow of the cameras—Buffy took a deep breath.

Half the screens before her remained black. They had been hastily shut off earlier in the evening after some of the Ragnarok technicians had recalibrated the positions of the cameras to which they were connected. At each of the five other monitoring stations in the security room, the corresponding screens had been shut down.

Unbeknownst to Buffy, the man beside her, who was staring with a sullen intensity at the board in front of him, had been instructed by the Prophetess herself to turn on each of the four dormant cameras at predetermined times. Yogi Mom had been quite specific about when they were to be reactivated, down to the precise second, calibrated to Greenwich Mean Time.

Buffy checked her synchronized watch. She felt weary to the very core of her being.

It was probably the lateness of the hour. Since she had come to Ranch Ragnarok, all members of her acolyte shift were required to go to bed at precisely nine o'clock each night. It was now past midnight, and Buffy was bleary-eyed.

She yawned loudly, rubbing her bloodshot eyes. The acolyte at the adjoining monitoring station shot her an angry look. It had been his job to guard Ragnarok against any and all evil infiltrators, and the racoon-rims around his bloodshot eyes were testament to the fact that he took his job very seriously.

She gave him a lopsided smile by way of apology and turned her attention back to the screens.

The other guard harrumphed in displeasure and began drumming his fingers on the metal console before him. He glanced at his watch.

It was almost time.

FIVE MINUTES AFTER he'd left his car, Remo encountered the first night patrol.

The man leading the group of ragtag soldiers was

the same one he and Chiun had encountered the last time he had penetrated Ranch Ragnarok.

The man held his AR-15 menacingly before him. The rest of his patrol did likewise. Remo counted eight in all.

Remo tipped an ear toward the forest and listened. Still more soldiers came stomping through the thick woods, some nearby, others farther away. Since the nearest patrol was brandishing weapons—Remo could tell by the way the soldiers carried themselves—he had to assume that the others were armed, as well.

This time Remo was absolutely certain he hadn't tripped any motion detectors or been spotted by any cameras. He had been extracareful since leaving his car. Every time he sensed the hum of electrical equipment, he cut a wide swath around the offending piece of technology.

So why were the soldiers out in force?

Remo figured he'd stumbled into the middle of some sort of night training exercise.

He had to remind himself that these men weren't innocents. In spite of the promise of universal love they preached, these Truth Church crusaders had killed at least one FBI agent and possibly dozens of their own cult members.

Regardless of their reason for being here this night, they were unlucky enough to find themselves between Remo and Esther Clear-Seer.

The eight soldiers moved loudly through the woods. The leader had positioned himself in the middle of the pack, thinking that he would be better protected from attack with the rest of his command surrounding him. Two of the others had been part of the original group that had collected Remo and Chiun, and one of these fanned out before the rest, taking point.

Remo slid silently behind a tree, and waited for the men to approach.

The path veered sharply to the right, and for a moment the pointman dropped out of sight of the others.

Remo reached a hand out from behind the tree and wrapped his fingers around the barrel of the rifle. He pulled.

The soldier had no time to react. His feet left the path and he disappeared into the woods, still clutching his weapon. There was a short snap—no louder than a breaking twig—and then nothing more from the limp sack of camouflage-dappled meat.

Remo used the butt of the rifle to stuff the body into the hollow of a fallen log. It felt like tamping powder into an old-fashioned cannon. Most of the man fit, and those parts that didn't Remo covered with a few strategically placed handfuls of pine needles.

As the body of the patrol filtered down the path, Remo slid back into the shadows, circling around behind them.

The soldiers had started to miss the pointman. Some were puzzled, while others were beginning to grow fearful. One of the men began to recount how they had encountered two men in the woods not long before who seemed able to appear and disappear at will.

The patrol leader ordered silence and feigned a lack of concern. But Remo could smell the fear building up around him like an odor of bleach.

As the Ragnarok patrol picked its way through the spot where the pointman had vanished, Remo slipped up behind a pair of soldiers at the patrol's rear. With a single swift, fluid motion he reached out and wrapped his fingers around the tops of their spines. He exerted pressure. Bones creaked and snapped under the pressure. And before the men had time to cry out, their spinal columns snapped free of their skulls. Two bodies collapsed like discarded marionettes in Remo's outstretched hands.

He drew them silently back into the woods, their boots dangling free of the ground.

Their disappearance went unnoticed for only seconds.

"Where's Adams and Caine?" the patrol leader demanded.

The remaining five soldiers looked fearfully about.

"Maybe they're taking a leak," a man offered nervously.

"Abel is gone, too," another muttered soberly.

A quick head count revealed that there were now only four of them.

"Where did he go?" the leader demanded.

"I don't know," a soldier said, hanging back by the sentinel pines. "He was next to me, and then he was just gone."

"Like Wainwright," another soldier announced.

A moment later the group didn't need a head count. What had started out as eight strong had now become two.

"Freeze in your tracks!" the patrol leader commanded with a burst of nervous rage. He pointed a stubby finger at the lone remaining soldier. "I order you to remain where you are!"

But when he made the mistake of blinking, he realized with a feeling of sinking horror that he was all alone in the forest.

This time the moment the last soldier disappeared, the patrol leader thought he heard the faint rustle of leaves.

Sweat drooled down his cork-blackened features.

Suddenly a face loomed before him. It was smiling broadly.

And it was familiar.

"Hi," Remo said brightly. "Remember me?"

THE RACCOON-EYED MAN counted down the seconds on his watch and, when the proper time came, he flicked two toggle switches on the board before him, saying, "Now!"

His dormant monitor screens lit up with the same pale green phosphorescence as the others.

On her own suddenly active screen, Buffy saw the death blow land.

The assailant's thick-wristed hand seemed to move in slow motion toward the patrol leader's chest. The soldier attempted to swing his weapon around at the intruder. But his movements appeared sluggish compared with those of the thick-wristed man. That's when Buffy realized the intruder only gave the appearance of moving slowly.

The patrol leader realized the same thing a split second later.

Buffy watched the Ragnarok soldier drop silently to the wooded path. Only then did his attacker turn toward the camera.

Her look was as surprised as his, for she recognized him as one of the strange duo Esther had sent her to greet once before. Now he was back. Buffy wondered who he was and what he had done to warrant a full-scale alert.

The camera was set into a cleft in a nearby aspen tree, and the man on the screen glared up at her through the wireless connection. His hard, high-cheekboned face was a thundercloud. He seemed upset at being caught by the camera's unflinching eye, but his initial anger soon melted away.

He then did something that sent a chill up Buffy's spine.

There was no audio feature, which made the weird, green-cast spectacle all the more surreal.

The man stood rigidly beneath the camera, bowed once, as if receiving thunderous applause, and then proceeded to dance a little soft-shoe for his unseen audience. When he was through, he bowed once more before he abruptly hefted the body of the soldier that had lain next to him throughout the entire scene. Without preamble he launched the corpse at the camera.

As if the lifeless shape could hit her, Buffy flinched. The screen filled with a jumble of gray static.

"My monitor's gone off-line," Buffy announced.

She glanced over at the adjoining monitor station. It showed a different angle. But it was the same thick-wristed intruder.

Raccoon Eyes jumped as a rotted log flew up toward his camera. Just prior to the point of impact, a second before the next screen became a hissing square of static, Buffy was certain she saw a pair of legs sticking out of the log's jagged end. On all of the monitor stations around the bunker, two screens hissed angrily at the worried Ragnarok acolytes.

Whoever this stranger was, he was dangerous. And he was coming their way.

REMO HAD QUELLED his initial anger at being detected.

He wasn't upset so much because he had lost the element of surprise, though that was cause for concern. A Sinanju assassin was never caught by surprise. No, Remo was angry at himself for allowing the camera to spot him in the first place. Something that amateurish wasn't supposed to happen.

Chiun would have been livid had he known. But Remo doubted if even the Master of Sinanju could have avoided the pair of surveillance cameras that had been suddenly trained on him.

Remo was sensitive to all electronic equipment and especially so to the many high-tech devices commonly used by security forces to detect enemies. In this case the cameras that had found him had been inactive when he first stepped into their range of vision. In this state, they were about as threatening to Remo as empty coffee cans. For this reason he had failed to note them. When they suddenly whirred to life, it was too late to move. It was almost as if they had known the precise moment he would be standing in front of them.

The cameras had been set up several yards apart on the same side of the path and were arranged so that even if one missed his movements, the other would catch him.

They couldn't possibly have known he was coming again, Remo thought.

Remo kicked the remnants of the nearest camera deep into the woods. The other camera, though smashed, still hummed quietly beneath the body of the Truth Church patrol leader.

Remo considered his situation.

The worst that had happened was that he had lost the element of surprise. No big deal. With all of the Ragnarok guards crawling through the underbrush, that probably would have been inevitable before he had reached the ranch.

So what if Esther Clear-Seer knew he was coming? It would give her time to make her peace with the Devil before he sent her off to her final reward.

Remo glided down the path toward the Truth Church encampment, every sense keyed up to maximum alertness. No one was going to catch him unawares again.

"DID YOU PICK UP the signal, Prophetess?" Raccoon Eyes asked anxiously.

"Yes, we did." Over the speakerphone Esther Clear-Seer's voice vibrated like a bass violin string. "Are the rest of the cameras ready?"

"They are," he replied.

"Do a systems double-check. Make sure we get those pictures back here."

"Yes, ma'am," he said. "And Yogi Mom?" he added, timidly.

"What is it?"

"Is this an agent of the Old Evil One?"

Her reply hissed angrily over the line. "Don't bother me with that crap now. I'm trying to save my ass."

With that she severed the connection.

The others glanced at Raccoon Eyes during the awkward silence that ensued.

"The intruder must be in league with the Antichrist," he said with a solemn grimace.

The others nodded, and returned to their stations.

Buffy's eyes hadn't strayed far from her own monitors. Only the two screens were out, and she watched the others in concern as the ghostly images of Truth Church patrols trekked back toward the ranch. Esther must have given the recall command over their radio headsets.

The intruder didn't appear on any of her monitors, but Buffy assumed he was heading toward the ranch, as well. The acolytes were closing in behind him, sealing off his escape route like so much living caulk.

She chewed her lip nervously as she watched for the mysterious man to reappear on her monitor screens.

Beside her, Raccoon Eyes turned his attention to the digital clock mounted at his monitor station.

The toggle switches to the two dormant cameras, as well as a third scarlet switch, sat enticingly within his reach.

REMO PAUSED at the edge of the forest.

The patrols were concentrating in the woods behind him. Nothing stood between him and the Ranch Ragnarok perimeter fence except one hundred yards of Wyoming greasewood prairie.

From high atop the nearest guard tower, halogen flood lamps raked the barren ground. While the beams played back and forth along the forest's edge with earnest diligence, they never quite managed to pin Remo.

He spotted four other towers, two to the south, the other due west. The lights from these moved relentlessly back and forth, as if searching for someone. For him, Remo understood.

He felt more than heard the hum from the electrified fence and Remo decided that he had better think of an alternate route into the compound. While a defense of this nature wasn't generally a major obstacle, he was in an unusual position. Those inside were alerted to his presence and he couldn't afford the few vulnerable seconds he would have to spend working on the electrified metal.

Remo waited until the spotlight beams broke at their farthest point in opposite directions before he emerged from the protective concealment of the forest. He slipped quickly across the small expanse of prairie to the nearest guard tower.

The tower exterior was rough and chalky. The structure had been built out of cinder blocks skimmed over with several coats of concrete to eliminate any hand- or toeholds between the heavy bricks.

Remo pressed his palms flat against the concrete surface and flexed his fingers. His loafers left the dry earth as he established a kind of suction and repeated the motion with his hands, pushing both inward and upward simultaneously. Spiderlike, he began ascending the tower.

There was a nest of razor wire encircling the concrete silo some three feet below the railed upper platform. Remo paused for a second, letting the pressure of his right hand and toes hold him in place. He snaked out his free hand and took a pinch of wire between thumb and middle finger, making a snapping motion.

With a tiny pop, the wire sprang apart, falling limply in two neat sections.

Remo moved up between the dangling wires and oozed over the tower rail like so much black smoke.

He was met by the startled eyes of four Truth Church acolytes. Two were operating the spotlights, and the other pair had been peering out toward the woods where the first Ragnarok patrols had already begun moving in a parody of stealth from out of the forest.

The two guards on lookout duty hastily trained their rifles on Remo. Unfortunately for them, Remo had positioned himself in such a way that the guards found themselves standing on either side of their target, so that to open fire each guard would be forced to mow down the other.

Sure enough, that gave them pause.

While they were puzzling over how to proceed, Remo snatched a rifle barrel in each hand and, with a quick, jerking movement, crossed his forearms. Each man lurched forward. The force Remo exerted was enough to drive the business end of each extended rifle into the face of the man opposite.

Both men looked as if they had suddenly and inexplicably sprouted a shiny new AR-15 from the bridges of their noses. The bodies collapsed in two khaki heaps.

The guard manning the nearest spotlight made a move to unholster his side arm. With a casual backhand slap Remo fused the chunk of metal into his pelvis.

To stifle any outcry, Remo then took him by the back of his British-style ribbed black combat sweater and jammed his head into the center of the spotlight lens. The glass beneath the outer cage of wire mesh cracked, along with the guard's skull. The body twitched its last as the beam from the broken spotlight faded from bright white to a timid orange glow.

The remaining guard recoiled from the bodies of his fallen comrades and, reflecting on his situation, did the only sensible thing he could think to do. He jumped.

Unfortunately for him, his pants snagged on the broken strand of razor wire. He hung upside down, flailing. As he struggled to free himself, he unwittingly swung into the electrified hurricane fence.

Zzzzappp!

"Yarrrghh!"

When his charred remains dropped from the smoking fence moments later, his horrified scream trailed off into a gurgling hiss.

Remo glanced over his shoulder. About forty armed Truth Church guards were skulking across the greasewood toward the electrified fence.

Cursing inwardly, he hopped the three stories from the tower into the Ragnarok compound.

"WHAT'S HAPPENING out there?" demanded the voice of a Truth Church security monitor. His video screens had just captured the carnage at the guard tower. In the strange green twilight of the cameras, he saw the smoking pile of garbage at the base of the three-story block of concrete. Only when he spied a pair of combat boots sticking from the glowing mass did he recognize the charred lump as one of his fellow monitors.

"It's him," Raccoon Eyes said with horror-filled

certainty. "It is the Evil One himself. He's coming for all of us."

As he watched the hordes of silent green guards swarm out of the woods, he swallowed hard. On another screen he saw a guard deactivating the gate near the burned remains of the tower guard. The other soldiers nearby covered their mouths to ward off the stench.

Raccoon Eyes could almost smell the sickly stench himself. The cameras captured several guards vomiting as they caught their first whiff of burned body.

"This is the end," Raccoon Eyes said to himself. His weary eyes seemed to recede farther back in their sockets as he glanced sickeningly at the remaining dormant toggle switches. He knew he didn't want to see that deadly face again, but he had a responsibility to his church.

With weakened resolve, he refocused his attention on the digital clock. Wouldn't be long now, he told himself.

Beside him Buffy Brand watched her monitors in silence.

REMO SENSED the presence of electronic-surveillance equipment within the compound. There were heat sensors and motion detectors immediately beyond the perimeter fence, but those were not placed beyond a twenty-yard distance from the guard tower. The subtle vibrations Remo felt now came from additional security cameras.

From the number of cameras he counted in this zone of the compound alone, it was pretty clear that Yogi Mom didn't put a lot of faith in her own disciples. He thought it was odd that he hadn't sensed this many cameras on his last penetration. Probably dormant during daylight hours, he decided.

Not a twig snapped, nor did any dried leaf crackle as Remo slid through the darkness, a silent shadow among shadows.

It wasn't any conscious thought that told him there was a pole-mounted camera to the right up ahead; he simply knew it was there. So he faded into the shadows, and out of the camera's limited range.

The camera whirred on its anchoring bridge of metal. A sound like fingernails on a blackboard scratched across Remo's ultrasensitive eardrums. He scrunched his face up at the noise. Didn't these Truth Church wackos own an oil can?

By the time the camera—guaranteed by the manufacturer to be completely silent—had squeaked, buzzed and rolled its way back in a return arc, Remo was already twenty feet beyond it.

He found the next one not quite as noisy and continued moving through the tufts of burned-out scrub brush toward the main cluster of buildings. Behind him Remo could hear the throng of advancing Ragnarok guards. And there seemed to be some kind of movement up ahead....

Remo was wondering how he was going to ice Esther Clear-Seer and get back to his car without having to take out the entire Truth Church congregation when a pair of surveillance cameras simultaneously snapped on ahead and off to his right, capturing him between them.

Remo became very, very still.

"What the ding-dong hell?" he muttered.

And in the nearby security bunker, hell was on someone else's mind, as well.

"HE'S PENETRATED the compound," gasped Raccoon Eyes. "The heathen has violated our sacred soil."

Not far from him, Buffy Brand hovered around one of the rear consoles, which featured the thick-wristed man who had wiped out the patrol in the woods. In the strange twilight of the night-vision camera, the man's deep-set eyes were two angry smears of black in a macabre green skull.

Raccoon Eyes made certain that the signal was being routed back to the temple monitors even as he watched the terrifying image on his own screen.

He had helped install most of these cameras himself earlier in the evening. This pair had been as carefully positioned as the rest—one on a watertower, one on a flagpole just above the windsock. They should have been completely undetectable—but the man whom he had dubbed the Evil One had spotted them the instant they had been turned on.

Frantically, he opened the line to the temple. Esther grunted her acknowledgment.

"He's here," Raccoon Eyes announced in a frightened voice.

"I know," she snapped back.

He heard Esther barking orders into the radio headsets just before she severed the connection with the security bunker.

Raccoon Eyes looked at the others in the room. Some were praying quietly to themselves. Others merely stared dumbly at the monitor screens, not comprehending the horror about to overtake them.

There didn't seem to be enough people in the cinder-block room and Raccoon Eyes glanced around, trying to force from his mind all thought of impending doom. For an instant the image of the Evil One vanished as he realized why the room looked emptier.

Buffy Brand was nowhere to be seen.

IT WAS JUST LIKE BEFORE. First the cameras had been off, then they were on.

Remo had been trained to recognize and deal with any kind of threat, potential or real. But, just as in the woods, the cameras hadn't been a threat.

What Remo's senses had disregarded as a lump of metal, plastic, glass and circuitry suddenly hummed itself into a camera, and it was already too late for him to get out of the way.

It was as if the Ranch Ragnarok cameras knew exactly where and when he would show up.

But suddenly the cameras became the least of his worries.

Across the field stretching before him, dozens of high-intensity spotlight beams blazed to life. All were trained directly on him.

They had caught him again.

Remo would have sensed what was about to happen had the lights been manned, but these were operated remotely. There must have been thick cables trailing off to some central location that would have eliminated the usual telltale nervousness that telegraphed the intentions of human operators. The ambush was effective precisely because no human being on the scene was responsible for throwing the switch.

But that didn't mean there weren't people there.

There were two dozen of them lined up just beyond the spotlights. They popped up as if from nowhere. Probably spiderholes or trenches.

When he focused his eyes to filter out the distracting brightness, Remo let a cool smile crease his set features. He would have laughed, but this would be unprofessional.

The men were set up in two overlapping semicircles beyond the lights in a variation of the old British method of attack that had lost His Majesty the Colonies in the Revolutionary War.

The first dozen were lying on their bellies between the lights and the main outbuildings of the Ragnarok complex. The other twelve were kneeling on one knee behind the first line, filling in the firing gaps between the outer row. All had relinquished their AR-15s and substituted shotguns, which were trained on the lean man standing vulnerable in the brilliant glare of the line of spotlights.

Remo thought quickly. There were more men moving in from the rear than there were waiting up ahead, and ahead was where he would find Esther Clear-Seer.

Remo took a step toward the spotlights.

All at once the peaceful Wyoming plain lit up with a coruscating eruption of deadly automatic-weapons fire.

18

The first high-velocity volley exploded through the blinding wall of light like dozens of tiny solar flares.

Through the spotlight glare, Remo could distinguish twelve distinct flashes erupting from the first row of gunmen, followed closely by another dozen explosions from the gunmen in the second row.

Everything happened in a blur of sound and fury.

The multiple attack was obviously designed to confuse Remo. He'd dodge the initial volley, and, in avoiding it, step into the second wave of deadly metal fragments. It was clever, in a rudimentary way, but it was also very, very presumptuous.

Instead of dodging the first shots, Remo moved toward them, ducking and skittering in the manner he had learned during his earliest years of Sinanju training.

A deer slug burned past his right earlobe, making the air sizzle.

A split-second jog to the left, and Remo avoided a spreading wall of buckshot.

It was a clever tactic to mix shells in with slugs. While single bullets were easier to dodge, the shot created an obstacle that almost forced him into the line of deadly fire.

His hands, lightning fast, shot out in a flashing blur, driving a hard wall of compressed air before them— and two slugs deflected harmlessly into the Wyoming night.

Twisting and spinning his way through the deadly hail, Remo looked like a contortionist who'd turned tennis player, lobbing back bullets with an "air racket."

He got halfway to the double rows of gunmen when a muffled radio command ordering the next round of fire reached his ears through a lull in the din. Two dozen fingers immediately depressed on triggers.

Remo knew the attack pattern now. Every other man in the first row was buckshot, while those in between were bullets. The second row had been arranged exactly opposite the row of kneeling men so that its firing pattern complemented that of the first line.

A tight smile of confidence riding his face, Remo moved steadily forward as all twenty-four men unloaded their weapons on his lean frame.

His smile evaporated almost immediately.

Remo knew then he had made a deadly miscalculation. The missiles launched at him now were not the same.

It was as if the carefully planned first attack had given way to complete chaos. Shooters who had been firing shells now loosed buckshot, while some who had relied on shot now opted for the heavier slugs. But the tactical change was not just a mirror image of the first attack. The ammo redistribution was completely random now.

For the fourth time that evening he cursed inwardly for allowing himself to fall into a trap.

I screwed up, Remo told himself.

A single ball of metal was hurtling toward him where he expected buckshot. Remo surged left and rolled low—into a flying field of buckshot!

His legs stiffened. He sprang forward, angling right, ahead of the metal shot fragments pelting the dusty ground behind him.

Even as he closed in on the lights, Remo could feel his inner rhythm. It was off. Dangerously off.

More shooting erupted beyond the spotlights. The steady burp of automatic-weapons fire this time. Remo could differentiate between powder loads and muzzle-velocity sounds. This was an AR-15, the weapon of choice for the Truth Church.

No time to worry about that now. Five humming bullets came seeking his chest. Remo flattened himself on the ground to avoid them, then executed an impossible flip—like a pancake being tossed by a giant spatula—from his stomach to his back.

Three rounds of buckshot kicked up a cloud of dust at the spot where he had been a split second earlier. They made ugly *thucking* sounds chewing up the red clay.

More deadly slugs flew toward him, but the second wave appeared to be petering out. In fact, the rounds from the rogue AR-15 seconds before appeared to have missed him entirely.

Remo twitched to the left—and another volley flew harmlessly past.

The lights were now only a few feet away. He could feel the heat from their white-hot filaments.

A final shot whizzed toward him from between the

spotlights. A deer slug. Remo had only to lean to one side, and the bullet missed him by a healthy foot.

A second later he arrived between the lights and at the two rows of Truth Church disciples.

Some were busy trying to reload their weapons. Others lay prone in their firing positions. He'd worry about the shooters on the ground later.

The hands of those trying to reload shook as they scrambled to stuff shells into open breeches. Remo danced in between the two lines, cracking a temple here, shattering a sternum there. Broken shotguns dropped, scattering red paper shells like Christmas firecrackers. Stunned faces were mushed into the soft red clay.

When he was finished, Remo paused, ready to deal with the ones who should have jumped off the ground firing by now.

Except they didn't. They lay on their stomachs as if paralyzed. There were no preattack signals coming from any of them. In fact, no signals at all. The air was dead all around.

Remo crouched to examine one shooter. He lay on his back.

His flesh was inert. A fading warmth was seeping out of it.

The man was dead.

Remo flipped him over. A pair of crimson streaks painted the lighter patches of his camouflage jacket. Shot in the back.

Remo checked the others. All had been shot at close range; even some of the ones Remo had finished off had suffered additional minor flesh wounds, he discovered.

It had to be the work of the lone AR-15 that had opened up while Remo was busy avoiding the shotgun attack.

While he crouched beside the body of a fresh-faced believer, Remo felt an unaccustomed coolness at the back of his right knee. He turned his leg slightly and noticed a tiny rip in the fabric of his chinos. Pulling the material between thumb and forefinger, he discovered a second small tear. Both were the size of moth holes, and Remo realized that a single fragment of buckshot must have passed through the back of his pant leg during the second wave of fire.

All thoughts of the dead Truth Church disciples vanished as Remo wondered how he could possibly have been sloppy enough to allow a single fragment of shot to touch his clothing.

When he heard the questioning calls from the approaching Truth Church patrols, his gaze went to the perimeter fence.

The firing had kept the rest of the Ragnarok soldiers at bay. Now the spotlights were having the precise effect they were supposed to have. His pursuers lurked out among the harsh fans of light, staying in the shadows.

An army of holy killers, remote-controlled spotlights, phantom cameras. This assignment, which should have been simple, had gotten complicated. Remo wanted to finish it. Now.

Remo left the soldiers behind and headed for the cluster of concrete buildings, determination writ in his face.

RACCOON EYES HAD LOST sight of the Evil One when the shotguns started blasting.

He was surprised that he could hear the cacophony through the security bunker walls, and wondered if it was dug in as deeply as it should have been.

When the dull thuds of the shotguns stopped filtering through the insulating sand and packed earth, he knew that the Evil One was on his way.

But that didn't matter now.

His expression bland, his skin drained of color, Raccoon Eyes stared at the scarlet toggle switch on his control board.

"Come out, come out, wherever you are," chimed a happy voice from down the concrete hallway, as though humoring children.

The Evil One had penetrated underground!

The other men and women in the security room glanced nervously at one another. All had participated in the firing-squad-style murders of Truth Church dissenters—it was a requirement of Esther Clear-Seer that all church members not shy away from the blood of pagans—but the guns in their hands felt somehow heavier this night. In unison they lifted their weapons toward the open bunker doorway.

The digital clock read 00.38.32. It was in military time, equivalent to nearly 12:39 a.m., and Raccoon Eyes watched the seconds click rapidly past in tenths, the numbers a flashing red blur.

Nothing mattered any longer.

"Yoo-hoo!" a voice shouted from somewhere nearby. "Can Esther come out and play?"

He was getting closer.

Raccoon Eyes stared intently at the clock. His hand snaked out for the scarlet toggle switch.

00.38.53.

It didn't matter.

00.38.59.

Nothing mattered.

00.39.04.

Raccoon Eyes flipped the scarlet switch. An electrical current went zipping through shielded wiring, seeking a strategically buried cache of inert gray plastic matter.

And a thunderous explosion rocked the security bunker.

As TONS OF ROCK and earth collapsed behind him, Remo was forced farther into the tunnel. He found a safe spot at a reinforced angle, threw himself flat, then curled into a fetal position to protect head and vital organs.

A succession of smaller, echoing detonations came, sealing off all branching paths that snaked off to the surface from the main tunnel.

The last handfuls of dirt were tumbling in mini-avalanches down the piles of displaced earth when Remo got back to his feet. A cloud of choking dust rose into the tunnel's musty air.

Remo shook dirt from his dark hair as he surveyed the ruins.

He had descended into the subterranean bunker complex through the newly formed tunnel at the rear of Esther Clear-Seer's ranch. That belowground route was now blocked by a wall of solid earth.

All exit corridors at this end of the bunker complex

had been effectively sealed. Remo saw he had no choice but to move deeper into the underground world.

He moved along the chilly corridor, past room upon room of survivalist supplies, without encountering a single living soul.

Remo checked several of the larger rooms along the way and found evidence of other cave-ins. Every escape route in the center of the complex had been collapsed. Remo felt the same vague concern at being outguessed by Yogi Mom he had felt earlier. It was as if she could anticipate his every move. He didn't like that.

Targets didn't anticipate Sinanju. It was against everything Remo had been taught. This was all *wrong*.

Eventually he entered a newly constructed section of tunnel. The soles of his loafers made not a sound as they glided along the concrete floor.

The recirculated air tasted more stale the farther Remo went, and he recognized a familiar underlying odor that was growing stronger with each cat-footed step. It was the same rotten-egg smell that had clung to Esther Clear-Seer like a shroud; the same smell that had held enough significance for the Master of Sinanju to terminate his contract with Smith.

While Remo ordinarily wouldn't have let a single awful smell dictate his actions, he decided that the strangeness of his encounters at Ranch Ragnarok were too great to ignore. He proceeded with caution.

The tunnel ended in a series of concrete steps. Remo mounted them, entering the interior of the old airplane hangar that marred the church's slice of Wyoming real estate.

The sulphur smell was stronger in here.

Remo could sense movement in a large chamber at the far end of the building. Carefully he moved toward the room through the yellow haze and flickering candlelight.

There was a heavy woolen tapestry covering a cinder-block archway into the main chamber. Remo swept it aside.

The sulphur stench poured from beneath the tapestry in a plume of thick yellow smoke. The odor soaked into his clothing, and though he was ordinarily able to block out offending smells, he found that the pungent miasma insinuated itself into his nostrils like a serpent seeking food. Remo's eyes watered as he fought an unaccustomed gag reflex. It subsided.

The interior of the large chamber was well lit by dozens of brightly burning torches. Through the haze Remo noted an opening in the ceiling that served to let the offending smoke escape into the star-flecked night.

Atop a mound of rock that seemed to grow up through the center of the floor, were two women and a man. One of the females, who was quite young, was seated on a small wooden tripod. The girl swayed back and forth as if being shaken by some invisible assailant. The man and woman, each in their forties, stood patiently beside the girl.

"Right on time," the man said to Remo, glancing at his watch.

Remo recognized Mark Kaspar from his appearance on "Barry Duke Live." He also remembered that Smith had said he wasn't due to return to Wyoming until the day after tomorrow.

Esther Clear-Seer stood smugly beside Kaspar at the

top of the rocky hillock. At first glance the broken nose Chiun had given her as a parting gift appeared to have healed. But Remo could see the extra makeup she had applied beneath her eyes to cover the fading bruises.

Behind them Remo saw a remote security panel with several monitor screens spread across its face. They had been watching his progress as he passed through the various Truth Church traps. Of course.

The girl on the stool moaned loudly. There was something odd about her, and not just the way she twitched and jerked about. Despite the swirl of choking yellow smoke that poured up from a crevice in the rock beneath her, she breathed deeply. Almost like Remo himself.

But the girl was irrelevant.

"SHOW'S OVER," Remo announced, taking the first few steps up the rocky incline in one bound.

Kaspar smiled. "I rather think it's just begun," he said.

As Remo began to take another step up, the girl on the stool raised a Browning pistol, which had been hidden at her side, and fired a round at Remo.

On the steps below, Remo felt a slight tug at his right thigh.

His face broke into shock as he watched blood begin to ooze from the bullet wound in his leg.

He took a step backward as the second shot rang out.

The heavy slug, like the first, bore through the fleshy part of his thigh—this time on the left—exiting cleanly out the back. It cracked through the top of a lighted torch and into the cinder-block wall, sending up a puff of chalky dust and sparks.

Blood pumped from the second wound, darkening the fabric of the black chinos. His body was already reacting to the injuries, rushing to clot and seal the bullet holes.

Remo reeled on his feet, eyes all but uncomprehending. He shouldn't be shot. His training made him sensitive to every warning sign that preceded any kind of offensive strike.

It was second nature for him to be able to sense when someone was carrying a concealed weapon. People with weapons walked and stood differently. In this case the girl should have sat differently. Remo's instincts had detected nothing.

Yet suddenly there was the gun in her hand and the gun was spitting at him.

And that was when the girl on the tripod spoke.

"Sinanju is no more," rasped a voice that did not seem to fit. It sounded more like the voice of an old, old man. "You, Remo of Sinanju, are no more!"

A hollow, victorious laugh filled the chamber.

Esther Clear-Seer licked her lips nervously and backed away from the tripod. Her eyes darted between Remo and the young girl.

Remo took an uncertain step up the hill. His legs buckled beneath him, and he fell forward onto the carved stone staircase.

"Bold to the end, young Sinanju master," the girl mocked. "Your pitiful house of assassins does not lack bravery."

"Whoever you are," Remo growled, forcing himself back to his feet, "you're dogmeat."

The girl only smiled. "A pity the old one did not tell you of the prophecy. For when East meets West, the destiny of Sinanju will be forever changed. The end for you begins this day, for I have foreseen it."

"You have foreseen squat," Remo spit. He took another wobbly step up the rocky incline. His body was working hard to heal the wounds in his legs, and the diversion of energy was sapping his strength.

The girl's voice became hoarse with menace. "I command you now, yield to the Delphic oracle. Yield to Apollo's Pythia. Yield to me, Sinanju, or die."

The Browning was lifted again. A third shot rang out.

The bullet snarled for Remo's shoulder. It was another warning shot—more significant than any fired over his head. The placement of the shots was proof that at any time the girl desired, a round could be fired that would end Remo's life.

But this time Remo was prepared.

The girl's posture hadn't provided a clue that she held a weapon until the moment the Browning was first fired. The second shot had found its mark only because Remo had been caught off guard by the first. But now Remo understood that the girl was somehow able to fire without any subtle signaling of her intentions whatsoever, so that before she could pull the trigger again, Remo had focused his concentration on the weapon itself. The shooter was unimportant.

In Remo's mind the gun became the enemy.

Remo watched the gun. The trigger was pulled, again without warning. The third bullet zipped toward his shoulder.

The bullet that was now his enemy. The bullet could kill him.

Remo's hand darted up.

His index finger caught the spiraling lump of lead a millimeter away from his shoulder, and he flicked the fragment up with the tip of a diet-hardened fingernail. His other hand swung around, forming a cup over the slowing projectile. The deflected round began losing speed. Remo slammed both hands together, guiding the lazy movement of the bullet until its velocity was spent.

When it felt safe, he opened his hands. The bullet rested in the center of his outstretched palm like a captured bug. It was hot. A protective sheen of palm perspiration protected the skin from searing.

Carelessly Remo tossed the bullet to the ground and forced himself up the remaining steps to the platform. The girl fired a fourth time. Grimly Remo sidestepped the bullet. Moving in, he knocked the gun from her outstretched hand.

"You didn't predict this!" Esther yelled at Kaspar as she retreated to the farthest edge of the platform.

"Quiet, woman," Kaspar barked. His reptilian eyes stared unblinking at the Sinanju Master.

Remo raised his hand to deal a death blow to the girl on the stool, but the girl stared blankly at the distant wall. She didn't seem aware he was standing before her.

Suddenly her hand lashed out, striking Remo in the chest. And while he was shocked that he hadn't read the blow coming, there was no force behind it. The girl had no special training. She was harmless.

Remo placed her hand gently back at her side and,

lifting her by the shoulders, removed her from the small wooden seat.

"Don't go anywhere," he cautioned the others.

Remo steered the girl over to where he gently sat her down at the top of the rock staircase. He then turned his dark, menacing eyes on Esther and Kaspar.

Smith would be upset if Remo polished off Kaspar, too, but he couldn't leave now. Not a second time. He'd take care of both of them. Let Smith pick up the pieces later.

Esther looked down the sheer drop at the rear of the hillock. It was almost completely vertical for nearly two stories and ended in a final, drastic slope near the rear wall of the chamber. There was a strong chance she wouldn't survive a fall, but if this Remo came anywhere near her, she'd take the chance.

On the other hand, Kaspar seemed unfazed. He merely stared at the thick-wristed man, like a hungry cobra eyeing a rat.

Remo assumed that the yellow smoke was some kind of new drug that doped up whoever was sitting on the stool, making them susceptible to the commands of the Truth Church leaders. It was hardly effective, considering that the victim seemed unable to leave the smoky chamber, but they were probably trying to figure out a way to concentrate the potent yellow smoke.

As he passed the crevice, Remo noticed something that looked like an antique pottery crock sitting on an outcropping of rock.

He peered through the grate that sat above the fissure. It was definitely some kind of container. And through the haze of yellow smoke, Remo could see that the contents were glowing.

Without warning, a dense column of yellow smoke—as focused as the high-pressure spray from a fire hose—burst from out of the crevice and slammed Remo in the chest. He staggered, then went reeling.

Esther Clear-Seer's eyes grew wide with shock. "What the hell's going on?" she hissed to Kaspar. "I never saw that before."

Kaspar ignored her. He took a step toward Remo, his black eyes gleeful as he watched the younger man stagger back toward the edge of the hill.

Remo spun around drunkenly on the platform. The voice thundered loudly inside his head. It was the same voice that had come from the young girl, and yet it was different. It was louder now, more masculine. And somehow infinitely more frightening.

It sounded again.

East has met West. The prophecy is fulfilled.

A throbbing pain behind his temples grew intense as the voice spoke. Remo toppled backward, over the lip of the platform. He skidded on his back halfway down the rocky incline, the sharp rock surface tearing viciously at his T-shirt and gouging his flesh.

In spite of the pain, some lucid part of Remo's mind told him that he had inhaled something vile in the smoke.

That something was inside his mind. He felt like a drowning man, and when he looked up he saw the girl, sitting immobile where he had placed her. Her expression as she stared into space was dull and lifeless.

The drug. Whatever had affected the girl was now inside him. Remo charged his lungs with purifying air, trying to dispel the force that now raged in his mind, hoping to quell the voice within him.

Kaspar and Esther Clear-Seer now appeared at the top of the staircase behind the girl. Kaspar was grinning maliciously.

The girl sat before them, catatonic. They had made her like this. With his training, Remo knew that he should be able to fight off the effects, but she hadn't had a chance. And all at once something told him that this was the reason for the mysterious kidnappings in Thermopolis. He didn't know if it was the voice that told him or his own instincts; he simply knew it to be true with a perfect inner knowledge.

Remo gritted his teeth and resolved to make the pair of them pay dearly for each missing child.

Save all pity for yourself, Sinanju!

Remo covered his ears in pain. The smoke in the room seemed to be drawing down toward him, surrounding him in a thick yellow fog. He felt an odd tingling sensation in every nerve ending as the sulphur smoke weighed heavier around him.

"Consider yourself fortunate, Mr. Williams," Kaspar called down. "You were predestined to be the strongest of all the vessels of Apollo. Your body will serve as host to the second Delphi, the center of the world." Kaspar took a step down toward Remo. "Together we will change the course of history."

The rotten-egg smell intensified as the yellow smoke thickened around Remo. Something within him was fighting for possession of his body.

"The hell we will," Remo growled, and the voice that rattled up his smoke-filled throat was his own.

Kaspar started, shook his head with disbelief.

You are mine! the voice inside Remo growled. *You will learn to fear, Sinanju. For I will be your teacher!*

Remo could feel the smoke that swirled around him begin to seep into his every pore. There was something else, something intangible at the fringes of his mind. It was as if a second consciousness had invaded his very soul. It was vague and indistinct. A phantom presence toying at the periphery of his thoughts.

He could not allow it. He could not let himself fail.

With an overwhelming effort, Remo pushed himself down the rest of the rocky incline. He tumbled to a stop at the base of the hill.

As he pushed himself to his feet, he was vaguely aware of Kaspar's face distorted in shock.

Like a toddler taking its first shaky steps, his legs still oozing blood from open wounds, Remo took a hesitant step forward. He would not let the force within take over his mind.

He staggered to the side door. With a slap the heavy slab of metal sprang open. Beyond, crickets chirped loudly at the midnight sky.

"Where are you going?" Kaspar asked desperately.

Remo shot the small man a keep-away-from-me glance and stumbled drunkenly out into the black Wyoming night.

At the top of the Pythia platform, the flow of yellow smoke ceased, as if exhausted.

19

"Of course, Mr. Kaspar is deeply troubled by these latest developments. He feels particularly sorry for the children, if the allegations against T. Rex Calhoun are true. But we mustn't lose sight of the fact that, at the moment, they remain just that—allegations." Mike Princippi stifled an urge to grin. The early-morning press conference had brought back in a flood his old political feelings. It felt great to be in the limelight again.

Hands were raised in the sea of reporters at the National Press Building in Washington. Princippi pointed randomly at one.

"Any comment on T. Rex Calhoun's reasons for dropping out of the race for Senate?" the reporter asked.

"I know only what you ladies and gentlemen of the press have told me," Princippi lied.

Of course he knew why Calhoun had dropped out. It was a foregone conclusion—once Mark Kaspar had instructed Princippi to leak the molestation story to the Prince's old friends at the *New Democracy* magazine. Kaspar had supplied the names of the young victims—all now of legal age and more than willing to tell their stories to a press that had ignored them until now. Kaspar had also persuaded Calhoun's former psychiatrist to speak to the magazine about the candidate's most private sessions. He didn't ask how Kaspar had convinced the doctor to go public with his story, but he assumed it had something to do with that strange temple at Ranch Ragnarok.

"How did Mr. Kaspar find out about Mr. Calhoun's record?" a reporter inquired.

"Mr. Kaspar has a great many friends. He also has an uncanny ability to size up a person the moment he meets him. Truthfully it's possible that he surmised everything from seeing the man on television, then confirmed his suspicions through his vast network of business and political allies. His ability to get to the heart of things is really quite astounding."

Some in the press scoffed at that observation.

"Any further comments on the State Department confirmation vote today?"

"Just that Mr. Kaspar feels the President's nominee will be defeated," Princippi remarked.

"He has the votes, Mr. Princippi," the congressional reporter from BCN News said blandly.

"Mr. Kaspar feels the President's nominee will be defeated," Princippi repeated.

"Is it possible Mr. Kaspar is mistaken?"

"I have not yet known him to be wrong about anything," Princippi said flatly.

Laughter rippled out at one end of the briefing room, making Princippi glower. Someone muttered that Kaspar's first mistake had been choosing the former governor as a political ally.

"Are there any further questions?" Princippi asked haughtily.

"Will Mr. Kaspar comment on the disappearance of Senator Cole's daughter?" asked the CNN reporter.

The snickering in the room subsided.

Princippi's eyes gleamed craftily as he absorbed this unexpected information.

Without missing a beat, he answered, "Our hearts go out to the Cole family at this troubling time. That's all for now, gentlemen."

As he excused himself from the room, Michael "the Prince" Princippi was deeply troubled by this worrisome news concerning Senator Cole's daughter. If the story broke big, the little bitch could knock his first press conference in ten years off the front pages.

HAROLD SMITH SCANNED the kidnapping report of Lori Cole with silent concern.

The CURE computers automatically pulled the story off the UPI wire, triggered by the Thermopolis and Truth Church connections.

The Associated Press had been quick to pick up the report and had disseminated a rewritten version of the UPI story to its subscribers. It made all the morning news shows.

With a fresh angle on the Thermopolis kidnappings, it would not be long before the press descended like starving vultures on the sleepy Wyoming town.

Alarming, as well, was the fact that the mysterious player in all of this, Mark Kaspar, had left Washington unexpectedly the previous evening. Smith discovered that Kaspar had taken a late flight from Washington not long before Remo had departed for Wyoming.

On the small black-and-white television in his Folcroft office, Smith channel-surfed between the morning shows, looking for anything, any nuggets concerning Thermopolis or Mark Kaspar, and praying that Remo didn't show up in the background of any on-the-scene reports.

Two major networks carried stories about Kaspar's appearance on television the previous evening. One anchorman described Kaspar as both "charismatic and enigmatic" and alluded to the fact that the "man from Wyoming" was a secret adviser to a great many Washington politicos. He went on to quote a *Times/Mirror* poll that had been conducted among "Barry Duke Live" viewers the previous evening that showed seventy-two percent of respondents favored a Kaspar run for public office—with a margin of error of plus or minus two percent.

Smith was amazed that people were willing to go on record for or against someone who had been in the national spotlight for barely one hour. It seemed that in the new electronic frontier of politics, Americans were willing to commit themselves to any candidate or issue on the strength of hardly any information at all.

When the news segment ended, the newsman joked with the morning show's weatherman and perky co-anchor about Kaspar's prediction of failure for the President's State Department nominee that morning. He opined Kaspar had about as much of a chance of being correct as the weatherman had of growing hair. The weatherman, an overweight, middle-aged man swathed in a flaming red sarong and high heels, burst into tears.

As the weatherman blubbered and pulled the giant fruit-garnished hat from atop his bald pate, the fire-engine red phone on Smith's desk began to ring. Smith switched the television off, shaking his head slowly. The older he got, the less the CURE director found he understood modern American culture.

Smith picked up the hot line to the White House.

"Yes, Mr. President."

"What in God's name is going on out in Wyoming, Smith?" the President demanded, his hoarse voice angry.

Smith sat up rigidly in his cracked leather chair. "I beg your pardon, sir?" he asked.

"Calhoun dropped out of the race," the President began. "That means an even weaker opposition candidate going up against Cole in the fall. I have no complaints there. I'm running roughshod over Congress just as it is. But now I'm hearing Cole might bail out over this kidnapping thing. I want you and your people to get the hell involved in this thing. This smells of someone tampering with a senatorial campaign. We can't have that, unless it's my party doing the tampering."

Smith considered. Did he dare tell the President that CURE was already involved, at least on the periphery of what was happening in Wyoming? After a moment's consideration, during which he kept the leader of the free world on hold like some telephone salesman, Smith decided that it would be best for all concerned if the President was kept in the dark.

He cleared his throat before speaking.

"Mr. President, may I remind you that it is against the organization's charter to involve itself in domestic politics?"

"I know that, Smith. But, dammit, this crosses party lines."

"That may be, sir. But with Calhoun no longer in the picture, if the status quo is maintained, no party has a clear advantage. I cannot use our resources to ensure a Cole run."

"I don't think you have the full picture, Smith," the President said tersely. "You know about this Mark Kaspar?"

"I am aware of him."

"Well, I just got off the phone with the minority and majority leaders in the House. It seems Kaspar has done an end run around me on this State Department appointment. They're voting in ten minutes, and I've just been informed that my shoo-in is going to lose."

Smith pursed his lips. "Really." He tried to force indifference into his voice, but interest silvered his lemony tone.

"At least the members of my own party had the decency to let me know they were turning on me," the President went on bitterly. "The House Minority Whip hinted that Kaspar prodded Principi to use political leverage against him and a bunch of the others." The President sighed. "I wish I knew what it was, because I'd sure as hell use it now," he added.

Smith's mind leaped to the Zen and Gary check with the word "prophecy" scrawled on the memo line. He turned his attention back to the matter at hand.

"I sympathize, Mr. President. But as I said, CURE cannot become embroiled in a domestic political situation. If there is something else...?"

"No," the President said levelly. "But you might

want to keep an eye on Kaspar. At the rate things are going now, when you pick up this phone in a couple of years, he might be the one on this end of the line.''

The President hung up.

Smith slowly replaced his own receiver.

Mark Kaspar. The enigmatic little man seemed to be at the center of everything swirling around the Church of the Absolute and Incontrovertible Truth. And now the field was being cleared for a run for the Wyoming Senate seat.

As Smith worked to isolate a dozen separate trains of thought, his computer screen began to flash a silent amber signal.

The Folcroft system had picked up something relevant to the events unfolding in Thermopolis. It was just a stroke of luck that half an hour before, upon learning of the abduction of Jackson Cole's daughter, Smith had included the disappearances of the other young girls within the search parameters of the CURE computers.

As he read the information on his buried computer screen, Smith's leaden pallor grew darker with something almost bordering on excitement.

One of the kidnapping victims had been recovered one hundred miles away from Thermopolis in the dense woods of Hot Springs State Park.

And she was alive....

20

The chatter of human voices pushed slowly into his consciousness.

Remo opened his eyes. The room was small and sparsely furnished. He was lying on a single bed beneath a set of long, tightly closed venetian blinds.

There was another bed, still made, next to his own. Beyond that was a simple dresser, a chair and a console television. The set was on and was the source of the muted conversation that had awakened him.

The morris chair before the television was occupied.

Remo sat up, swinging his legs around to the floor. Despite a slight feeling of dizziness, the strange sensation he had experienced at Ranch Ragnarok seemed to have passed.

The person in the chair sensed Remo's movement and quietly shut the television set off.

"Welcome back to the land of the living."

Remo ignored the speaker, noticing for the first time the items atop the bureau. A bottle of hydrogen peroxide, a torn-open package of gauze and two spools of white adhesive tape. A small tin trash barrel beside the bureau overflowed with bloodstained rags.

He looked down. He wore only his shorts. His bare thighs were bound with tape and gauze. In the center of each bandage, halfway up his thigh, was a half-dollar-size spot of brown dried blood. Other bandages covered the minor wounds on his back.

"You're a medic now?" Remo asked the room's other occupant.

"I wear a lot of hats," Buffy Brand admitted.

"This was a nice thought, but unnecessary," Remo said, indicating the bandages. He jammed his index finger in under the tops of each bandage and slit down toward his knees. The gauze section underneath the adhesive popped free. Remo peeled off the rest of the tape, exposing the wounds beneath.

The blood flow had abated, and the bullet holes had collapsed into angry patches of congealed plasma. A pinkish pucker of skin burned around both entry and exit wounds.

Buffy tried to conceal her surprise at the rapidity with which the wounds were healing. When she had brought Remo to this motel only hours before, it looked as if the blood loss he had sustained could prove fatal.

Remo stood. His legs felt good and solid, though he still sensed something malevolent hovering at the murky fringes of his mind. He took a step toward Buffy.

"Hold it," she commanded. She lifted her hand from beside the chair, revealing a nickled revolver that she trained carefully at the center of Remo's chest.

"You brought me here and bandaged me up just to kill me?" Remo's voice was flat, but there was a spark of humor in his deep-set eyes.

"Maybe," Buffy Brand said, her voice unwavering. "If you don't do exactly as I say."

"Sorry," Remo said with an apologetic shrug. "No can do." In a flash he was across the room and at Buffy's side. Before her eyes could register the blur Remo had become, he plucked the gun from her hand.

"I've had enough of these things lately," he growled. And with that he wrapped his fingers around barrel and butt and twisted. With a creak of protesting metal, Remo wrenched the revolver into two large halves. He then tossed the useless sections onto the unused motel bed.

"Who are you?" Buffy asked, her seemingly unflappable exterior giving way to a moment of amazement as she goggled at the remnants of her weapon.

"Ace cub reporter Remo Olsen," Remo announced. "Here to uncover the truth behind the Truth Church. And you are?"

"Special Agent Buffetta Brand, Federal Bureau of Investigation," Buffy said. "And you are full of crap."

"Aren't most reporters?" Remo asked. "Besides, I don't see you waving around any ID."

Buffy allowed him a tight-lipped smile. "It's buried in the woods a mile outside Truth Church property. Yogi Mom likes to conduct spontaneous searches, and I don't think she'd appreciate it if she found out one of her disciples was government-issue."

"Probably not," Remo agreed.

"So, what agency are you with?" Buffy asked.

"I told you before. I'm not with any agency."

"No way," Buffy said firmly. "Not the way they were preparing for you last night. They've got you pegged as someone dangerous. And from what I saw on the surveillance cameras, they're right on the money there."

"I don't know how dangerous I am like this," Remo said, indicating his bare legs. "Is there any rule against interrogating prisoners in their pants?"

"They're drying on the shower curtain," Buffy said, indicating the half-closed bathroom door behind her. She slumped back down in the worn morris chair as he went to retrieve his chinos. "I washed the blood out as best I could, but I draw the line at sewing up bullet holes," she called after him. "I assume you don't want me to know what agency you're with. I'd prefer not to be in the dark, but I've been alone on this Truth Church thing for so long, I'll take all the help I can get."

"I don't know if I can be much help right now," Remo admitted as he came back into the bedroom. He had pulled his wrinkled chinos back on and he zipped up his fly as he sat carefully on the tacky motel bedspread. Buffy had washed the pants in the bathroom sink, and they were still a little damp.

"Suit yourself," Buffy said. "I infiltrated their organization nine months ago and I've been left in there ever since. I'm working on the warm-body principle right about now."

Remo took a deep, cleansing breath. He was beginning to feel dizzy again. His throat suddenly felt tight and scratchy. "I heard the FBI lost somebody at the Truth Church."

"My partner," Buffy said. "He disappeared last September. I think they shot him one night. But I haven't been able to locate the body. I'll have them dead-bang on murder when I do."

"What's stopping you from escaping?"

"Until now, it's been impossible to sneak out of the place. Has been ever since Kaspar showed up. They won't let anyone go into town by themselves. I haven't even been able to report in."

"The FBI's written you off, too."

"That might make my job easier," Buffy said, and there was a cool professionalism in her voice Remo appreciated.

Remo felt a wave of nausea, and he leaned his knuckles on the edge of the bed for support. A sensation like a thousand flea bites attacked his lungs. He began coughing violently.

"You want a glass of water?" Buffy asked, rising.

Remo raised a hand. "I'm okay," he said. But his heart was pounding. He hadn't coughed like that in twenty years. He tried to ignore the dizziness and nausea. "Any idea how they knew I was coming?"

Buffy shrugged. "These people are wacko, but they've made some uncanny guesses lately. I don't buy into any of this tarot card or tea-leaf nonsense, but there's something weird going on there. About ten o'clock last night, the place went absolutely crazy. I didn't know why. I just knew something big was up. At first I thought Justice was starting a Waco rerun and the tanks were about to roll. But it was just you."

Remo nodded. "What do you know about the building at the back of the complex? The one with all the yellow smoke?"

"It's Kaspar's domain," Buffy said. "Remember my telling you when you first showed up with the old man about a split between Kaspar and Esther? Since he arrived, Kaspar's been bringing the Truth Churchers back to the hangar. Whatever he's doing in there, he's managed to shift their loyalty away from Esther.''

"It's a drug," Remo said, remembering the yellow smoke.

Buffy nodded. "I'm not surprised. I avoided going back there myself. I've only seen Kaspar a couple of times. He keeps to himself in that building. Along with an endless parade of mysterious visitors.''

"I know about them," Remo said dismissively. "So you're saying Esther isn't in charge anymore?''

"Correct," Buffy said. "But that's not the half of it. While everyone else was setting up cameras and bombs for your arrival, I finally snuck a peek inside the temple. You've heard about the Thermopolis kidnappings?''

Another coughing spasm racked Remo's lean frame. He nodded as he blinked back welling tears. His eyes were becoming hot.

Buffy's face was grim. "I've only picked up the story a little at a time from supervised trips for provisions into Thermopolis. Esther doesn't allow newspapers, TV or radio inside the camp. You knew Senator Cole was from Thermopolis?''

"I got that impression," Remo managed to say as another coughing spell subsided.

"While you were sleeping, I've been catching up on the news," she said, indicating the television with a nod. Her voice grew grave. "Kaspar has kidnapped Senator Jackson Cole's daughter. There's no telling what this means, but it's big.''

"It means," said Remo, "that it's time to shut the Truth Church down.''

SMITH LISTENED attentively to Remo's report on the secure line to his Folcroft office.

"It's all tied in, Smitty," Remo said. "The Truth Church, Kaspar, the kidnappings. Now they've got Cole's daughter. I just don't know why."

"Leverage, perhaps," Smith said. "Kaspar employed dirt to remove T. Rex Calhoun from the race. It may be that he hopes to extort Senator Cole into stepping aside, with the senator's daughter as the lever."

"That's pretty far-fetched."

"It is possible that he hopes the kidnapping alone will be enough to force Senator Cole from the race." A sudden fit of coughing from Remo caused the CURE director to pause. "Are you all right?" Smith asked.

"Fine," Remo said, clearing his throat. He felt the malevolent presence lurking at the back of his mind. He sucked in two deep breaths to clear his mind. The ensuing wave of heavy coughing doubled him over on the motel bed.

"Are you ill, Remo?" Smith asked urgently. He couldn't remember the last time his enforcement arm had been sick. But the deep, rasping cough coming over the line sounded like that of a lung-cancer patient.

"Never better, Smitty," Remo said, but the sarcasm was lost in another series of muffled coughs.

Smith found himself involuntarily clearing his own throat. "In any event," he said, "it is clear that Kaspar is a danger that must be dealt with."

"I'd like to oblige you, Smitty, but I've run into a little problem out here."

"Explain."

As Remo went into the details of the previous night's events, Smith grew intrigued. He was shocked that anyone would be able to hurt Remo with a common firearm. But he was astonished that the Truth Church denizens once more anticipated Remo's impending arrival. When Remo told him of the girl in Kaspar's temple, Smith's tone grew more incredulous.

"The girl spoke of the Oracle of Delphi?" Smith asked after Remo had finished.

"And something about Apollo's Pythia," Remo added. "Isn't Apollo some kind of Roman god?" As he spoke, Remo felt something subtle and insidious slipping like an early-morning fog across the back of his mind.

"Greek," Smith corrected. "Apollo was the son of Zeus. He was the god of light who drove the chariot of the sun in Greek mythology. He was also the god who gave people the gift of knowledge of future events."

"You're kidding." Remo grew dizzy. His eyes were suddenly heavy lidded, as if he hadn't slept in a year.

"In ancient Greece, Delphi became the religious center of the empire because of the oracle there," Smith supplied. "Is it possible, Remo, that the intoxicating effects of this yellow smoke caused the Cole girl to speak as she did?"

"Possible?" Remo growled, trying to snap out of his mental fog. "Smitty, it was pretty damn obvious that's what was going on."

"What?"

Remo suddenly sat bolt upright on the motel bed.

He clutched the phone in his now sweating palm, making warm imprints in the plastic casing.

Something appeared before him. Remo wasn't sure if it was real or in his mind. It was a field of inky blackness spreading limitlessly in every direction.

"Sinanju is mine!" a voice that was not Remo's boomed from his throat.

"What was that?" Smith demanded over the line.

Smith could have saved his breath. The phone had slipped from Remo's fingers as he slumped, unconscious, to the bed.

Buffy Brand, who had remained in her chair across the room for Remo's entire conversation, jumped up to check his pulse. Satisfied that he was still alive, she lifted the receiver to her ear.

"Your man is hurt," she said.

There was a momentary pause on the line before a lemony voice spoke. "Who is this?" the voice demanded.

"It doesn't matter," Buffy said. "I'll give you instructions on where he is. You can have somebody come and collect him. I'm going back for the Cole girl."

This time the man on the other end of the line paused only a beat. "That is inadvisable," the lemony voice said. "If my man, as you call him, failed, it is unlikely that anyone else can succeed."

"It doesn't mean that no one else can try," Buffy Brand retorted.

But she spoke the words with more confidence than she felt. Buffy Brand had seen Remo in action. They didn't make them like Remo in the Bureau. Or anywhere else.

21

"What the hell were you thinking?" Esther Clear-Seer screamed. She had learned from CNN—which she picked up via satellite in her ranch house in spite of her strict ban on such devious outside influences—that the latest virgin she had harvested was none other than the only child of the state's senior senator.

Esther thought she had recognized the girl from somewhere. Now she realized that it was from the numerous campaign appearances she had made with her famous father, Senator Jackson Cole.

"You are distraught," Kaspar said indifferently. He had removed the tripod and the grate from above the rock fissure and was climbing down to retrieve the heavy rock urn. As she had since the previous night's events, Lori Cole sat rigidly on the top steps of the Pythia platform.

"Of course I'm frigging distraught!" Esther yelled. "You made me go out and collect one of the highest-profile kids in this backwater state! What, do you *want* me to go to jail?"

"I want you to stay in line," Kaspar said tersely. There appeared to be a crack in his usually unemotional facade. He hefted the heavy urn in his frail hands and was forcing it up to the top of the platform. He strained beneath the great burden.

"Stay in line?" Esther said. "What do you mean, stay in line? Didn't I go out and get you all the girls you wanted?"

"Didn't you resolve when you collected this one that it would be your last?" Kaspar said. Sliding the urn to the platform, he nodded toward the catatonic girl on the steps.

Esther's eyes grew wide in surprise. "How did you know that?" she demanded.

Kaspar shook his head. "You have no idea what we have unleashed here, have you?" he said, pushing himself back up to the platform.

"I haven't unleashed anything but a huge nightmare," Esther said. "Cole's daughter," she muttered bitterly to herself. "I never should have let you come in here."

"You were destined to be the one to help my master."

"I don't believe any of that hocus-pocus," Esther said. "Any deal I made with you was purely business."

"How fortunate for you, then, that your procurement of this vessel will allow you to continue our venture."

"You're going to hold this over my head, aren't you, Kaspar?"

"Only as much as it is necessary."

"And if I don't toe the line?"

"I would be distraught, as would you, if the authorities were to find out that your church was responsible for the abductions. Particularly the senator's daughter. As I understand it, he has many friends who are judges in this state. I'm sure they will be quite fair when the time comes to pass judgment on you."

"You bastard," Esther snapped.

Kaspar smiled tightly. "Can I assume we have a firm understanding?"

Wearing a look of pure hatred, Esther nodded sharply. She then stormed over to the far side of the platform.

Satisfied, Kaspar knelt before the urn. With great care he tucked the sleeves of his priestly robes up inside the body of the garment and, without hesitation, shoved his pale arms into the yellowish powder up to the elbows.

Kaspar closed his eyes.

After a moment of intense concentration, his eyes reopened. A concerned expression creased his brow. With growing anxiety he began feeling around inside the stone urn like a child searching for the prize at the bottom of a box of cereal.

When he at last pulled his arms from the yellow powder—now a moist, sticky paste from the natural steam of the rock fissure—his face was a rock. He brushed the thick yellow clumps from his forearms.

Esther noticed Kaspar's worried look, and though she wished it wasn't so, she knew that her fate was now tied inexorably to his.

"What's wrong?" she asked from the other side of the platform. She tried to force indifference into her voice, but it came out as shrill as a mouse's squeak.

"It is as I feared," Kaspar said, still kneeling beside the urn. "The essence of the Pythia has fled with the young Sinanju Master."

"What does that mean?"

Kaspar got to his feet slowly. "It means that Apollo has chosen a vessel." Kaspar stood.

"You mean that Remo nuisance?"

Kaspar nodded. "East has met West. The prophecy is fulfilled. But the young Sinanju Master is attempting to fight his destiny." He thought for a moment. "He must be returned to us."

"But we have no idea where he is," Esther said.

"At present, no," Kaspar admitted. He began pacing back and forth beside the open crevice atop the platform. "The services of Sinanju are quite costly," he reasoned. "Much more than most wealthy individuals are willing to pay. In all likelihood Sinanju is employed in some covert capacity by the United States government. It is there we will begin." He started down the stairs.

"This is a big country, Kaspar," Esther said. "The government is huge. Where are you going to start?"

Kaspar did not slow his pace down the rocky steps.

"At the top."

IT WAS EARLY EVENING and Smith's footfalls were the only sound in the basement corridor of Folcroft's security wing. Like the report of a rifle shot, each single step echoed sharply off the sickly green walls.

Smith couldn't remember the last time he had felt this weary.

He had just gotten off the phone with the President. The nation's Chief Executive had vaguely threatened to defund CURE if Smith didn't look into the political morass that Mark Kaspar had created.

A part of Smith had been tempted to tell the President that CURE was already on the case, but with the Truth Church situation still unresolved and Remo's status up in the air, he decided it would be best to leave matters as they were. Besides, it would be better for all concerned to let the President shut down the secret organization than allow him to believe that Smith could be used as a political tool of the executive branch.

In the end the President had hung up, unhappy with Smith, but willing to await developments.

Smith understood the President's anger.

Earlier that afternoon Mark Kaspar had appeared on CNN, ostensibly to comment on the failed assistant-secretary-of-state appointment. As the segment unfolded, Kaspar began hinting of even more tumultuous events unfolding in Washington. The little man revealed that the loss that morning of the State Department spot would be as nothing compared to the major political problems facing the President in Washington that very afternoon.

The resignations started at about 4:00 p.m.

Five congressmen in the President's party had held a joint news conference to say that they were resigning. Since the entire House was up for reelection in the fall, the resignation of these five players was a critical blow to the President's legislative agenda. It was probably already too late for the party to field viable candidates in these five crucial races, and so the President was looking to take some major hits in the House—the wing of Congress his party had hoped most to retake in the fall midterm elections.

Because of his obvious insider's knowledge, the three major networks competed to get Kaspar on their nightly news shows. He had appeared on two, both BCN and MBC, being interviewed in-depth by the networks' respective anchormen about the latest problems facing the president.

On both programs Kaspar had predicted two more major resignations before the evening was through.

By nine o'clock, eastern standard time, two ranking senators of the President's party had quit, each citing "personal reasons" for his unexpected decision.

Smith had run a computer check on all seven men and had traced several payments—through various agents—to the Church of the Absolute and Incontrovertible Truth.

It all came down to Kaspar.

Smith's thoughts immediately turned to T. Rex Calhoun and the child-molestation charges. Kaspar must have had information just as damning against the other legislators to force them to step aside so quickly. One of the senators had served in Congress for over thirty years.

Smith was thinking of the telephone call from the President as he approached the door at the end of the long corridor. It was odd, but as he raised his knuckles to knock on the thick metal panel, Smith realized that getting chewed out by the President of the United States was far less threatening to him than what he was about to do.

Smith rapped sharply on the door.

"Enter."

Inside the room the Master of Sinanju sat cross-legged on his woven reed mat. Smith allowed the door to swing closed behind him.

Chiun rocked back and forth, humming quietly to

himself. His ancient eyelids, as thin as the most delicate rice paper, were closed in meditation.

Smith cleared his throat. "Am I disturbing you,
Master Chiun?"

The old Korean's eyes remained closed. "Does the
bee disturb the delicate flower?" he asked. Of course
the answer was yes, but Chiun did not speak the words
as an insult. It was always good to leave the employ
of an emperor on the best possible terms. "Has your
mighty warship arrived?"

Smith hesitated. "I'm sorry?"

"The vessel that will return Remo and myself to
Sinanju."

"Ah, the submarine. There has been a slight, er,
delay."

Chiun ceased his subtle rocking motion. His parchment eyelids fluttered open.

"It has already been two weeks," he said, eyes nar-
rowing.

"It will arrive any day now," Smith assured the
Master of Sinanju.

Chiun closed his eyes and resumed the side-to-side
motion. "Then my heart soars that I will see my
homeland once again." His tone was colored with the
unmistakable message that he considered this meeting
with Smith finished.

"Master Chiun?" Smith asked.

Chiun checked his meditation chant. "What is it
now?" he asked impatiently. The rocking motion was
more forced as the Master of Sinanju labored to main-
tain a level of inner peace.

"I thought that I should prepare you...." Smith considered his next words carefully, as if revealing a secret shame. "Remo has been injured," he said quietly.

Chiun stopped rocking at once. "Explain," he said sharply.

"He has been shot," explained Smith. "Twice. He has also sustained a few minor injuries—multiple cuts and abrasions. I am not certain what else is the matter, but he suffered some kind of fainting spell when I spoke to him earlier today. I have arranged for his transport back to Folcroft."

Inwardly Chiun allowed himself a sigh of relief. This was obviously a transparent attempt by Smith to retain the services of Sinanju. Remo could not be shot. No full Master of Sinanju had ever been shot with a gun since the invention of the weapon, and Remo had become a full Master years ago.

"Poor Remo," said Chiun, shaking his head sadly. The white tufts of hair over each ear seemed to swirl with the subtle violence of the gesture.

Smith was surprised that Chiun wasn't more upset. The Master of Sinanju had long ago developed a paternal affection for Remo, and for his part, Remo looked on the old man as the father he never had. There was something unsettling about Chiun's easy acceptance of the situation.

"One of the Thermopolis kidnapping victims has been recovered," Smith continued. "I have had her rerouted to Folcroft. In our conversation Remo suggested some kind of new drug is being used on the Truth Church followers, which could explain Remo's fainting spell. We may be able to learn something from the girl that will help Remo. He will be here within the hour himself."

Chiun's hazel eyes locked on Smith's, freezing the CURE director in his tracks like a frightened deer in the blazing headlights of an oncoming car. He spoke only two words: "Truth Church?"

Wary of those two menacing eyes and of the deadly power behind them, Smith tensed. "Yes," he said hesitantly. "At my insistence Remo returned to the Truth Church yesterday."

The life seemed to drain from Chiun's face. "My son," he said softly. "He is truly ill?"

Smith nodded. "I am sure he will be fine," he said haltingly.

Chiun's hazel eyes flared like twin candles.

"This child you spoke of—was there an odor about her?"

"The girl from Hot Springs State Park? As a matter of fact, there was. A very strong sulphur smell. The doctors think that it may be a side effect of the drug she was taking. I have placed her in this wing, two floors above."

"The Remo with whom you conversed, did he hack?"

Smith frowned. This was a puzzling line of questioning. "Hack?" he asked, confused.

"Did he clear his throat thusly?" Chiun hacked loudly.

Smith shrugged. "Yes, now that you come to mention it, Remo *did* display coughing spasms. He mentioned that he had inhaled some of the drug-laden smoke."

"It is no drug," Chiun said, and there was a deep sadness in his voice. "What were the last words spoken to you by Remo?"

Smith considered a moment. "He said, 'Sinanju is mine.'"

Chiun's eyes strayed forlornly to the faded carpeting.

"We were to leave your employ." The words of the Master of Sinanju were soft and far away, bitter waves in a sea of regret. "Only a matter of days, and we would be free."

"The contract was still in force," Smith countered. "I was within my rights to send Remo back on assignment."

"Do not speak to me of rights," Chiun hissed. "My son is lost."

Smith cleared his throat uncomfortably. He understood Remo and Chiun's relationship, but he also understood his job. And that job involved placing his two operatives at risk whenever missions required it.

Smith assumed his most reasonable tone of voice. "Master Chiun, if Remo has become infected with something at Ranch Ragnarok, it is possible that we can find a cure. His fainting might only be a result of blood loss, nothing more. I will let you know when he arrives. If he is ill, I am certain he will appreciate a visit from you."

Smith issued a farewell nod and left the room.

For a long while after he had gone, Chiun sat motionless on his coarse tatami mat. He no longer hummed.

"THIS WAS one of the greatest days of my life," Michael Principi enthused over the telephone. He had coordinated with the networks to get America's latest political guru, Mark Kaspar, on television as quickly as possible to comment on the departures of the various congressmen and senators. Unbeknownst to all but the highest elected officials under the Capitol dome, Principi was also the man who had placed the phone calls that had forced the seven men into premature retirement. All of these machinations were engineered by Mark Kaspar himself, behind the scenes. As he listened to Kaspar's voice from Ragnarok, he knew that more was to come.

"You are not having a problem with access inside the Beltway now?" Kaspar asked.

"Are you kidding? They're scared shitless not to talk to me," Principi said joyfully. "The power boys are afraid I'm going to give them the same whammy I gave to the President's allies today."

"It is good that they fear you," Kaspar droned.

"Good, bad, what do I care?" Principi said. "Just so long as they fear. So what's all this about anyway?" Kaspar had given him the dirt he needed to unseat the "Capitol Hill Seven"—as the media had dubbed the departing members of Congress—but had yet to give him a reason for the action. Privately, he suspected Kaspar was weakening the current administration in anticipation of the next national campaign. Everyone knew the vice president was considered virtually an heir apparent.

"I want you to place some discreet phone calls to the highest-ranking members in both houses of Congress," Kaspar instructed. "Find out if they possess any knowledge of the Master of Sinanju or his protégé. Particularly the whereabouts of the younger Master."

"Wait a minute, let me get a pencil."

While Principi fumbled around his Washington

hotel room, Kaspar glanced impatiently at the Pythia chamber.

He wore his street clothes, having left his white priestly vestments in an outer room. No sense in dressing for ceremony since his Master was no longer present.

Even the tripod was empty. Esther Clear-Seer had sequestered the latest virgin vessel in a sealed antechamber.

The bare brick room felt empty and cold.

"I'm back," Michael Principi's whiny voice announced over the cellular phone.

Kaspar detailed his instructions slowly, making certain Principi repeated every word back to him.

"Okay, I'll ask around," Principi said once he had copied down the information.

"Make it clear that I will smile favorably on anyone who is able to give me information concerning the young Sinanju Master. Encourage them to go to the highest authority if necessary."

"Will do."

"You've done your job well so far, Prince," Kaspar said by way of encouragement. He could almost hear Principi beaming over the phone.

"You know, Mark, you embarrassed the President a lot with that State Department thing this morning," Principi said, getting back to what he felt was the day's most important business. "I have the results of a poll they took after the vote. Your name-recognition factor has jumped up to the high thirties. That's not bad for someone who just yesterday was a political unknown. And I can guarantee you that your appearances, coupled with these resignations, are going to push you higher up in the public awareness. You're building a strong platform."

"First things first," Kaspar said. "If I do not find the one I seek, I am destined for failure."

"Then we better find this guy," Princippi responded, sobering. "Because I can tell you from experience, failure sucks."

22

The ambulance passed through the iron gates of Fol-croft Sanitarium a little after 9:00 p.m. The white-and-blue vehicle circled the meticulously landscaped traffic island at the main entrance, stopping before the lone figure who stood waiting like a ghost in gray.

The attendant in white uniform and orange jacket climbed from the cab. He walked to the rear of the vehicle, the gravel driveway crackling beneath his shoes. He lugged a clipboard beneath his arm, which he handed to the sour-faced man in gray.

"You sure you want this one?" the young man asked, chewing languidly on a huge wad of gum.

Harold W. Smith had already begun signing the sheaf of forms jammed under the clipboard's metal fastener. He felt his heart skip a beat. "Is something wrong?" he asked, looking over the tops of his glasses as he signed another sheet.

The attendant laughed. "Just that this nutcase trashed the first ambulance the company sent to fetch him." The young man was like a rusty faucet that, once it was pried open, could not be stopped.

As Smith hastily filled out forms, the other launched into his story. "First he tells Buck—that's the other driver—that he wants to ride up front. Buck says no way. Company policy. Fine, everything's hunky-dory. Buck barely makes it out on the highway from La-Guardia before it starts raining.''

"It hasn't rained in six days," Smith said levelly.

"It wasn't raining water," explained the driver slowly, turning the wad of gum over in his mouth. "It was raining stuff. You know—blankets, plasma bottles, tongue depressors. Finally Buck spots the oxygen tanks and gurney come sailing over the roof. When he looked in the rearview, he saw your psycho ripping the back door off the ambulance.'' The ambulance driver paused and singled out one of the forms on the clipboard.

"That one is for the door, and the one below is for the damage this guy caused when he threw it over the ambulance roof. It took out the right front tire and shattered the axle.''

"Yes, fine," said Smith unhappily. He signed the final forms hurriedly, handing the clipboard back to the driver.

"I heard how these crazies can be superstrong sometimes," he added. "But, man, throwing something as heavy as an oxygen tank over the roof of a moving ambulance? I hope you got a sturdy rubber room, Doc.''

Smith followed the ambulance attendant to the rear of the vehicle, and the young man unlocked the door, taking special care to stand clear in case the lunatic in the back let loose with another tantrum.

The door came open.

And the rear of the ambulance was empty.

"What the—?"

The driver climbed up into the back of the large van

and began digging through boxes and peering behind assorted medical equipment.

"Where is my patient?" Smith demanded anxiously.

"Hiya, Smitty," a familiar voice said.

Smith spun around to find Remo leaning casually against the side of the ambulance, his hands jammed deep into the pockets of his torn chinos.

"Lose someone, pal?" he called airily toward the rear door.

The driver stuck his head out of the back of the ambulance. "Hey, how'd you get out there?" he asked.

"I opened the door and climbed out of the cab," Remo said, a smile of utter contentment spreading across his harsh features. He pointed to the ambulance cab. The passenger's door was hanging open. "Be sure and tell Buck how you waived the 'no front riders' rule." He coughed quietly into his balled fist.

This was more than the driver could comprehend. "But you were in back," he sputtered. He removed his cap and scratched his head pensively.

"If there is any further damage," Smith said quickly in a rare display of generosity, "be sure to send any additional bills to Folcroft."

He grabbed Remo by the arm and hustled him up the steps.

Wearing a look of utter bafflement, the young man closed the rear door of the ambulance and climbed back up into the cab. As he leaned over to close the passenger's door, he noticed that the seat was pushed forward slightly. When he glanced behind it, he found a wide hole had been ripped in the sheet metal separating cab from body. He hadn't noticed it from the back because it had been blocked by an equipment-laden shelf unit.

He looked up at the building. The mental patient had already disappeared inside the sanitarium with the doctor. The attendant stuffed a new stick of gum in his mouth as he considered the damage to the ambulance.

Finally he shrugged, started the engine and circled back around to the main road. He had resolved to let whoever signed out the ambulance after him take the blame for the damage.

After all, how was he going to explain this to his supervisor?

"WHERE'S CHIUN?" Remo asked.

Smith was stooped, carefully examining the bullet wounds in Remo's legs. "The Master of Sinanju is in his quarters," he said vaguely.

The scrapes and bruises on Remo's arms and back had long since healed, Smith saw. His system was now working furiously to repair the internal damage caused by the Pythia's bullets.

"I kind of figured he'd meet me out front." Remo sounded disappointed.

Smith stood. "This is remarkable, Remo," he said. "Your wounds are healing so rapidly I would swear they occurred weeks ago. The scabs have even dropped off."

"Right," Remo said disinterestedly. "Smitty, you did tell Chiun about the yellow smoke?"

Smith's steady gray gaze was drawn away from the injuries. "I informed him before your arrival."

"And?"

"He wishes to meet with you downstairs."

Remo cleared his throat. "Bet he's pretty steamed."

Smith did not respond. He didn't feel it was his place to tell Remo that the Master of Sinanju had seemed more sad than angry.

"Chiun *did* seem concerned by your cough," he admitted.

"Not half as concerned as I am," Remo said. He poured himself a glass of ice water from a nearby frosted metal pitcher and downed the liquid in one gulp.

"You have recovered from your fainting spell," Smith said.

Remo shook his head. A minor coughing spasm racked his thin frame. "You have an unerring ability at stating the obvious, you know that, Smitty?" he said. "Besides, it feels like whatever knocked me out could come back any time."

Remo made a face. "It was strange. The last thing I remember in Wyoming was talking to you on the phone. I don't know what was in that yellow smoke, but it knocked me for a loop. I woke up on the plane. Guess Buffy must have told you where to find me, huh?"

"The girl from the motel," Smith said, nodding. "What does she know of our operation?"

"Nothing," Remo answered. "She probably saved my life. Besides, she's a Fed."

Smith grew interested. "The missing FBI agent?"

"She didn't look very missing to me," Remo said.

Smith considered telling Remo that the girl had returned to Ranch Ragnarok to try to free the Cole girl, but decided against it. He didn't want CURE's enforcement arm risking another trip west until they were certain of what they were dealing with.

"She must remain the FBI's problem for the time being," he said instead. "Right now we must put all our efforts into identifying the drug you inhaled. You described a sulphur smell?"

"The place stunk of rotten eggs, if that's what you mean."

Smith nodded. "Typical of sulphur. It is quite pungent. Perhaps there's something to learn from the Forrester girl."

Smith led Remo out of the examining room and down the corridor to a windowless room at the end of the security wing.

On the room's only bed a young girl, not quite in her teens, lay motionless beneath a thin cotton sheet.

"She was discovered by some campers in a forest near Ranch Ragnarok," Smith explained as they entered the room.

"One of the missing girls?" Remo asked.

Smith nodded. "The fourth," he said. "And the last to disappear before Senator Cole's daughter. They must have released her when they went to collect the next girl."

Remo watched the young child in the bed breathing rhythmically, oblivious to all external stimuli. Remo himself had a daughter, and even though he rarely saw her, he knew how he would react if he found out she had been treated like Allison Forrester. He vowed to make Mark Kaspar and Esther Clear-Seer pay dearly for what they had done to the innocent young girls of Thermopolis.

A strong smell of sulphur exuded from her unconscious body. Smith pulled a pearl gray handkerchief from an inner coat pocket. He placed the bunched cloth over mouth and nose in a vain attempt to block out the offensive odor.

"Since her arrival, I have had a battery of tests run," Smith said, gazing down at the prone figure. "CAT scans. An MRI. All results point to near dormant synaptic activity. It is as though her brain has been completely wiped clean."

"The smoke?" Remo asked softly. He had slid a folding chair close to the bed and sat down beside it, his forearms resting on the retractable metal restraining bar. He breathed in long sips through his mouth so the stink wouldn't affect his olfactory receptors.

Smith nodded. "All children are born with some level of cognition. Even in utero a fetus is conscious of its surroundings—but all of our tests have shown that this girl has regressed beyond that limited level of awareness. Her responses to external stimuli are back beyond prenatal. We even had to close her eyes for her. She didn't seem to know how to do it without help."

Allison Forrester was a pretty young girl, and while Remo watched her sleep on that strange bed so far away from her home, he thought she looked like some long-forgotten princess from a fairy tale, waiting for a knight in shining armor to revive her with a kiss.

Remo gently pushed a lock of auburn hair from her forehead. The girl stirred, as if awakening from a long slumber. She smiled as she stretched her arms beneath the sheets.

Smith took a step forward, lowering his handkerchief in surprise. "What's happening?" he asked.

Remo looked baffled. "I'm not sure," he said.

He put his arm above the girl once more. She stretched again, rotating her shoulders as if she was about to awaken.

This time Remo detected a faint movement from over his own bare forearm. He peered closer and saw something that looked like steam rising from his skin. A ghostly phosphorescence. And it was yellow.

All at once the eyelids of the Forrester girl snapped open. Her mouth opened, making rubbery shapes in a desperate attempt to speak. But no sound came out.

The yellow exhalation from Remo's arm gathered and coalesced, hovering like an early-morning fog over the girl's bed. With deep, gasping breaths the girl began to breathe in the yellow mist, like a smoker craving airborne nicotine.

She fell back to the bed, her vacant eyes suddenly content.

Smith was about to say something when the girl spoke.

"Sin-an-juuu..." The voice was that of a long dead soul crying out from beyond the grave. Smith shuddered at the eerie sound. "Sinanju," she wailed. "East has met West. Your destiny will be fulfilled."

Somewhere in the back of Remo's mind, the malevolent presence resurfaced. It had been there all along, flitting at the edges of his thoughts. But as the girl spoke, he could feel the other consciousness grow in strength.

As he stared through the yellow haze, an image suddenly appeared in Remo's mind—the same one he had seen in the motel room in Wyoming.

It was as if he were seeing something projected on the wall of the small hospital room. He saw a limitless black expanse at the center of which two figures stood. He did not know how, but he knew that one of the figures was purely malevolent. The other figure stood immobile in his mind, paralyzed perhaps by fear. As the bizarre tableau played on in silence, Remo saw the figure of evil move toward the second, docile creature, the villain's hands raised as if to do battle.

Remo tried to focus closely, attempting to see the combatants more clearly, but the vision started to disintegrate.

All at once the blackness drained from his sight, and he was again in the Folcroft room. The Forrester girl lay before him, eyes open, breathing softly.

He felt a hand on his shoulder.

"What is it, Remo?" Smith asked in a hushed voice.

Remo closed his dark eyes once, squeezing hard. Perspiration oozed from every pore. He leaned on the hospital bed. "I don't know," he admitted. His breathing became labored and he panted, trying to catch his breath. His throat felt raw and swollen.

"Is this like the last fainting spell?" Smith asked.

"Fainting spell?" Remo turned on Smith as if the director were out of his mind. The room was dimming. He realized that the yellow sulphur smoke had somehow expanded. It was as if he were looking at everything through a veneer of yellow gauze. The rotten-egg stench filled the room, clogging his nostrils. He had forgotten to breathe through his mouth.

"You were out for more than five minutes," Smith said.

"What are you talking about, Smitty?" Remo said.

The smoke in the room was heavy and its sheer thereness crawled with subtle menace. He felt as if there were just enough good oxygen in the room to keep him alive. No more.

"After the girl spoke, you seemed to fade off. The smoke you see was produced somehow by your own body during that interval. Perhaps you absorbed it through your skin at the Truth Church ranch."

Remo began to protest. The words died in his throat.

Both men watched in wonder as the faint yellow haze began to pulsate with the regularity of a steady beating heart. The room gradually brightened as the incandescent fog grew with each passing second.

Remo felt the sensitive hairs on his arm lift and tingle. The strange force within his mind stirred, stretching as one awakened from an ancient slumber.

THE YELLOW SMOKE ROSE slowly toward the center of the ceiling as if it were being drawn into a black hole. Smith's blinking gaze followed it. In a matter of seconds, it had formed an odious, swirling mass that completely obscured the dingy acoustical tiles above.

The glowing cloud throbbed with a regularity that was at once familiar and frightening to Remo, for he knew that the pulsing of the living cloud matched the beating of his own heart.

It hovered there, like an octopus of mist drawing its tentacles tightly about it.

Without warning, the swirling cloud gushed down

from the ceiling. The thick mass of smoke surged into the gently rising chest of Allison Forrester.

At its touch the girl twisted unnaturally. Her head arched back into the hospital pillow, and her mouth shot open, her cracked and swollen tongue darting forward in pain. The force within the yellow cloud passed through her thin hospital nightgown to vanish within the girl's straining bosom.

Mouth agape, Smith looked from the girl to Remo and back to the girl again, trying to comprehend what had just transpired.

Allison Forrester sat bolt upright in bed. She turned to look at Remo. But the eyes that gazed upon him were not the eyes of Allison Forrester. They were as black as beads of liquid tar.

"Why do you resist?" The voice was old and very reasonable. The eyes remained malevolent, and Remo knew that they belonged to the demon force within his mind. "You have only to ask the one you call 'father,' and all will be made clear to you. East has met West, young Sinanju. It is no use resisting. The sun god will have what is his."

The girl's hand snaked out, gripping Remo's forearm. He felt the yellow smoke pass back through his skin like a slow jolt of electricity. Remo broke free.

The girl dropped lifelessly back to the bed. The violence of the motion tore the intravenous tube from her arm, and the end slapped hollowly against the metal support pipe. A small puff of yellow mist curled from her nostrils to vanish in the fetid air.

Remo stepped back, horror distorting his features. The presence had reasserted itself within his mind, stronger than before. He could feel the power of the Delphic oracle swelling like a tumor within him.

Smith was shaking his head in disbelief. "What does all this mean?" he asked breathlessly, unable to reconcile all he had just witnessed with anything he knew to be real.

"I don't know," Remo said tensely. "But I think I know who will."

Like a man under sentence of death, he trudged resolutely to the door.

23

The Master of Sinanju sat morosely in his Folcroft
quarters, the skirts of his white mourning robes pulled
tightly around his bony knees and tucked neatly away
beneath his sandaled feet.

Chiun had not stirred from his simple reed mat for
hours. A great sadness filled his heart as he awaited
Remo's dreaded return.

Around the room the light from more than two
dozen squat white beeswax tapers played among the
dusty pleats of the heavy woolen drapes.

The Master of Sinanju had prayed to the souls of
his ancestors for guidance in this terrible time, but no
inspiration touched his receptive essence. The
thoughts crowding his mind were too deep and troubling.

He didn't know if he could face what had once been
Remo.

Chiun had spent this final hour of solitude berating
himself for this, his ultimate failure. He had failed
himself and his son, along with the tiny fishing village
that relied on them both.

Chiun was to blame for not forcing Remo to listen
to reason. If he had related the legend of Tang, Remo
might have saved himself. Remo would have under-

stood. Then they could have shaken the dust of this barbarian nation from their sandals, and gone off to ply their trade in other, more fortunate lands.

But the curse of Tang prevented all of that. The inevitability of what had been foretold, at a time when this so-called Western civilization was in its infancy, had overtaken all.

East had met West.

And another, darker part of his soul knew that if Remo had now become as he suspected him to be, then the Master of Sinanju could not allow his adopted son to live. It was, above all, this knowledge that weighed so heavily on Chiun's frail shoulders.

A shallow copper bowl of incense sat on the floor before him, and when the Master of Sinanju heard the unmistakable sound of Remo's feet gliding up the hallway, he spun a long taper between his fingers and touched the burning wick to the incense. The contents of the bowl flashed to life.

Chiun pressed his fingers together at the taper's tip, extinguishing the yellowish flame. Thus prepared, he stared stonily at the heavy metal door. And waited. For all had been foretold.

Remo tapped lightly.

"Little Father?" he called softly.

"Come in, my son," Chiun said, voice as thin as a reed.

Remo pushed the door into the room. The flickering candlelight on his bony face gave him the gaunt aspect of a houseless specter.

Chiun beckoned with a skeletal finger. "Seat yourself before me, my son."

A second mat had been spread out on the carpet

before the Master of Sinanju. Remo sank weightlessly to the floor.

Remo raised his nose at the smell of the incense. "Sheesh, what are you doing—burning alley cats?"

Chiun ignored the remark. "You are not well," he observed.

Remo gave a halfhearted shrug. "I've been better," he admitted.

Chiun nodded in understanding and stared at the incandescent center of the incense pot. "The sulphur smell is quite strong," he said.

A great sadness clung to his teacher, and it deepened Remo's anguish to know that it was he who had placed this burden upon Chiun's thin shoulders.

A silence existed between them for a time. Neither man spoke. Finally Remo cleared his throat.

"What is happening to me, Little Father?" he asked quietly.

"What do you feel, my son?" Chiun countered.

"There's something inside me. Inside my brain," Remo said with difficulty. "It feels like it's taking over my mind. Every time it forces its will upon me, it gets stronger." He rotated his thick wrists in absentminded agitation. "Chiun, I don't know if I can keep fighting it off."

Eyes slitting, Chiun nodded. "The prophecy is fulfilled," he intoned. His voice was hollow and distant.

"The legend of Master Tang?"

Chiun looked up from the incense bowl. "It grieves me, Remo, that I did not sooner impart this tale to you." His mouth grew grim. "But we who are one with Sinanju understand that it is not possible to avoid destiny."

"Tell me about Tang," said Remo. It was the first time in his life he could remember asking to be told a Sinanju legend.

Chiun stroked his wispy beard. "It is quite an interesting tale, Remo," he said. "It is not terribly old, either—a trifle over two thousand years by Western dating." As Chiun settled back to retell the ancient legend, a profound sadness marked his web-wrinkled countenance.

"Master Tang was possessed of a quality most rare to Sinanju Masters, Remo," Chiun began. "A quality, in truth, rare in members of our ancestral village."

Remo leaned closer, very interested of face.

Chiun hung his head, as if relating a personal disgrace. "Master Tang was a dullard," he whispered.

"That's a quality?" Remo asked.

"Qualities are measured in extremes," explained Chiun. "To gauge the worth of something, it must first be set beside a thing of worthlessness. And so it was with the dullness of Tang, measured against the brilliance of all Masters who came before."

Remo's brow puckered in puzzlement. Chiun went on.

"Just as it is true that qualities are measured in extremes, it was also true that Tang was a most extreme individual. Now, it is written that the Master who trained Tang was skillful and swift, and when it came time for him to choose a successor, many curried favor but none could perform to his satisfaction." Chiun closed his almond eyes. His voice became that of another. "Woe to Sinanju. Woe to the Master. None are worthy. So the line must end. The babies would have to be cast into the sea. For that is what the women of

Sinanju were forced to do when work and food were wanting. They threw the infants into the icy waters of the bay, pretending they were sending them home to be born in better times—but this was just a fable to console themselves. For what they were doing was the unthinkable. Woe to the Master, for it was his labors which sustained the village—and it was his failure that would end a tradition already three thousand years old. Oh, how sad a fate for Sinanju, and for the Master Paekjo, who was known as 'the Swan,' because he plied his art with the grace of a swan in flight.''

Remo wondered if swans were all that graceful but kept his mouth shut.

"Master Paekjo toured the village, his head held high, for he was, after all, still Reigning Master of Sinanju. Everywhere his foot alighted, he was greeted with jeers and stones. The women of the village did spit upon his cloak and hurl abuses upon him. The children threw dirt and rocks at his back, shouting after him that he had failed the village of his ancestors and that he should send himself home to the sea, and other calumnies. The men of the village, rightfully fearing the wrath of an angry Master, fled to a nearby village where drinks of fermented grains were dispensed and loose women from Pyongyang sold themselves.''

"Those people were scum," said Remo bitterly. "He should have wasted the whole ungrateful lot of them."

"Ah, but waste them Paekjo could not," said Chiun, lifting an instructive finger ceilingward. "For it is written that the Master cannot raise his hand against a member of the village. And, alas, he was both protector and provider, and understood that the people's anger stemmed from a fear of the future.

"So this was to be his final tour of his beloved Sinanju, for while the coffers in the House of the Master were full, due to his tireless labors, with no heir they were fated to run empty. This is a sad fact of life, Remo. The best Paekjo could hope for would be to leave forever his beloved home and ply his trade in foreign lands until his bitter end days, and thus save the infants of his reign from the cold waters of the West Korea Bay, and so preserve his good name in the Book of Sinanju."

Chiun's tight-squeezed eyes relaxed. His pupils, touched by candlelight, shrank to ebony points.

"This, Remo, was the reason for his final tour."

Remo nodded. A Master lived for his place in history—the only thing that survived his passing.

"But on his way from the village," Chiun resumed, "Paekjo did notice something wallowing in the mud and ordure at the outskirts. A child, weak of limb and dull of senses. An idiot-youth, abandoned by a lesser family, who daily scrounged for scraps and rice hulls for sustenance. And the Master's heart filled with pity. For it was for this child, and others like him, that all Masters of Sinanju plied their deadly trade.

"Seeing this foundling, Master Paekjo turned to those who dogged his footsteps, vilifying him. And his countenance grew wrathful. The women, taken aback, ceased their shouting, clasped their abusive children to them in fright. These slatterns did cry and beat their breasts, rending their garments. And the words they shouted were these—'O wise and benevolent Master. Do not be angry with us, who did question thy perfection. For we are but women.'

"And the Master fixed his steely gaze upon these ingrates and he spat, 'Women of Sinanju, begone! You who were not able to breed a cup worthy to receive the ocean that is Sinanju are as worthless as the children who cower at your hems. Your cowardly husbands hide from my sight and grow fat under the beneficence of my toil, yet their seed is like a mongrel's waste—plentiful and valueless. Hear me now. Though your lives are filled with shame and sloth, though the very sight of you is painful, the Master of Sinanju and his successor will continue to fill your unworthy bellies.'

"At this, the women gave voice to their confusion. 'But you do not have a successor, Master,' they cried. And Paekjo fixed them with an iron stare, intoning, 'I have today chosen a pupil that is more worthy than all others in the village, and it is he.' At that the Master pulled the bewildered idiot-child from the mud and cradled him in his arms."

"Tang," said Remo.

"Yes," Chiun said somberly.

"I thought you said he was a braggart, not a dullard."

"The two terms are not mutually exclusive," sniffed Chiun. "I have heard you brag. Heh-heh-heh." And though Chiun would ordinarily revel in such a witticism, this day his laughter sounded hollow.

The tense look on Remo's face shattered Chiun's cackle. He continued the story.

"On that long-ago day, Master Paekjo detected deep in the eyes of young Tang a certain promise. And while this promise was far from that of the least Master who had come to Sinanju up to that time, it was still superior to the clay available to him.

"Under the patient and determined guidance of his Master, Tang learned. The day finally came for Tang to assume his role as Master of Sinanju, and when this day arrived Tang the Dullard was assigned the simple task of protecting a minor assemblyman—which was another name for a Greek nobleman—in the town of Bura in one of the far Greek provinces.

"While not a glorious task, Tang approached it with an enthusiasm normally discovered only in the very young or the very stupid. The noble was old and weak and had made many enemies during his years of public life, which is not only not unusual in a Greek, it is something that is expected in their politicians.

"Now, this noble had enemies who lusted after his assembly seat. These enemies whispered behind the old Greek's back that he would die on a certain date in a certain way because an oracle had predicted it to be so. And it was with the promise of gold and fine bolts of silk, slaves and fabulous jewels, sweetmeats and confections and many gallons of fine wine that the noble did hire Tang to protect his life from danger until the ordained hour had passed. To this, Master Tang agreed.

"Now, even Tang at his most obtuse knew that oracles were merely fabrications meant to frighten men. They were nearly always ambiguous and never reliable. So Tang took his place at the nobleman's right hand for a period of one month. And when the day of doom foretold by the oracle was at hand, Master Tang slipped into the Greek's bedchamber under cover of darkness and spirited him away, secreting him in a cave several miles distant until the death hour had passed.

"At daybreak Tang returned the noble to his home. This man was so overjoyed to have cheated certain death, he offered Tang the hand of his loveliest daughter in marriage. Tang declined the offer, saying that his lot was a marriage of duty and obligation to his tiny village. So he bade farewell to the noble and his daughter who was, in point of fact, far from lovely. The girl was ugly and white and a Greek, and it was for these three reasons that Tang did not wish to wed her, for while he was an idiot, Tang was not completely stupid. He returned home to Sinanju, there to rest from his travels."

"That's it? End of story?" Remo asked, perplexed.

"Of course not," Chiun rejoined. "When the day the noble was prophesied to perish came around again—Greeks for some reason repeating their days—word reached Tang that death had struck in the foretold method. In a vile bathhouse where all manner of perversions took place. This on the exact date, one year later, as prophesied by the oracle. While the cause of death was ascribed to heart failure while in the act of pederasty, word was spread that the elderly statesman had been killed in battle against Xerxian forces, an all-too-common lie created to mask an ignominious death among Greek nobles. No one believed the story, save the nobleman's trusting daughter. The very one whom Tang refused to take as his wife. And this daughter traveled in secret from the house of her uncle in Thebes, to Delphi in Phocis, there to visit the famed Pythia who had prophesied the demise of her father.

The girl thereupon had vanished—a victim of roadside thieves, according to the slave with whom she had traveled.

"Now, Master Tang, being an idiot, was troubled by these things. Instead of considering himself fortunate to have earned a large payment despite what some might consider a technical failure, a nagging pressure filled his heretofore empty head, entreating him to return to Greece to avenge the death of his former charge."

"His conscience," offered Remo.

"His stupidity," explained Chiun. "The noble was already dead and Tang was already paid. What need was there for him to run halfway around the world on a fool's errand? But this is what Tang did.

"Tang returned to Greece and made his way to Phocis and Delphi, there to confront the priests of the Pythia, the *peristiarchoi*. Tang assumed, as only a fool would, that the priests had been paid by a rival noble to predict the death of the old man, whereupon the death was arranged, leaving the all-important seat in the assembly open." Here Chiun broke from the narrative and leaned over to Remo. "I say all-important, Remo, because that is how it is written in the histories. But I tell you that nothing white people do is ever important. This is a myth perpetuated by whites about whites to make themselves feel more worthy in one another's futile estimation."

This stated, Chiun returned to his tale. "The all-important seat was empty. A charge of Sinanju was dead. So Master Tang sought retribution in the place where the prediction had originated. This is a logic not uncommon among idiots."

"Delphi wasn't where the hit order came from?" asked Remo.

"There was no order," Chiun said.

"So why was the guy killed?"

"He died of natural causes."

"So why the fuss?" asked Remo, exasperated. "He just happened to die on the right day. It was a coincidence, right?"

"Wrong," said Chiun. "It was foreseen by the Pythian oracle at Delphi."

"But you just got through telling me that these people were fools for listening to oracles."

Chiun's hazel eyes grew heavy of lid. "Up until that time, no oracle had been known to speak truth."

Remo felt a lurking presence flit through his mind like a fugitive shadow. He suppressed a shudder.

"But the Delphic Oracle *could* predict the future," Chiun said gravely. "And alas for Sinanju, it was the dullard Tang who made this discovery." He returned to the story. "Not knowing the truth behind the nobleman's death, Tang fell upon the priests of Delphi to avenge his murder. Ignorant of all but vengeance, Tang slew the priests of Delphi."

Chiun raised his arms in pantomime, his long ivory nails flashing like daggers in the fitful candlelight.

"*Thwap!* His hand shot east, and a body fell. Snap! His hand flew west, and another's life was snuffed. Many in number were the priests of the Pythia. But Tang, dull though he was, littered the temple floor with their hapless corpses. Through the storm, Tang did shout, 'You have dared discharge one whom it was my duty to protect.' Tang tore through the temple, reaching the very inner chamber where the mythic Pythia sat atop her tripod. A horrible-smelling smoke filled the large room, pouring from the rocky crevice over which the Pythia sat. And it was in this chamber that strange thoughts began to crowd the vacant mind of Tang, seeking to control his mighty rage.''

At this, Remo sat up. For a moment the alien presence in his own mind seemed to still. Almost as if it heard Chiun's words.

''But the tendrils that touched the dull mind of Tang slithered back into the circling yellow sulphur smoke. And Tang, in his idiocy, did shout up at the Pythia, 'What is this place of demons that fills my mind with thoughts of death?' And the Pythia on her tripod—her long black hair covering her face—did writhe and twist on her seat as if to do herself harm. And this child of the smoke called down in an unearthly voice, saying, 'Tang, you of simple mind are not a worthy vessel of Apollo's essence, but hear you this. When the time has come for the dead night tiger of Sinanju to walk the earth, East will meet West and the destiny of Sinanju will be forever changed. This I have foreseen and this is the legacy I bequeath you for that which you are about to do.''

Remo frowned. According to Sinanju legend, Remo was the dead night tiger, the avatar of Shiva, the Hindu god of destruction. Chiun went on.

''Tang flashed to the top of the Pythia's platform. As the smoke burst into searing yellow flame around him, he spirited Apollo's Pythia to safety, for even Tang's thick mind recognized it was the smoke that made the child what she was. Only after he had carried her from the temple did he push her shining black hair from her face. And, lo, he beheld the nobleman's daughter, who had been offered as bride tribute. Deep was his anger that the girl should have suffered such a fate, for her mind, like Tang's, was empty of thought. In his rage Tang approached the temple and, with hands more powerful than iron and swifter than the eye could follow, he set to work. For one full day he labored, demolishing walls beneath his fists, pounding rock to powder. After his work was done, not one stone stood upon another. It is said, Remo, that an earthquake destroyed the temple at Delphi, but it was in truth the wrath of Master Tang. Tang stood back and admired his handiwork, for such is what children do when they wreak random ruin.

"And once he was satisfied, Tang left Greece forever, taking with him the idiot girl who could neither speak nor think. A perfect match were these two, and though unable to perform the duties of a proper wife, she did live for many years. Her grave is still tended in my village, although on the far side of the garbage dump because she was, after all, a foreigner."

Chiun settled back and folded his arms across his chest, signifying that the story was finished.

"So Tang beat the oracle," Remo said. The shadowy thing in his mind began to stretch its tendrils across his thoughts.

"The temple was rebuilt not long after," Chiun explained. "The Delphic oracle gave many prophecies long after the death of Tang."

"So what's the moral?" asked Remo. The dark image of a battlefield that he had seen in the Forrester girl's room appeared like a mirage behind Chiun. Remo stared at the surreal scene.

"There is no moral, but that I should not have

waited for Smith to transport us from this country of Tang-like fools. For now it is too late. For you and for me. But especially for you, my son."

Remo felt the first strains of panic tugging at his stomach. "But there is something I can do about this, right?" he asked.

The combatants reappeared on the battlefield in his mind. Somewhere in his consciousness, Remo felt the mocking presence of the Pythian oracle.

Chiun shook his head slowly, the wisps of white hair decorating his head and chin doing a drifting dance in the darkened room. "I know of nothing that can help you, my son," he said. "East has met West. We are of the East, and Delphi was the West in the time of Tang. It is the will of the sun god."

In Remo's mind the malevolent combatant was poised and ready to strike down its weaker rival. He felt the force of the Pythia crawl over him like an icy fog.

Remo was losing the battle. He needed some normalcy, a compass to orient him. Something to root him in reality. "So why was Tang a braggart?" he asked, trying to pull away from the strange, otherwordly realm intruding on his vision.

"When he returned to Sinanju, Tang told the villagers that he had grappled with a god and had won. This story he repeated to the end of his days." Chiun shook his head sadly. "But he did not win, my son. Woe to us, he did not win."

Remo could no longer hold up the dam he had built in his thoughts. The malevolent force of the Pythia's consciousness burst loose, pouring through his mind in a sickly warm flood. And like a helpless victim in the raging river of his own thoughts, Remo was swept away into the darkness.

24

Telemachus Anaxagoras Kaspurelakos had always known that he was destined for greatness, and he didn't shy away from sharing this knowledge with those he met. Since Telemachus had no friends, his family was forced to endure the theories of his future ascendancy to power. And since most of that family lived on the other side of the Atlantic, Papa and Mama Kaspurelakos were the ones who had to suffer most through their young son's delusions of grandeur.

The winds of fate had blown his parents from their native Greece just after the Second World War, and the Kaspurelakos family had eventually settled in the familiar-sounding town called Thermopolis, Wyoming. It was there young Telemachus was born and spent his formative years.

His mother had gone to work in a local bakery, rising at four in the morning so that she could make enough to school young Telemachus to look and act like the other American children. Telemachus's father was a natural politician, having served in public life for many years in his native land. But in the early 1950s, America found it difficult to accept an ugly little man with hairy ears and an accent thicker than a vat of feta curd sitting on the local city council. And so the elder Kaspurelakos found work as a cobbler.

Young Telemachus settled into his life in the United States of America, content in the knowledge that, humble beginnings aside, his future was as bright as Apollo's shield.

But the future had other ideas.

Telemachus steered a treacherous course through the Wyoming school system, graduating early from high school in the spring of what should have been his junior year. It was of no consequence to him that when he received his diploma on that sunny Sunday afternoon, he was as friendless as he had been his first day of kindergarten. After all, great things lay in store.

Down at the bakery Mama had gone on double shifts, and Papa—now proud owner of a cobbler shop—had redoubled his tireless efforts to finance Telemachus's continuing education. The young man would be the first of their family to receive a college diploma.

With no social life and few extracurricular activities to distract him, Telemachus graduated from the University of Wyoming with his B.A. in two and a half years. He then told his aging parents that he wanted to stay on in school to receive his Master's. A good education, he argued, was the surest way for him to achieve his ultimate goal of national prestige and power.

Once his next educational goal was met, Telemachus Kaspurelakos, who now went by the more American-sounding "Mark Kaspar," had informed his parents that he wanted to stay on in school to get his B.Sc. His father had just celebrated his seventieth birthday and looked forward to Mark's graduation so that he might at last retire from the shoe shop. Arthritis had forced his mother to leave her job long before, and the patriarch of the Kaspurelakos family had worked night and day to fund his only son's ever rising college tuition.

With a weary sigh of resignation, the senior Kaspurelakos returned to the sweltering back room of his tiny shoe-repair shop. Family was family. And Mark was the future of the Kaspurelakos family.

The father died a month into Mark's next semester.

Young Mark—in truth not quite so young any longer—was devastated. At his father's funeral, he begged his grieving mother to return to the bakery, but his pleas only made the poor woman's mournful wails all the louder.

Without the financial support, Mark couldn't afford to hide out in the halls of academia. This realization terrified him. For the truth was, in spite of all the grandiose talk of his future greatness, Mark Kaspar hadn't a clue what he was going to do with his adult life.

Mark ultimately convinced his mother to surrender the proceeds of the sale of the Kaspurelakos shoe-repair shop so he could continue along his march to glory. At that point the old woman was only too willing to give in—anything to get her son out of the house.

Money in hand, Kaspar returned to the world in which he had squandered his adult life. He got a job as an English professor at a local state college.

Truthfully the only driving ambition Mark Kaspar owned was a compulsion to further the myth that Mark Kaspar possessed any ambition at all. He was, ultimately and in spite of his own delusions, intellectually lazy and bereft of any marketable skills whatsoever. He never recognized this, however. Everything wrong in his life could always be blamed on some external factors. It was the worst kind of self-deceit, but Mark Kaspar had practiced it skillfully all his life.

And so it was for fifteen years that the young man with the glorious dream of some ill-defined future languished in a mundane job. As the days stretched into years, his early assuredness of his own destiny devolved into a visceral hatred of all that had cheated him of the life he deserved.

Until the day a quirk of fate pushed him onto the path of greatness that he had wandered from.

To impress the faculty dean, Kaspar had signed on to teach a summer course in archaeology. It was a fledgling department, and Kaspar hadn't quite studied the course requirements when he agreed to add it to his schedule. But it meant tenure. And tenure meant job security.

A month later he was in Greece.

His class had been signed up as part of an international student team set loose at the site of a new dig in the ruins of ancient Delphi.

The students—some natives of Greece, others from the U.S., Great Britain, France, Belgium, as well as a handful from as far away as South Africa and New Zealand—attacked the pile of rubble with spoons and brushes. Representatives of Greece's archaeological-affairs office dug in right beside the students, and the careful, studied excavation was soon a bustle of activity.

Mark Kaspar surveyed the work area from a distance, slumped sullenly in a folding beach chair beneath a heavy, sweat-stained pith helmet.

The work went on for the better part of a month. Kaspar grew increasingly sullen as the permanent stains beneath the arms of his jungle jacket grew stiffer and encrusted with salt.

"My life is not supposed to be like this," he growled.

As his time in his ancestral homeland wore on, he spiraled deeper into his self-made pit of misery.

But just before the dig was to end, something happened that would change the course of Mark Kaspar's life forever.

A new chamber was discovered at the ruins of the temple to Apollo on Mount Parnassus. At first this was less interesting to Kaspar than his next decent American meal, but the team leaders acted as if they had stepped miraculously into another time.

The students beamed, while older members of the dig handed out bottles of warm wine. The discovery was talked up as of greater importance than it actually was, for although that sort of find occurred with some frequency, whenever a new chamber was discovered it was treated as if it could contain treasures as important as the Dead Sea Scrolls. Besides, the children were leaving in a week, and their Greek hosts wanted to make them feel as if they had participated in something more important than sifting teaspoons of sand through wire-mesh screens.

It was too late in the day to continue working. Once the last wine bottle was drained, everyone agreed to meet shortly at the tavern in town to continue the celebration. They would return to the site at dawn.

They hugged and shook hands and, with the camaraderie of shared hardship, the entire group marched proudly down the hill, arms draped over one another's shoulders, and singing. Their raucous cadences boomed across the ancient rock-strewed hills, making polyglot echoes.

Once they were gone, the site of Apollo's former temple was as lifeless as it had been the day after the last worshipful Greek supplicant had come to pay his respects to the sun god over two millennia before.

Almost as lifeless.

As the jubilant crowd passed down the road and out of sight, a lone pith helmet bobbed into view behind a pile of overturned stone.

Once he was certain everyone was gone, Mark Kaspar slipped down to the excavation pit. It was marked with poles tied at the end with bits of flapping white cloth.

Mark didn't see what the big deal was. It was nothing but a hole in the side of a mound of scrub-covered dirt that might have been dug by a giant prairie dog. Beyond that there wasn't much to see.

Kaspar noticed that someone had left a flashlight near a pile of empty wine bottles beside the mouth of the cavern.

He never knew what compelled him to get down on his hands and knees and crawl through the dirt and stone chips into the midnight black opening. But a minute later he found himself crouching inside a chamber that had not encompassed a human inhabitant since before the time of Christ.

Mark still didn't see what was so fascinating. He

played the dusty flashlight beam around the cramped room.

It was man-made, obviously. The ceiling was cut of large, rough-hewn stone. The walls, as well, were stone. The floor was dirt. Kaspar guessed that the room had filled with sand over the years. It was possible that the original floor was much farther below.

As Kaspar examined his surroundings, he noticed that the stones in the wall and ceiling were strangely marked. He had heard that the temple had been destroyed by an earthquake around 400 B.C. and he reasoned that the rocks had probably been shattered and then salvaged for the rebuilding. But the pitted areas in the stone were odd. Kaspar peered at the markings. Each came in a series of four. As he studied them closely, he realized they looked almost like...knuckle marks.

As he moved along the interior of the chamber, examining rock after rock, each etched with the same knucklelike indentations, Kaspar's curiosity heightened. Several yards in he stumbled upon something of recognizable historical value.

It was a large stone urn, still intact.

It rested on a rock shelf and was half-buried in two thousand years' worth of settled earth. Excitedly Kaspar brushed the dirt away with his hands, exposing a stone exterior that was decorated with delicately intertwined serpents.

Kaspar's mind fired.

He knew that Greece was once a powerful civilization. He knew that historically, powerful civilizations were always, always very wealthy. And he knew that he had discovered something in the ruins of an ancient temple from what, in its day, had been the most powerful civilization on earth. And in that ancient urn had been placed something mysterious that someone back then thought valuable enough to store for safe keeping.

Ignoring all protocol for a discovery of such magnitude, he pulled the lid from the top of the dust-covered urn.

And in the sickly beam of the flashlight, Mark Kaspar thought he had unearthed an ancient pot of pure gold.

With a shaking finger, he touched the glistening yellow substance.

His hopes were immediately dashed.

It was powder. A pot full of some ancient spice, probably.

In disgust Kaspar started to replace the heavy stone lid.

All at once he felt something slither into his mind.

The sensation shocked him. He dropped the lid to the ground. It landed on a slab of rock and its edge chipped off a dozen small stone pieces.

Kaspar watched in wonder as the yellow substance in the urn began to glow brightly in the center of the ruins of Delphi. The strange, powdery residue on his hand flared up in sympathy.

And a voice inside his mind spoke to him, and it said, *You have returned, my* peristiarchoi. *Your great future is at hand.*

And he accepted the truth of the voice in his excited mind.

When Kaspar left the ruins, the shelf on which the

ancient urn had sat for more than two thousand years was empty.

THE SPIRIT of Apollo's Pythia was weak in the yellow powder.

Kaspar found it necessary to enhance the strength of the oracles by artificially steaming the powder, just as had been done in the hills of Greece all those years ago.

Back in America he began harvesting virgins himself, at the urging of his unseen master. The first was a freshman in his English class. He used her in the spare bedroom of his attic apartment and, when she was of no further use to him, he drove her out into the night like a stray dog.

The last Kaspar had heard, she had been institutionalized, her mind a gibbering blank. But that didn't matter to him. The girl was no more than a vessel. Something to be used and discarded by his master.

There were other vessels as the years wore on. Kaspar was forced to move from city to city. The Pythia always provided for him, and he never had cause for any bitterness at the life he had been chosen to lead.

Fate had led him to Delphi. And it was fate that led him back to his home in Wyoming. It was here, in a dingy boardinghouse room in Thermopolis and through the utterances of the gymnast Pythia—the girl he would eventually bring with him to Ranch Ragnarok—that he finally learned of his great destiny.

America was a nation where many had gotten out of touch with its Judeo-Christian roots. New Age mysticism and faith healing had taken the place of a monotheistic religion. The Pythia foretold that the greatest of all Western nations would become the seat of Apollo himself in the dawn of the next millennium. And Telemachus Anaxagoras Kaspurelakos, the high priest of Apollo, would be the herald of the great new era.

You are destined, Telemachus, it said, *to rule the land in which you dwell.* The prophecy had sent a chill up his spine.

But it was only fitting that the god of the new American theocracy have a proper place to reside, a place from which it could spread its influence to the powerful and influential.

Esther Clear-Seer's ranch was the perfect choice.

Esther had founded the Church of the Absolute and Incontrovertible Truth with her husband during the 1970s. When he had passed away, she had nearly bankrupted the entire church by trying to cash in on the faith of all of her worldwide members. She thought that if she bilked her entire membership in one fell swoop, she could live like a queen for the rest of her life. And so, even as the United States and the Soviet Union were beginning to ease nearly fifty years of tension, Esther had created Armageddon in her own mind.

She had made a young fortune in the single venture but lost out in the long run. After her predicted apocalypse failed to materialize, members of the International Truth Church finally figured out that they had been had. Church membership dropped off dramatically, and what with all the bills she still had to pay, Esther found that her anticipated windfall was only a passing breeze.

It took years to rebuild an acolyte pool productive enough to sustain her lavish life-style.

When Mark Kaspar showed up at her door with his ancient urn and uncanny stock-market predictions, Esther thought at last she had hit the mother lode.

With greed, power and corruption to unite them, Mark Kaspar and Esther Clear-Seer were truly a perfect match. And the Pythia's plan for the future of America moved along with flawless rapidity.

There was only one small problem.

MARK KASPAR DIDN'T KNOW why the President of the United States hadn't yet responded to his threats.

Former governor Michael Princippi had assured Kaspar that the leaders of the President's party had informed the Chief Executive that more congressional resignations would follow if the young Sinanju Master wasn't turned over at once.

In actual fact the sorry truth was that without the Pythia, Kaspar's threat was hollow. He only had minor dirt on two other members of Congress, and the nature of the charges was survivable in the new permissive political climate in America. What Kaspar had done was fire all of his seven major salvos at one time, hoping sheer numbers would force the President to turn over Remo and thus return the essences of Apollo and his Pythia.

But official Washington had so far refused to take the bait.

"He's got to respond," Michael Princippi insisted. He wrung his hands as he paced anxiously.

They were in Kaspar's office in the corner of the abandoned hangar on the Ranch Ragnarok site.

"Now that you're a bona fide candidate, he can no longer ignore you," Princippi added worriedly.

Kaspar had taken out the proper papers and filled out the necessary disclosure forms several weeks before. In a brief statement to the press that morning, on the heels of the congressional resignations, Mark Kaspar had declared himself an official candidate for the United States Senate.

"He is doing just that, my friend Michael," Kaspar said, leaning back in his leather chair.

A rap at the door was quickly followed by Esther Clear-Seer herself, who didn't wait for permission before marching into the office.

"I just caught one of the acolytes trying to take off with Cole's daughter," she announced. She didn't acknowledge Princippi's presense.

Kaspar leaned forward, peeved. "What happened?"

Esther shrugged. "No big deal. I had the guards take care of her. She was yelling her head off about being a Fed, but she didn't have any ID in her room." She shook her long raven tresses. "I don't like this, Kaspar. It's getting too weird around here."

Kaspar seemed distracted by some vague, distant thought. At last he exhaled deeply and slapped his palms onto his desk.

"Mr. Princippi, would you excuse us for a moment?" he asked.

Miffed, Princippi nodded his respects while shooting a frosty glare at Esther Clear-Seer as he left the room.

Once Princippi was gone, Kaspar asked, "You saw my press conference?"

Esther nodded. "Senator Mark Kaspar. I would

have figured that was beneath you." She seemed too weary to give the remark a biting edge.

Kaspar smiled. "All in good time," he explained vaguely. "You realize that with or without the Pythia, I still have a schedule to keep." A casual shrug indicated that Esther understood something was going on. "There are issues that must be dealt with now," Kaspar explained. "The Senate race being one of those things."

"You better run one hell of a campaign. Cole just went on CNN, vowing to stay in the race, 'come hell or high water.' Unquote."

"I am aware of his intentions," Kaspar said. "I had hoped the peril to his daughter would be enough to force his withdrawal. But the Pythia's prediction was strangely vague on that point."

"Pity for you," Esther said with an unsympathetic grin.

Kaspar smiled back. "Mr. Princippi has been on the phone with the senator's advance man to arrange a meeting for the two of us. We are, after all, now the leading candidates for the office. When our meeting is over, I want to be certain that I am the only candidate left in the race."

"You want to off Jackson Cole?"

"It is rather crude," Kaspar admitted with a shrug. "But at this point we haven't much of an alternative. It could be days, even weeks, before the one from Sinanju succumbs to the power of my master. It is imperative that I win this race so that my ultimate destiny can be fulfilled."

Esther sighed. Since this creepy little man had shown up, she had found herself involved in assault, kidnapping, extortion and murder. And now she was being set up to assassinate a senator of the United States of America.

It was as if Kaspar had been born to play power politics. And she had no choice but to go along for the ride.

Esther sighed. "Just tell me what you want me to do," she said resignedly.

25

Smith learned of the impending meeting between Mark Kaspar and Senator Jackson Cole in a news story that was sandwiched awkwardly between a segment on dog grooming and an in-studio "Mr. Chow" wok demonstration.

The story was brief. As well as mentioning his daughter's abduction and the fact that he was neither going to give up hope for her safe recovery nor allow the tragedy to dictate the rest of his life, the story also stated that Jackson Cole was a resident of Thermopolis, Wyoming, and that the senator would be making his regular public appearance at his hometown's annual spring fair. Political neophyte and pundit Mark Kaspar was also scheduled to appear at the same public event.

When the story concluded, Smith placed a call to the White House.

He didn't know what Kaspar's game plan was, but he knew that Senator Cole was at risk every moment he spent near Mark Kaspar and his Truth Church acolytes.

The President picked up on the fifth ring.

"Mr. President, are you aware of the meeting between Mark Kaspar and Senator Cole?" Smith asked.

"What about it?"

The President sounded cold, and Smith realized he was still upset over their previous phone conversation.

"I do not believe it would be prudent for the senator to meet with Kaspar at present," Smith explained.

"Is this political advice, Smith?" the President asked frostily.

Smith silently adjusted his tie and pressed on. "I have reason to believe Mark Kaspar is a dangerous individual."

"You're telling me?" the President said sarcastically. "I've been taking the press and party flak for two days straight over these resignations. Now my staffers are telling me the boys on the Hill have been getting some pretty mysterious phone calls from Prince Princippi."

"Phone calls?"

"Apparently his boss is looking for someone named Sinanju or something. Princippi is about as subtle as a mud pie in the face. He suggested to my colleagues on the Hill that they take the matter up with me. Can you believe the gall of this guy? And no one can dig up anything on this Sinanju. Probably some fringe special-interest group is my guess."

Smith swallowed his horror silently. Kaspar was trying to use the President to flush out Remo. Fortunately, though the Chief Executive had used the services of his two operatives in the past, he had never heard or did not recall the name Sinanju. A blessing for CURE.

Smith pursed his lips. "I believe the man is bluffing, Mr. President," he said after regaining control over his voice.

When the President asked him how he could be certain, Smith reluctantly explained the Ragnarok connection and how each of the seven men who resigned had visited the ranch on at least one occasion.

"There are only two other congressmen who have had contact with Kaspar in the past three months," Smith added. "And it seems reasonable to assume that if he had anything incriminating on them, he would have targeted them also."

"Or he's got something so toxic he's holding back until he needs to strike a death blow against my administration," the President suggested worriedly. "We've been doing nothing but damage control up here for the past two days."

"That is not my impression, Mr. President," Smith said. "I believe Kaspar's hand is played out. There was an incident involving one of my special people. I cannot go into the details, but as a direct consequence Kaspar has become desperate enough to try to contact you, even if it is through a surrogate. And I do not need to remind you, sir, that desperate men sometimes do desperate things. I urge you to persuade Senator Cole to reconsider this joint appearance with Kaspar."

The President lost his cool attitude. "You sure about this, Smith?"

"I am certain Kaspar is dangerous."

The President was silent a moment. "I'll call you back shortly," he snapped.

He was back on the phone within fifteen minutes.

"I personally contacted the senator's office," the Chief Executive reported. "Cole's administrative assistant informed me that the senator is adamant about maintaining his normal campaign schedule, even if it means attending the Hot Springs State Fair at the same time as Mark Kaspar.''

Smith politely thanked the President for his cooperation and hung up the phone. He spun around in his cracked leather chair and stared out at Oyster Bay on the other side of Long Island Sound, his face pursing like a wet leather glove.

He had few options now.

Remo was nowhere to be found. He had vanished not long after visiting Chiun the previous day. Smith only knew Remo had left after a Folcroft guard reported seeing someone matching Remo's description slipping across the grounds late that night.

Chiun had become even more withdrawn after the disappearance. He hadn't mentioned the phantom submarine to Smith in more than a day. The Master of Sinanju simply sat immobile in the center of his Folcroft quarters, eyes closed, deep in meditation.

That left only one CURE operative for field work.

With great reluctance, Smith unlocked the bottom drawer of his desk. In an old cigar box tucked deep in the back of the drawer behind a stack of dummy sanitarium files, Smith found his old Army-issue Colt automatic.

He collected his battered leather briefcase and tucked the automatic in a special side pouch that was impervious to airport X-ray machines. Always cautious, Smith slipped a plastic laminated card in his wallet identifying him as airline security and thus legally entitled to carry a firearm on a plane.

Smith reserved a seat on the next flight to Wyoming, then shut down the Folcroft computers.

HE MADE ONE STOP before leaving the building.

When he entered the room, Smith noted the candles and incense bowl of the previous day were gone, presumably packed away somewhere in the mountain of steamer trunks awaiting transshipment to North Korea. The heavy draperies were open, and dirty sunlight filtered grudgingly through the white translucent windows set high up in the concrete walls.

Chiun sat on the floor in the middle of a diluted patch of sunlight. The old man's eyes remained closed as Smith shut the door behind him.

"Master Chiun?"

"It is customary to knock," he informed Smith.

"I am sorry," Smith replied. "I thought you should know that I am leaving for Wyoming within the hour."

"You do not need my permission," Chiun said, thin of voice.

Smith felt a minor chill. The old Korean was usually effusive in his compliments to the man he called Emperor Smith. But now he was cold and distant. Chiun was at his most dangerous in these moods.

Smith cleared his throat and changed the subject. "There has been no word from Remo?"

Chiun's eyes squeezed more tightly as a cloud of worry passed across his aged brow. "I have not seen my son since yesterday," he admitted. "However, I have been attempting to locate him."

Smith frowned. Chiun had not left this room since the previous evening.

"Locate Remo?" Smith blurted. "How?"

Chiun sighed deeply. And for the first time that day

opened his eyes. His stare was as barren and frigid as an Arctic winter.

"Why is gold the color gold?"

"Is that a riddle?" Smith asked.

Chiun merely stared.

"Gold is simply...golden," Smith offered.

"You would understand what it is I do even less," said Chiun, as if this settled the issue once and for all. And with that, the wizened Asian closed his eyes and refused to speak further on the matter. The whereabouts of Remo were a problem for Sinanju and would be dealt with by Sinanju; that seemed to be the Master of Sinanju's unspoken thought.

Smith got the message and backed quietly from the room. He would have neither Remo's help nor the help of the Master of Sinanju on his trip to Thermopolis.

Long after Smith had gone, Chiun remained immobile in the basement room, hazel eyes shut like trapdoors.

His desperate quest for his lost pupil continued.

NO HUMAN BEING WAS present when the shadow emerged from the sea of posttwilight darkness. Therefore no man saw the black shape slide effortlessly through the gates like a silent fog.

Like a knife the distinctive wail of a frightened lemur sliced through the cold, dead heart of the night. The sound set off a chain reaction of complaint.

Nearby gibbons and spider monkeys howled when the shadow drifted past.

Gorillas propelled themselves swiftly away on leathery knuckles, finding safety behind trees and in straw-filled corners, as far distant as possible from the wisp of moving darkness.

Farther away a dozen lions roared in terror at the night as a small herd of elephants trumpeted and stomped in fear beyond their heavy walls.

The shadow moved through turnstiles and past rusting metal railings. The lock on an unmarked rear door shattered as it passed. Fragments from the door handle skittered off in a symphony of metallic clinks, landing in large part beneath a pair of vacant benches and under a boarded-up vendor's cart.

The shadow passed inside.

The building was warm, the corridor suffused in the dull white glow of a single recessed light. A sudden hand movement shattered the light casing, and the bulb exploded in a spray of delicate wedges. The glass tinkled softly to the floor in the wake of the passing shadow.

The corridor led into a large chamber that had baked in the daytime sun. It still held the faint trace odors of hundreds of sweating men, women and children.

The main pathway in the center of the chamber was lined on either side by metal railings, the height and design of which vaguely resembled horse rails in an old Western. Beyond the railings, high Plexiglas panes cordoned off large cubicles from one another and offered a view inside each of the giant glass cages.

Most of the creatures within the boxed-off sections of glass didn't move as the shadow passed them by. Some did slither in lazy S-shaped paths through patches of transplanted grass and shrubs. Still more were looped around the branches and trunks of artificial or transplanted trees, but the movements these made were barely perceptible to the naked eye.

The shadow passed the cages of the cobras, asps and rattlesnakes without slowing. It found what it wanted in the final blocked-off pen at the far end of the main visitor's room on the other side of a sheet of one-inch-thick Plexiglas.

A plaque set below the exterior window was etched with the legend P. Molurus. Below that, in smaller letters, was written Indian Python.

The thing that had been Remo Williams paused before the sheet of heavy reinforced Plexiglas.

Remo could see himself in the glossy reflective surface of the glass-walled python cage, but everything seemed strange and distant. It was as if he were a faraway spectator to his own actions. His face, crawling with shadows, was a hollow-eyed death's-head.

When the demon force had taken over his mind, Remo had been helpless. He saw the image of the malevolent combatant that had raged within him since his encounter at the Truth Church ranch strike out at the more docile form. He did not know if the blow had struck home, but at the point when the outstretched hand of the evil combatant would have landed, both creatures had fled from his vision.

The dimensionless black plain on which they had stood was with him still, but it was now vacant, devoid of any life.

The moment they had vanished, Remo Williams had died, as well.

He remembered the look of anguish on Chiun's face when the old man realized that he had lost him to the Pythia. He recalled vividly his flight from Folcroft. He remembered skulking through the streets of Rye like some mongrel dog.

A full day of restless wandering for the soul that now controlled Remo's body had passed. And he had watched it all from a surreal vantage point, back behind his own eyes.

Superimposed above all the images flashing before him was the vacant black battlefield. Remo had the intense feeling that there was something lurking over the alien horizon. Something more deadly than the spirit of the Pythia now controlling his actions.

The reptile house at the Bronx Zoo reappeared before him in a haze. His own face in the window of the python tank was washed-out and lifeless. A skull clinging to a thin mask of flesh.

A hand flew out before him. Remo recognized it as his own. It struck the side of the tank, and a vertical crack appeared beneath the tips of his slashing fingers. The thick Plexiglas split into two neat halves, and the thing that controlled Remo popped one side from its frame and set the heavy sheet of glass on the floor beside the tank.

A sudden hop, and he was gliding wraithlike through the cage. The leaves from a dozen different transplanted subtropical bushes brushed silently against his shins as he moved.

It was humid inside the cage, and the thing that had taken possession of Remo smelled the air like an alert hunter.

Behind it and unseen, something large and dark uncoiled from the low-slung branch of an artificial tallow tree.

Remo somehow knew what was happening. The

mingling of minds had produced a dim form of understanding within him.

It was the snake. The snake held some kind of significance.

He saw visions, more images across the limitless black plain.

The evil combatant returned, but this time he was alone. He appeared almost as an infant in this vision and he wore on his back a quiver full of arrows. In his hand he held a golden bow.

All at once there appeared before the young combatant a great serpent. It moved to attack the boy. Quick as a flash, the youth's hand sought a quivered arrow and launched the deadly missile into the head of the massive creature. The small warrior repeated this motion again and again, spearing the hapless creature with arrow after arrow until at last its great pointed tail flopped lifelessly to the ground.

It was dead.

The image vanished. Remo was again in the reptile cage.

The serpent. Its death was somehow part of a rebirth.

But not of the Pythia. It was the rebirth of something much vaster. Something far more terrifying. Something hunkered down over the far side of the horizon of his mind.

As his thoughts returned in the cage, some lucid part of Remo's brain told him that something was at his ankle.

Like a spectator to his own actions, his head looked down, allowing Remo to see what his body had felt.

A fat, gleaming brown rope was wrapped around

his right leg. It was banded and spotted in hues of chocolate and mud.

The thing moved and Remo fell.

Palm fronds slapped against his forehead. Remo landed face first in a tuft of tall sawgrass.

A cool pressure surrounded his waist.

The slow, crushing sensation didn't faze the presence of the Pythia in Remo's mind. As the snake's scaly coils slid up around his chest, it remained calm. As if the python sought this cold encounter.

As the unblinking head looped higher, the massive body rippled almost imperceptibly while wrapping its neck around Remo's throat. He felt a growing pressure against his windpipe.

The python, purchased from an East Indian zoological society, was over thirty feet long and had not eaten in days. While it was normal for a python to attack smaller animals, it wasn't unheard of for a snake as large as this one to attack and suffocate something Remo's size. Especially when hungry.

The creature's amber eyes looked directly into Remo's own as it constricted its muscular coils harder.

With every exhalation, the python squeezed Remo's rib cage. Every intake of breath that followed was shallower and less charged with oxygen than the one before. Inexorably the python's shrinking body was starving Remo's lungs of the one element that fueled the sun source that was Sinanju.

Oxygen.

The alien force in Remo's mind seemed almost to mock the efforts of the huge reptile. As the snake strove harder to crush the breath from the warm-blooded mammal trapped within its constrictor coils, the demon within Remo slowly extracted a hand from the living bonds.

Remo watched as his own hand swatted the creature's flat head, almost as if the Pythia was remonstrating a badly behaved pet.

Immediately the python's coils dropped into loose ropes. It flopped to the cage floor.

Shedding the last clinging coils, the thing that possessed Remo stood.

In the thicket of carefully tended jungle, the reptile stirred. It had only been stunned. The flat, blunt head swayed back and forth, as if adjusting to the vibrations it felt through the bottom of the cage.

Remo felt himself step over the snake. The head lifted slightly and turned toward the new movement. He felt a tingle of evil jubilance in the pit of his own stomach.

Remo sensed what was really happening. The demon within him was only playing with the giant snake. It intended to toy with the creature, and when the entertainment value had at last been exhausted, it would slaughter the python in fulfillment of an ancient prophecy. This was somehow the final step toward the ultimate perversion of Remo's body. An inexplicable rite of passage.

And Remo felt a deep, helpless shame that his perfect body was being corrupted by this ancient demon.

He could not allow it to happen.

The snake slithered about his ankles once again. This time the demon within Remo anticipated the attack. He didn't fall.

While the inner presence was concentrating on the

external pressure of the predator snake, Remo willed himself loose.

The thick hide wrapped around his chest.

Remo forced himself outward, pushing back to where his mind belonged. As he concentrated all his energy on a single, minuscule effort, he imagined sweat appearing on some internal brow. It was a small thing. But it would be proof that Remo was not totally helpless.

The snake pulled itself up around his neck and bobbed unsteadily in a gawking position a foot before the pale white face of its prey. A long flat tongue darted hungrily from its lipless mouth.

Remo pushed outward. Farther, farther.

The snake brought its alien snout closer. The huge coils below tightened.

With a phenomenal effort of will, Remo forced his index finger to twitch. The movement was quick and sharp. He felt the rough texture of the snake's hide against the pad of his finger.

He *felt*.

There was a flare of surprise from the presence within him.

Remo pushed again—hard. His hand twitched spastically. It rubbed along the interior of the coiled snake.

Something close to panic rose from the spirit of the Pythia within him. It was an inner remonstration. The Pythia had frittered away precious time when it should have first concentrated all of its efforts dispelling the last vestiges of consciousness from its latest vessel.

The rebirth was incomplete. To become the true Pythia, it had to kill the snake. And if the Pythia failed,

Apollo could not assert his presence in the modern world.

Both hands moved freely now. The shoulders rolled in a shrugging motion, pushing the snake down farther.

The spirit of the Pythia had underestimated Sinanju. Underestimated its power because of the weak-minded Tang so many years before.

The Pythia had assumed that the Remo-vessel was as corruptible as the others. But his training in Sinanju had made Remo stronger.

It could not fail its master, not now. Not when it was so close.

The Pythia forced its will upon its vessel once more.

Remo's hands wrapped around the python's throat. The Pythia squeezed.

The thin, merciless reptilian mouth dropped open as the creature gulped helplessly for air. It thrashed its head, but could not prevail. The giant tail swung around defensively, looping around Remo's ankles.

Remo had had possession of his body only briefly. With a murderous lunge the demon within him had reasserted itself. It felt as if his spirit had been knocked backward into his own mind. Remo concentrated harder, trying to assert mastery over his own body once more.

As the life ebbed from its heavy, limp frame, the tail of the snake began twitching reflexively. It was dying. And Remo was the instrument of its death.

Remo suddenly felt the huge thing he had sensed on the other side of the bleak internal horizon loom into view. The thing was giant. It strode across the barren terrain of his thoughts like a colossus. It was nearly larger than his mind could conceive, greater than his consciousness could encompass. It was a vague mountain of pure evil. And it was moving toward him.

At that moment Remo realized that it would not be possible to defeat the thing within him in this place. He could quell it, stall it. But it could not be beaten.

Not while it still dwelled within him.

It would first need to be removed.

With a sudden desperate leap, Remo forced his spirit outward. In a flash of blinding energy he was in control of his body once more.

His limbs jolted at the sudden surge of energy in his muscles, and Remo, still wrapped in the loosened coils of the deadly python, dropped in a heap to the cage floor.

In a struggle that wasn't visible externally, but that exploded within him with a force more powerful than a supernova, Remo seized his essence from the spirit of the Pythia, taking hold of his own mind like a tenacious climber scrambling for a handhold above the precipice of his own darkest fears.

Desperately he held on to his body with his mind, with his will, with his very soul.

The snake, jarred loose by Remo's actions, relaxed its coils from around its slender prey, to slither off into the leaf-choked shadows, apparently deciding that its meal was no longer worth the effort needed to conquer.

Sweating and shivering, Remo climbed to his feet.

His mind had touched that of the creature within him—and he now knew what it had intended all along.

The Pythia was as much a servant of Apollo as the

vessels were servants to the Pythia. And the giant evil thing that had moved toward him in his thoughts was the spirit of the sun god himself, ready to take possession of Pythia's latest vessel.

East would meet West within him.

Remo felt the mocking presence at the periphery of his thoughts once again and knew it to be Apollo.

He couldn't beat him. He had quelled the spirit of Apollo for now, beaten the Pythia twice in as many days, but he couldn't fight this battle over and over again. It had taken all his inner strength to stave off the Pythia this time. Next time Remo couldn't hope to win. Not until he banished the spirit that lurked within the darkest recesses of his own mind.

The spirit had slithered into his mind via the smoke and steam of the Pythia Pit, and instinct told him that any hope of separating their intertwined minds resided in the rocky hillock of the modern Delphic temple far to the west.

Remo would have to return to Ranch Ragnarok.

His jaw set in grim determination, Remo jumped down from the cage.

Behind him the torpid python slept peacefully in the shadows.

In a darkened basement room on Long Island Sound, a pair of hazel eyes opened with a start.

The only sound to stir in the room in more than six hours was that of the heavy door opening and closing.

26

Kaspar was standing atop the Pythia platform in his pale priestly vestments.

This was odd, thought Esther Clear-Seer. He hadn't worn the strange pagan robes since the young Sinanju Master had fled into the night two days before.

Kaspar glared angrily at Esther as she mounted the stairs.

"What is this?" he demanded, pointing.

Behind him, sandwiched between two burly Truth Church acolytes, was Buffy Brand. The young girl looked pale and shaken.

"This is the sneaking Fed I caught with Cole's daughter," Esther explained, forcing a steady tone. She noted with surprise that Lori Cole was seated once more atop the small wooden tripod. All that was missing from the strange scene was the noxious yellow smoke. A column of vaporous steam rose up from the rock fissure. That was all.

Kaspar tapped his foot impatiently. "She is still alive," he said, extending an index finger toward Buffy.

"Oh, I didn't tell you?" Esther returned blandly.

"You told me you killed her."

Esther shook her head. "I told you I took care of

her," she corrected. "And I did. And what were you doing snooping around the bunkers?"

Kaspar grew angry. "She escaped," he hissed at Esther. "We were lucky one of the patrols stumbled upon her."

It was Esther who was angry now as she turned on Buffy. She thought she had locked the girl securely away in a tiny punishment cubicle in one of the rear bunkers. Perhaps the girl might have compatriots on the Truth Church grounds, she thought. "How did you get out?" she demanded.

Buffy refused to respond. Her mouth was twisted shut in defiance.

Esther turned back to Kaspar. "It doesn't matter anymore," she said firmly. "She didn't escape."

"The young one from Sinanju was able to escape in spite of his injuries," Kaspar countered. "I am wondering now if it was this little spy who aided him."

Esther suddenly remembered the two rows of dead Truth Church guards who had ambushed Remo within the Ragnarok compound. The video cameras and explosives that night had been intended to disorient the young Sinanju Master named Remo and lure him back to the Pythia Pit. Esther had been surprised to find that so many of the guards had been shot from behind. They didn't have video on the incident. She assumed that Remo had captured a weapon and assassinated the acolytes himself.

"So what if she helped the guy escape?" Esther said, knowing that it did indeed make a great deal of difference. "He hasn't blabbed to the FBI yet. He's probably lying dead somewhere out in the greasewood scrub.''

"You are a fool," Kaspar snapped.

"Not as big a one as you are," Esther replied calmly. "Look, it would be better for us in court if we kept this one alive."

"That's good advice," Buffy said, glaring at Kaspar. "The two of you are finished."

Buffy had given up struggling long before. Her hands were bound with thick rope cords, and her wrists were bloodied from trying to twist herself free. The Truth Church acolytes squeezed her biceps in their meaty fists. She subsided.

"Now, now," Esther remonstrated. "Remember the Book of Samuel, wherein we are instructed by our Lord to turn the other cheek."

"There is no Book of Samuel," Buffy said flatly. "And I prefer Revelations." She began quoting. "'And the beast was seized and with it the false prophet. And these two were cast alive into the pool of fire that burns with brimstone.'" Buffy's stare bore into the blackened soul of Esther Clear-Seer, and when the young woman smiled her perfect smile, it was sincere.

Esther shivered involuntarily. The Feds these days were getting creepier and creepier.

"Okay—you win. Go ahead and kill her," she muttered to Kaspar.

"No," Kaspar said. "She is to be a sacrifice to my master…"

Esther arched a very black eyebrow. "Graduated from goats, have you?"

"And *you* will perform the sacrifice."

Esther waved the suggestion away. "I don't stoop to slaughtering goats or lambs," she said. "Have one of the acolytes do it."

"You will perform the ritual, for it was you who saw fit to hide this spy from my sight. Perhaps this will help you to better grasp your earthly obligations."

Esther bit her tart tongue. No point in arguing. Just kill the girl and get on with her life. She dared not tell him that she had driven out to Hot Springs State Park and released the last Pythia into the wild like a captivity-bred condor. Her mind was shot, and she'd probably die from exposure. But if she survived, Esther could always claim at the trial she tried to help the girl out.

"Do you want me to do it now?" she asked, controlling herself.

Kaspar shook his head. "It is not the appointed time. Are your acolytes in readiness for the senator's reception?"

Esther nodded. "Everything's set. After today I doubt they'll be my acolytes any longer. No way can the Truth Church survive the hell about to break loose in Thermopolis."

"Oh, it will survive," Kaspar assured her. "When my master returns to us, we will unleash power greater than any seen on this planet in two millennia."

Kaspar turned away from Esther and began fussing around the tripod and the Cole girl. "Go supervise the operation," he said dismissively. "Be certain that nothing goes wrong."

Esther had decided not to ask how Kaspar knew for certain that his master was returning. But as she crossed the platform, it came to her.

She could see down through the grate beneath the small stool. The stone urn had been replaced on the outcropping of rock within the jagged crevice. And Esther saw with alarm that the yellow powder within it was *glowing*.

HAROLD W. SMITH had locked his briefcase in the trunk of his rental car before hiking more than three miles to the center of Thermopolis, Wyoming.

He guessed by the choke of cars parked at the outskirts of town and the increasing noise as he got closer to Arapahoe Street that the Hot Springs State Fair was a big event in this part of the state. But still Smith was surprised by the sheer numbers of people who had migrated to what was just an ordinary sleepy Western town.

Compared to the state fair, the rally held for Senator Cole a few weeks earlier looked, in retrospect, like an anemic Rotary Club meeting.

That was not to say the earlier event hadn't been large for a town Thermopolis's size. It was just that the state fair was something everyone in the area could enjoy, election year or not.

The downtown area had been blocked off to all through traffic. Dozens of large green-and-white-striped tents had been propped up in the park across from city hall. Some straddled the asphalt strip on Arapahoe Street between the small brick library building and the new post office/minimall.

Hundreds upon hundreds of people were crowded into the vicinity of Arapahoe between Cottonwood Street and Beartooth Road. The park was clogged with a sea of bobbing heads.

There were still a great many Cole banners flapping gaily in the seasonably cool breeze. Signs in support of the senator hung on telephone poles as far as the eye could see. One had been slung down the side of the four-story office building adjacent to the city hall, but few people paid them any attention. This was a day to forget about politics.

There were no Calhoun posters in sight—the few who had hung signs in defiance of the overwhelming support for Senator Cole having lost their nerve since their candidate dropped out of the race. A coming grand-jury investigation into the molestation charges didn't bolster partisan confidence any.

As Smith moved uncomfortably through the sea of pedestrians, he thought it odd that there seemed to be almost as many Mark Kaspar posters in the crowd as there were Jackson Cole placards. In a few acts of random political zealotry, some had been stapled over Cole posters. But most were mingling within the body of the crowd, carried on poles by roving ideologues. It seemed to Smith he could not walk ten feet without bumping into noisy Kaspar supporters.

On the posters Mark Kaspar's face showed an uncharacteristic grin from a larger-than-life center square that was framed on three sides by a patriotic red, white and blue border. Beneath the picture on a block of white, large stenciled letters proclaimed Mark Kaspar, Man Of The Era.

His supporters carried Kaspar's reptilian face around determinedly on the ends of their sticks, annoying the hometown crowd who overwhelmingly supported the popular incumbent senator.

Smith asked around and found that Cole had not yet

made his appearance. When asked where the senator might be, a few people pointed vaguely in the direction of a potbellied man in an out-of-style polyester suit and a big foam campaign hat.

Smith found, upon questioning the man, that he was mayor of Thermopolis and that, even though he wasn't really supposed to tell anyone, he'd let Smith in on a little secret. The senator was in the last closed-off tent beyond the peanut vendors.

"And he better get out here soon," the mayor enthused. "This is a big, happy hometown crowd. Great place for a politician to press the flesh. Damn great place." Someone called out to him, and the mayor made a beeline back to the Buckhorn beer booth.

As he hurried to the last tent, nearly colliding with one of the pole-carrying Kaspar supporters, Smith wondered how many other people the mayor had spoken to.

At the tent Smith found his path barred.

"Excuse me, sir," a Cole staffer said firmly. "No admittance to the general public. But I'll convey your support to the senator." He tried to steer this gray-flannel supporter away from the flap of the senator's tent, but found that he would not be moved.

Smith produced a card that identified him as a member of the United States Secret Service and held it beneath the upturned nose of the senator's staffer.

The clean-shaved young man checked the card scrupulously. He then looked the unhappy-looking man in the nondescript gray suit up and down critically.

"You're a little old for Secret Service, aren't you, Pops?"

"It is not your place to make that observation,"

Smith said forcefully, as if to explain away his advanced years. Experience had taught him that most things said with authority were accepted without question. He returned the ID to his pocket.

''Guess not,'' the man said agreeably. He was nervously scanning the crowd, concerned the senator's tent would be overrun if he left his post for a minute.

Smith glanced at the crowd. Although there appeared to be more Kaspar signs gathered at this end of Arapahoe Street than anywhere else, no one seemed much interested in the last tent. In point of fact, it was the presence of the overly vigilant staffer who had planted himself outside the closed flap that seemed to have attracted the most attention.

When the staffer was finally persuaded things would not fall apart if he abandoned his post for a few seconds, he led Smith inside.

The atmosphere within the tent was not quite that of a political nerve center. About a dozen people milled about. Some local politicians in sweat-stained suits, taking their jobs on the Thermopolis city council far too seriously; a few Cole aides; a couple of the senator's friends—local business people who had stopped to wish him well and ended up chatting among themselves.

Senator Jackson Cole was in his shirtsleeves, sitting cross-legged on one of the several dozen metal folding chairs that had been left in the tent for his convenience. Most were folded and leaning up against a rickety old table, but the senator had found himself a nice spot on the trampled grass floor to unfold his seat. He was scanning a few sheets of fax paper through a pair of granny-style bifocals. He looked like a balding condor in cowboy boots.

"Senator Cole," Smith said, stepping away from the tent flap.

The senator glanced up, seemingly annoyed at the unfamiliar voice. He gave his nervous assistant a displeased look.

"It's okay, Senator," the young man explained, motioning to Smith. "He's Secret Service."

Cole looked at the proffered card suspiciously, then returned it to Smith.

"So what do you want?" he asked. His voice suggested a perpetual peevishness, and a slightly protruding lower jaw caused him to whistle softly when he pronounced the letter *s*.

"The President was concerned for your safety, sir," Smith said. "With the strange circumstances surrounding this campaign so far, he thought it best you have some kind of protection."

"So he sent you?" Cole said with a tired chuckle. "You look like you last saw duty under ol' LBJ."

"He was concerned," Smith repeated, unfazed by the senatorial dig.

Cole removed his glasses and wearily massaged his eyelids beneath large bony fingers.

"You're a couple days too late. You realize that, don't you, Smith?" he asked.

"I was given a full briefing before leaving Washington," Smith replied. "I am sorry about your daughter."

The staffer visibly winced. It was obvious the campaign staff had been avoiding the subject of the kidnapping.

Cole looked up at the Secret Service agent with something bordering on respect.

"Appreciate the good thought," he said.

Smith hunched awkwardly beneath the sloping green-and-white stripes of the tent roof. His eyes were determined gray flecks beneath his rimless glasses.

Cole nodded to Smith. It was a gesture of respect, as much as one of appreciation. He stood up, grabbing his suit jacket from the folding chair.

"Let's go out and kiss some babies," he announced with a tight smile.

As he ushered his nervous aides and the Secret Service agent from the tent, in his heart Jackson Cole wished more than anything that he could kiss his own baby again.

27

Remo hailed a taxi at the airport.

At first the cabbie was reluctant to drive as far as Thermopolis. The round trip would take a couple of hours minimum, and besides, the fare in the back seat had a hacking cough that sounded like he belonged in a TB clinic. It didn't help that he also reeked like a pile of sun-ripened eggs.

Remo had persuaded the cabbie to change his mind by peeling hundred-dollar bills from the thick roll of cash in his pocket. When the man ceased griping and started drooling, Remo stopped peeling.

Every route into Thermopolis was tied up for some kind of festival, Remo saw. The driver had been forced to take a dozen detours before they finally turned onto the familiar road that led out to the Truth Church ranch.

The taxi deposited Remo near the blinking yellow light, and Remo slipped into the woods as the car drove away.

Remo encountered no patrols as he moved onto one of the wooded paths that led up to the main ranch compound.

The guard towers at the perimeter looked abandoned.

As he approached, Remo sensed no hum from the electrified fence. Just deadness. It was just as well. He was in no mood for acrobatics.

Coming to a side gate, Remo stepped up onto a square of raised concrete in which an anchoring hurricane fence pole had been sunk. He gripped the pipe in his hands and pulled. Concrete dust exploded around his shoes like clods of trampled dirt. With a protesting cry of metal, the pole wrenched free of the mortar.

There was a steady snap, snap, snap of metal fence links as Remo pulled the pole back toward him. When he was finished, Remo rolled the chain-link section around the pole and dumped it off to one side. It clung limply to the next upright post, bouncing slightly.

As he stepped through the newly formed gate, Remo was startled by a voice behind him.

"How fortunate for you that the power was not on," the voice said.

Remo wheeled.

The Master of Sinanju stood beside the guard tower, a blot in a crimson kimono. His bony hands were tucked inside the voluminous sleeves, which lay across his belly.

"How did you find me, Little Father?" Remo asked quietly.

"I followed the smell," Chiun explained simply.

Remo nodded. For some reason the strong sulphur odor around him had grown more powerful since the incident at the zoo.

"You shouldn't have come," Remo said, shaking his head slowly. "I don't want this thing inside me attacking you, too."

"I am safe," said Chiun. "It is you the sun god seeks."

Remo smiled darkly. "So, you here to give me a pep talk?"

Chiun's eyes thinned. "I am here because I am here."

Before he could reply, a sudden coughing spasm shook Remo.

"It is worse?" Chiun asked, face quirking up in concern.

The fit of coughing abated. Remo nodded. "A little," he admitted, wiping tears from his watering eyes. Something seemed to drain from him at this small effort. All at once he gripped his head in his hands in a burst of frustration. If only he could shake the presence within him.

"I don't think I can beat this thing, Chiun. It's already too powerful." When he looked into the old man's eyes, the tears on Remo's face were no longer the by-product of coughing. "I'm sorry I let you down, Little Father," he choked out. "I wasn't strong enough to fight it."

Remo turned away. He wanted to hit something. He wanted to throw something. He wanted to rip something apart and shred it with his bare hands. Anything to quell the feeling of loss and utter helplessness welling up inside him. Instead, Remo found himself staring sullenly at the hard-trampled earth at Chiun's black-sandaled feet.

Chiun's wrinkled visage had grown stiff. "I will not hear this foolishness, Remo. You have let nothing down but your guard. Despite the tumult in your mind, your essence lives." He lifted his bearded chin proudly. His scrawny neck extended like a turtle's from its shell. "Hear this now, my son. Every day you breathe brings glory upon the House of Sinanju. You do not let me down, because I will not allow this."

In spite of the mocking presence in his mind, a swelling pride at Chiun's words took root within Remo.

"I will do my best, Little Father," he said, bowing to his Master.

"That is what I expect from you," Chiun replied with a nod of satisfaction. "For having been trained by the best, only the best resides within you."

"So, you going to wait here for me?" Remo asked. He feared this might be the last time he would ever see Chiun. A part of him did not want the moment to end.

Chiun shook his head. "I must now join Emperor Smith in town."

"Smitty's in Thermopolis?" Remo asked. "Why?"

Chiun shrugged. "The day I understand Smith is the day I surrender sanity," he said. "But I have an obligation to my emperor." He started across the expanse between the fence and the woods, but paused after only a few feet. "Remember, Remo, the spirit of Apollo resides in the smoke. Be wary of it always."

They both seemed on the verge of saying more, but at last they bowed with respectful heads, then turned to their respective paths.

A few hundred yards from the first concrete building, Remo looked back. Chiun had already reached the edge of the forest. A moment later he was gone.

As he scanned the empty plain, Remo's eyes

alighted on one of the vacant guard towers. Where were the Truth Church guards?

He made hard fists and spun back toward the buildings.

"Be careful, Little Father," he said softly to himself.

And somewhere in his mind he thought he heard Chiun's voice warning him to do the same.

"So, WHAT ARE YOU, like Clint Eastwood in that movie?"

Smith raised a narrow grayish eyebrow. He was, of course, aware of the actor, but he had not seen one of his films in more than twenty years. He shrugged his incomprehension at the young Senator Cole staffer.

"You know, the one where he played the over-the-hill Secret Service agent?" he reminded. "I figured you must have seen it a hundred times."

The staffer had been stung by the way the senator had warmed up to Smith. He knew that in some circles it would be considered a pretty trivial thing to be worked up over, but in Washington entire careers had been built on things far less petty.

The staffer bobbed along annoyingly beside him as Smith attempted to survey the crowd. As far as the CURE director could tell, about twenty thousand people jammed Arapahoe Street, and so far he had only seen two uniformed police officers.

If an attack came, he would be alone defending Senator Cole.

The senator appeared to be unfazed by the crush of people. He worked the crowd like a consummate professional, calling many people by name.

Smith didn't know what he was looking for, but his old instincts were alert. He sensed there was some kind of danger lurking just out of sight in the crowd.

As Senator Cole grabbed a few outstretched hands, his entourage moved deeper into the packed corridor of humanity that lined the street.

Smith's eyes scanned the crowd on either side as they went, carefully keeping things in view.

If he had looked more carefully behind, he would have noticed several Mark Kaspar campaign posters had drifted up, and were now following a safe distance in their wake.

REMO DIDN'T BOTHER with the bunker tunnels. He had gone straight to the old airplane hangar on the adjacent lot.

The goat pen he had seen on his first visit to the ranch was less full this day. The animals bleated in fear at his approach.

Remo rounded the back of the building from the direction opposite the one in which he had escaped—with Buffy Brand's help—earlier in the week. It was because he had not left by this route that he had not seen the pile of rotting carcasses.

Remo almost fell into it.

A shallow pit had been dug, but was nearly obscured by the mountain of dead goats piled on this side of the hangar. The ground around the pit was damp with oozing fluids.

The remains of Kaspar's sacrificial animals.

Pounds of powdered limestone had been shoveled onto the pitiful bodies. But no amount of lime would have masked the horrid stench. The stink of rotten flesh attracted all manner of scavenger insects. The air teemed with thick black swarms of flies. They bred in the naked eye sockets of the small corpses, and the oldest of the bodies were covered in part by wriggling white maggots.

Carrion flies buzzed and swirled around his head as Remo moved toward the hangar's side door. He steadied himself as he took hold of the handle.

The separate consciousness within his mind seemed poised to attack. He didn't know if opening the door to the Pythia chamber would unleash the floodgates once again. It had taken nearly every bit of strength he had to overthrow the presence of the Pythia back in the zoo.

And what of Apollo?

Remo didn't know if he was up to another conflict with the lesser entity of Apollo's emissary. The power of the sun god would surely be too great to withstand.

His only chance—a hunch really—would be to bound up to the top of the platform and to attempt to expel the spirit residing within him into the steam emanating from the fissure before Apollo could take full control of his mind. For Remo knew if that happened, the battle would be lost.

Nerves tight, Remo flung open the door and leaped into the Pythia chamber.

The noxious yellow smoke overtook him immediately.

A fresh cloud of the sickly sulphur fog belched up from the crevice like ash from a jaundiced volcano. It flowed around the room, slipping into every corner, enveloping Remo like an enticing shroud.

He grabbed the door frame for support.

A voice cried out.

"Remo!"

His head swam. His vision blurred. He was seeing everything around him in a whirling kaleidoscope of overlapping images. Remo looked up, eyes seeking the point where he thought the voice had come from.

Buffy Brand was manacled at the top of the rocky hill. Her ankles and wrists were snapped securely in twin sets of iron shackles. The leg irons were fastened to the stone platform by a heavy length of chain.

Remo felt the spirit of the Pythia washing over the dams he had built up in his mind. It was like a violently roiling flood, sweeping away a helplessly inadequate levee made of twigs and sand.

He focused on the bottom step.

Must get to the top.

Remo took a few clumsy steps into the chamber.

"Get out of here, Remo!" Buffy yelled.

He didn't know where the voice came from this time. It was Buffy once again, but the disorienting effect of the swelling tide in his brain was worsening with every step. He couldn't tell if she was before him or behind.

His foot touched the first step.

The footfall was somehow soft and echoey. And far away.

Another step.

The black battlefield returned in Remo's mind. This time the bleak sky of the vision, which had been black, as well, was painted in sickly smears of bloody red.

The third step.

The combatants appeared. One vicious, the other docile.

Over the horizon a black shape grew like time-lapse photos of the birth of a mountain.

Remo forced himself up. Must make it to the top.

He took the next half-dozen steps in jerky, uncertain strides, twice almost tumbling backward. Charged by some unseen electrical force, the yellow smoke crackled in minilightning bursts all around him. Remo bulled through it all.

Somehow, some way he reached the top.

The Cole girl. Somewhere in his mind Remo recognized her for who she really was. She sat on the tripod, glassy-eyed, face dead of all emotion.

Buffy Brand was to the girl's right. She stared at Remo with frightened eyes and babbled some warning that he couldn't understand.

The world swam around him in swirls of colored light.

He moved across the platform.

The presence was seeping through Remo's disordered mind once more.

It was strangely comforting this time. Somehow here, in the Pythia Pit, it was soft and inviting, rather than something he should fear. It was something to accept. To embrace.

The thing that told him he should fight was small and weak within him. It was easy to ignore that stubborn part of his mind.

East had met West. It was his destiny.

Through drunken eyes, Remo watched someone else step out from behind a tapestry at the far end of the platform. A little man dressed in strange robes. He was uttering incantations that Remo couldn't understand. For a brief instant he thought he should recognize the man, but in his drunken state he couldn't tell. Remo ignored him and moved toward the tripod.

The Cole girl rose at his approach.

As if in some prearranged ritual, she moved aside as he stepped on the metal grate that traversed the rocky fissure.

Smoke poured from the crevice as thick as that from an oil-well fire.

It was his destiny. East had met West. There was no sense fighting destiny. Especially his own.

Carefully Remo took his seat on the tripod of Apollo's Pythia.

The white-robed man whom Remo thought he should have recognized stepped in front of him. He wore a wicked smile as he stared coldly into Remo's dilating pupils.

On the battlefield of his mind, Remo watched the fierce combatant strike a final, terminal blow against his docile opponent. And for the first time Remo saw the face of the victim. As the body fell to the barren plain, Remo saw that the combatant's face was his own.

And in that minuscule part of his mind that he could still call his own, Remo bade a silent farewell to his father and teacher, the Master of Sinanju.

HAROLD SMITH didn't know what he had done to rankle Senator Cole's assistant, but he wished there was some way he could take whatever it was back. The young idiot was becoming a nuisance.

"When was the last time you fired a gun, Pops?"

The question was asked with a malice bordering on glee.

Smith continued to watch the crowd surging around them as the senator chatted with a group of older women near a booth that was stocked from top to bottom with rag dolls, patchwork quilts and a dozen other handmade items.

"I am regularly recertified." Smith didn't look at the young man as he spoke.

"No, did you ever fire *at* someone?" the staffer asked. He seemed to consider this a kind of witticism, for there was a humorous, self-congratulatory glint in the depths of his eyes.

"That is not something I wish to share with you," Smith replied. He noticed a woman standing over by one of the concession stands who was eyeing the senator strangely. She had a kerchief wrapped around her head, and wore a pair of dark sunglasses so large they made her look almost like an oversize insect. Was she looking this way or wasn't she? Smith couldn't tell for sure.

A moment later she had turned away, becoming fixated on something on the other side of the pavilion.

Probably just trying to find a lost friend, Smith decided, and continued scanning the crowd.

There certainly were a lot of supporters carrying Mark Kaspar signs beneath the tent. Some of them had to crouch so that the long poles didn't get caught against the festive, multicolored tarpaulin roof.

They seemed to be converging in Cole's general area.

Smith turned his attention back to the woman in the sunglasses.

What was it about her? She was somehow familiar....

She seemed to be nodding to a cluster of supporters carrying Kaspar signs. Never uttered a word, but it appeared as if those she nodded to understood some unspoken command.

As she stepped from the cover of the tent back out into the bright sunlight, it suddenly occurred to Smith where he knew her from. He had seen her face several times while he was researching the Church of the Absolute and Incontrovertible Truth. She had even worn the same sunglasses in one picture.

Esther Clear-Seer.

The people with the signs supported Mark Kaspar. And they had surrounded Senator Jackson Cole on all sides.

"At your age, you probably need help loading the magazine, huh?" the Cole staffer was saying.

The young man chuckled at his own comment. The chuckle mutated into a choked gurgle when the part of his brain that controlled the laughing function was rudely disrupted by a small piece of soft lead that had traveled at great velocity from the other side of the tent.

The staffer's forehead exploded outward. Then the sound of the gunshot registered on this end of the tent. Dollops of blood and sticky gray brain sludge splattered across a quilt depicting meticulously sewn scenes of early Wyoming pioneer life.

The staffer fell to his knees, his mouth sagging in shock. Before he had even hit the asphalt, Smith had drawn his own gun and, crouching like a football lineman, threw one gray shoulder into the back of Senator Cole. The force propelled Cole through the open wooden archway of the quilting booth. When a second shot rang out, Smith threw himself atop the senator.

A fat woman Cole had been speaking with was struck in the shoulder by the bullet. It spun her around like a confused dancer without a partner. She dropped heavily to her ample bottom, stunned. A fountain of red burbled up from beneath her smart cotton blouse.

Screaming erupted all around. Most people had frozen in shock when the first shot rang out. By the second they were shocked out of their shock. The crowd under the tent scrambled in all directions.

Behind the cover of the small booth, Senator Cole sat stunned and blinking like a stupefied ostrich.

No time to check on him now. As he and Cole had ducked for cover, Smith registered the Kaspar campaigners drawing weapons from beneath their candidate's smiling face. They had been concealed in the hollow centers of the poles on which they had carried their posters.

The front of the booth was draped across with a sheet of wide crepe paper. Smith tore a hole large enough to see out across the main body of the tent.

Pairs of nervous legs went scampering close by. Not much farther away he could see an advancing group of armed men. Smith aimed his automatic at the closest gunman and pulled the trigger.

A satisfying explosion came from the heavy gun. The bullet struck the first man dead center in the chest. He toppled backward, his rifle clattering away from his twitching fingers.

The rest scattered like roaches, taking cover behind the dozen other carnival stands that stretched across the far side of the tent.

The burp of an automatic weapon preceded a shower of bullets across the open face of the booth where Smith and Cole were hidden. Fabric from shrapnel-torn quilts exploded in every direction, blowing wildly from the various impact points before settling softly to the asphalt floor.

A gunman appeared over the top of one of the concession counters. But before he was able to squeeze the trigger on his AR-15, Smith loosed two more shots. The gunman flung up his arms, then he sank behind the counter. He didn't appear again.

"Who is it?" Cole hissed. "Who's trying to get me?"

Smith was surprised that the man sounded so calm. Probably still in shock.

"I believe they are members of the Truth Church, Senator."

Cole screwed up his leathery face in confusion. "The cult?" he asked.

Smith had no time to respond. Two other members of the Truth Church were moving out from behind the raffle stand. They moved from folding chairs to tables, and when they were close enough, Smith fired his last three shots at the pair. He only hit one.

Jamming a hand into his jacket pocket, Smith fumbled for the spare ammunition clip he brought with him. But even as he did, he knew that if the gunman had continued moving forward he wouldn't have time to reload before the assailant made it to the booth.

Smith had just rammed the clip home, and was yanking back on the slide, when he saw the barrel of the AR-15 appear over the counter of the booth above their heads like the snout of a curious anteater.

Another second, and the barrel would be aimed at them. A second after that, Harold W. Smith and Senator Jackson Cole would be dead.

But those two seconds were precisely two seconds too long.

A shrill voice ripped the deathly still air.

"Hold, vassal of evil!"

A blur of crimson whirled across Smith's field of vision.

Before he knew what had happened, the rifle had vanished back over the top of the counter. Smith again peeked out through the hole in the booth, and he saw the gunman lying facedown on the ground, his own weapon jutting from his back like the dorsal fin of a shark.

A wizened face appeared over the counter.

"What are you doing here!" Smith exploded. "Where is Remo?"

The Master of Sinanju's eyes grew heavy of lid.

"Normally, when one preserves the life of one's emperor, the skies rain soft gold, not hard questions," Chiun said aridly.

Smith pushed himself up to a crouching position. "There are other assailants here," he warned Chiun.

"I will deal with such ruffians," Chiun said. "I have cleared a path so that you may lead your charge to safety." He gestured back in the direction from which he had come, behind Smith.

Smith glanced over his shoulder. He saw a motionless leg lying at an unnatural angle through the nearby rear tent flap. Close by lay a trampled Mark Kaspar poster.

Without another word Chiun moved toward the center of the tent.

The other members of the Truth Church, emboldened by the absence of return gunfire, had come out of hiding and were again advancing on Smith's position.

Like a fiery red dervish, Chiun swirled into the center of the mob.

One gunman, then another, raised their weapons to fire upon the Master of Sinanju. But it seemed as if he was never where they expected him to be. And as they redirected their fire, trying to fix their bizarre target, one by one they began dropping.

Smith watched for a moment. Only when he was certain that Chiun had crowded the remaining gunmen inside did he urge the senator to his feet. The two men scurried, crouching, out the rear tent flap to safety.

ESTHER CLEAR-SEER had watched the attack from a safe distance outside the tent.

The crowds had swarmed around her when the shooting started, but by this time most had fled screaming to safety. Aside from her Truth Church acolytes, Arapahoe Street was all but deserted.

She had no idea who the old guy with Cole was, but when she heard the last of eight bullets fired and didn't hear another as her men approached the booth, she was certain that the senator was finished.

And then the Asian had surged out of nowhere, arms high, face a thundercloud of righteous wrath.

He was the same old Asian who had come to her ranch with that Remo. The one who had broken her nose. The one Kaspar called the Master of Sinanju.

Esther had looked forward to seeing that old fossil again. She wanted to teach him a lesson that would never let him contemplate again blackening both all-seeing eyes and impacting her holy sinus cavities.

And it was just fine with her if her loyal acolytes did all the maiming and bone busting for her.

The old man was quickly surrounded. He disappeared under the bigger and taller bodies that closed in with slow, steady menace.

Esther Clear-Seer smiled. This would be worth waiting for.

When the bodies of her Truth Church acolytes began dropping around the feet of the old man, she changed her evil mind. It might be better for her own personal safety if she watched the proceedings from an even greater distance, after all.

In a blind panic Esther Clear-Seer turned and ran after the last remnants of the fleeing crowd, and her ears filled with the ugly, too-familiar sound of bones breaking and shattering.

28

At first the blackness was complete.

But then slowly, almost imperceptibly, scenery began to resolve from the darkness around him. Shades of gray appeared as the ink of total blackness bled away, illuminating some areas, highlighting others.

The flickering mirage congealed into a familiar setting.

It was the expansive plain on which the two warriors had battled. As the lighter shades of gray took hold in the lowering sky, Remo knew now that it was no longer the scene of his tortured visions, but the actual field itself. He didn't know how he knew this.

As he walked along, Remo felt the solid earth beneath his feet, breathed the air of the strange perpetual twilight.

Were he to walk a hundred yards or a hundred years, he would never be able to tell.

The plain was perfectly flat and bare. He detected no vegetation, no animals. As far as the eye could see, there was not even a solitary stone. Just more of the same bleak, barren expanse stretching limitlessly off to the unreachable point where land met sky.

And the sky itself seemed nothing more than a vacant extension of the land. It was a sky without sun or stars or moon. Without life.

Remo walked on to a point that he knew instinctively to be the center of the plain. He had no idea from where this knowledge came, but when he reached the middle, he stopped and turned.

And there behind him was the weird figure who had struck down the helpless combatant of his thoughts.

Remo could see the warrior clearly now, though his mind still couldn't reconcile the image. A creature dressed in yellow smoke, the foul exhalations of the pit. Remo knew it to be the Pythia.

Their roles now were reversed. Remo could see the giant looming shape of his prior visions floating at some indistinct point in the distance. He realized on some primal level that this was where he should rightfully be. Apollo had assumed control of his body, and the Pythia now stood guard against the threat from within.

That threat was Remo.

The figure of the Pythia raised its hands and took up a menacing posture.

"Night tiger of Sinanju, you continue to fight." It was a statement of fact.

Remo stood his ground. "I do," he replied.

"That which you consider your soul should have fled into the Void when my master assumed his predestined place in the world of mortals. If you fail to leave of your own volition, Sinanju, it is within my power to destroy your essence for all eternity. You will know neither pleasure nor pain nor hope nor sorrow. You will not be wept for, for you will not have existed. Is this your desire?"

This creature had mocked him in his thoughts, usurped his mind, spirited him from the physical world into this hellish twilight. And now it threatened to rob Remo of his soul if he didn't go peacefully into the Void.

It offered him a simple choice…but Remo was prepared to make neither. He instead chose that which the Pythia did not offer.

In the vision in his mind, Remo forced himself to smile.

"Take your best shot, smoky."

And a deadly hand lashed out at Remo's indomitable form.

ESTHER CLEAR-SEER WAS breathless when she burst into the Pythia chamber. She began gagging on the thick sulphur smoke as she tried to suck down lungfuls of air.

"That old Sinanju guy is in town," she panted to Kaspar, repressing her gag reflex at the noxious stench.

Kaspar, poised expectantly at the apex of the Pythia platform, was indifferent to Esther's report. "It does not matter," he said with a wave of the hand.

"Like hell it doesn't," Esther said, mounting the stairs. She noticed Lori Cole sitting off to one side of the platform. "When I took off, he'd already taken out at least a dozen of my crack acolytes. It took me three years to build my following back to this level, and you've got me sacrificing all of them like lambs in one afternoon. Plus I think Cole got away."

This news nearly got a reaction out of Kaspar, but at that moment the eyes of what had been Remo Wil-

liams fluttered open. The head moved around, as if
testing the bones and muscles of the neck for the first
time. The eyes this time seemed more focused than
those of the others who had straddled the wooden tripod.

Kaspar appeared to be fascinated by every movement the man on the stool made. Esther realized that
she wasn't going to get any sympathy out of him for
the great setback the Truth Church had suffered that
day.

"So he came back after all, huh?" she said, nodding
to Remo.

When Kaspar looked back at her, his eyes were
moist with barely containable joy. "He has indeed
come back," he said reverently.

"Yeah, well...right." Esther shot a baffled look at
Buffy Brand, who was still manacled beside the crevice. But the young girl was staring fearfully at the man
on the stool.

And what had once been Remo spoke.

"I live," Remo pronounced to Kaspar in a voice
that was not his. "East has met West. The prophecy
is fulfilled."

And the eyes of Apollo incarnate looked with fiery
satisfaction on the modern world.

THOUGH THE SMOKE of the Pythia's body appeared
insubstantial, Remo's hands felt as though they were
striking solid flesh and bone.

It was not as it had been in his mind.

Here, in this netherworld of his own thoughts, unen-
cumbered by distractions of the natural world, Remo
stood on an equal footing with the Pythia.

More than equal footing.

A fist snaked out with lightning speed from the cloud's left node. Remo deflected the blow easily. His own hand shot out, connecting sharply with the creature's midsection. The sound of expelled wind came from the Pythia, and Remo didn't know if in this strange ethereal plain he was seeing things as they really were—or fashioning in his own perception responses that were easier for his mind to understand.

He only knew the Pythia was injured.

The thing had been attempting to block him from passing over toward the spot where Apollo resided, but it now staggered to one side.

Remo's hand snapped out once more, and again it landed where the thing's belly should have been. Another gasp for air, and the Pythia weaved farther to one side. It raised its hands defensively.

It was almost too easy. Remo brought the side of his hand in a chopping motion against the temple of the Pythia.

The creature dropped to the plain, gasping for breath in a desperate, feeble gurgle.

Remo stepped beyond the stricken form. Apollo waited beyond.

KASPAR'S DELIGHT was boundless. Esther stood dumbly behind him. They faced the new Pythia.

"Your humble servant waits breathless to perform your earthly bidding," he said obsequiously. "I am eager to rule this land in your name."

The thing within Remo gave the appearance of looking down on Kaspar even though, seated, it was a good foot below the little man.

"All will be as my servant predicted," the voice said sonorously.

"The prophecy?" Kaspar said, licking his lips anxiously. "I will govern the land in which I dwell?"

"All will be as I have foreseen."

Kaspar couldn't contain his ecstasy. This was no longer the Pythia he spoke to. The servant of Apollo had been banished to some unimportant corner within the vessel. These words were spoken by the sun god himself—and they confirmed that he would rule the United States of America.

"I am humbled by the gifts you have bestowed upon me, my master," Kaspar said, bowing. "The sacrifice we now make is a homage to your ineffable greatness."

He pulled the ceremonial dagger from the scabbard at his waist and, turning, summoned Esther Clear-Seer to him.

Esther wasn't sure what was going on, but she understood enough to know that it was something more vast and powerful than she had ever encountered. Dumbly she walked over to Kaspar and took the proffered knife. He gestured to Buffy Brand, and like an automaton, Esther began walking stiffly over to the girl, all the time never taking her eyes off the creature on the tripod.

Buffy, as well, was fixated on the man on the stool. But as Esther approached, knife in hand, she began struggling fearfully, trying to pull away. The heavy chains at her wrists and ankles prevented her from moving.

As Esther raised the knife, ready to bring it slashing down and across Buffy's throat, a sudden scream distracted her. When she turned, she saw the mouth of what had been Remo opened in shock. The cruel face was a mask of rage and hate.

Kaspar stood before the tripod, surrounded in furious puffs of sickly sulphur smoke, a look of helpless confusion creasing his narrow features.

Before Kaspar could say or do anything, the head of Apollo slumped back to the body of its host vessel.

"LITTLE MAN FROM SINANJU, you think you can best Apollo?" The voice was filled with anger and scorn.

Apollo appeared on the plain the instant Remo had stepped past the prone figure of the Pythia. He barred Remo's way.

The sun god wasn't as huge as he had appeared in the previous visions, but he was a powerful being nonetheless. He towered several feet above Remo. A giant among mortals. Around his shoulders was draped a cloak of fire, and across his back was slung a quiver filled with golden arrows. In his hand he held a mighty longbow. His face was a radiant bronze shield crowned by hair the color of sunshine. The eyes were reddish gold.

Wordlessly Remo took a step forward.

A hand flew faster than Remo's eyes could detect. Up, around, behind. A golden blur raced from the center of the bowstring.

Remo felt the arrow strike his shoulder. It thumped him back a pace, throwing him off stride. A second arrow flew, striking just below the first. He tried to take another step, but a third arrow, then a fourth and fifth in rapid succession knocked him back in place.

The arrows continued to fly. Each time Remo was

sure the quiver must be empty, another deadly missile hurtled through the air of the netherworld.

His body was racked in pain. Blood flowed freely from hundreds of open wounds. Through it all, Remo did not fall. He refused to.

When the pain became too great and Remo was certain that his mind could no longer endure the torment of this other world, he suddenly felt another presence explode in white-hot brilliance in his thoughts.

It was something that was vast beyond his comprehension, but it didn't belong to the sinister creatures that had inhabited his thoughts of late. This was a presence that was neither evil nor judgmental, but was, incongruously, fierce and violent all the same. It was a force so powerful that it could not be reconciled to the modern world.

And it was familiar.

The force took over his will, but didn't attempt to obliterate Remo's consciousness. He remained a detached spectator, as he had been in the previous battles—but to a lesser degree. He was still his own self—yet now that self had become part of a greater whole.

And the force within him spoke and it did say, "Foolish minion of Greece! Save your simple tools of destruction for the ignorant who fear and serve you."

And in his mind Remo's hand swept down and yanked the arrows from his body as though they were nothing more than feathers. When he again looked up, he was on a level with the creature before him.

"I will have my due," Apollo sneered. "Atonement for the destruction of my earthly temple by the fool

Tang. It is as I have foreseen—East has met West. The night tiger belongs to the gods."

The being within Remo threw back its head and laughed loudly at the endless black sky. "East *has* met West, fool," it spit. "But *I* am fulfillment of your prophecy."

Apollo grew angry of tone. "Who is this who speaks to me from the mind of my Sinanju vessel?" he demanded.

And the voice within Remo intoned, "I am created Shiva, the Destroyer—death, the shatterer of worlds. The dead night tiger made whole by the Master of Sinanju. Prepare to pay with blood, corrupter of my avatar, Shiva Remo."

He advanced on Apollo, hands floating before him like questing python heads, ready to strike a deadly blow.

And in this place of immortals that knew neither time nor space nor dimension, the spirit of the sun god felt fear.

"WHAT'S HAPPENING?" Esther Clear-Seer asked fearfully. The knife was forgotten. She had dropped it at the feet of Buffy Brand when the voices started emanating from the mouth of the vessel on the tripod.

They were strange and alien voices. Loud and fearful. A struggle was taking place somewhere within the heart of the vessel. The body twitched in tiny spasms as cries of pain and anguish issued from its mouth.

All at once the sounds ceased, and the body became still once more.

Kaspar shot a worried look at Esther Clear-Seer, who had backed fearfully to the top of the stone staircase. He stepped closer to the tripod, afraid that some unseen internal force had destroyed the integrity of the vessel. Remo's dark head was still slumped down on his chest, and there appeared to be no breathing coming from the vessel. Carefully Kaspar took a thick wrist in his hand, seeking a pulse.

The head suddenly rose. A pair of dead black eyes lifted, then bore into Kaspar's soul.

"Boo," said Remo Williams in his own voice.

Kaspar jumped as if shocked by electricity. He tried to pull away, but Remo had grabbed him by the arm. Kaspar stood rooted in place atop the metal grate as Remo got to his feet.

"This is not possible!" Kaspar yelled. He could feel the bones of his wrist shattering beneath the pressure of Remo's viselike grip. "My master prophesied my greatness! I will govern the land in which I dwell!"

"That is true," Remo said, and the smile that spread across his features was one of cruel joy. "But the land you govern is your own grave."

And with that Remo swung his other hand around and clapped it firmly atop Kaspar's head. As he held Kaspar in place with one hand, he pushed downward with the other.

In all, it took less than a minute. Remo made certain that Mark Kaspar was conscious until the last possible second. Kaspar's screams as his legs were shredded through the grate of the Pythia Pit grew more frenzied as his pelvis and torso passed into the crevice beneath.

It was as if he were being swallowed up by some breed of rock-dwelling shark, and the screams subsided as his heart muscle passed out the far end of the grate in three distinct sections. When it was all that was left, Remo pressed down with the sole of his shoe on the skull, delivering Kaspar's brain with a final, feeble snap into the belly of the dwindling yellow smoke.

He turned on Esther Clear-Seer.

She had watched, horrified, the whole time Kaspar was being shoved like a blob of pasta through a noodle maker. But when Remo turned his deep-set eyes on her, she began stepping backward down the stairs. Her hands lifted defensively.

"He made me do it all," she said desperately. "I didn't even want to kidnap the girls. I thought it was stupid. Bad for business. He made me do it. He was the devil and he made me do it!"

Remo hadn't moved. He stared at Esther as she continued inching down the stairs.

"You kidnapped the girls," he said flatly.

"Hey, it was just another way to make a buck," she said. Behind Remo she noticed that the yellow smoke began to pour more freely from the crevice beneath. She bit the inside of her cheek, stalling for time. Remo still hadn't moved. "I'm just a businesswoman at heart," Esther said with a shrug.

The smoke had gathered behind Buffy Brand, whose eyes were zipping back and forth between Esther and Remo. She never saw the thick yellow fog even as it shoved through her thin blouse and disappeared with her. The girl's back suddenly arched as if she had been stabbed between the shoulder blades. A glazed expression settled across her features and, without any warning, she threw the metal chain that bound her wrists around Remo's exposed throat.

Esther had been backing down the stairs slowly, but

when the chain bit into Remo's flesh, she stopped completely.

Remo didn't struggle. He simply reached up and snapped one of the metal links. The two halves of the broken chain slithered uselessly over his shoulders. He broke the chain at Buffy's legs and lifted her away from the rocky crevice, setting her carefully atop the platform.

Esther took this as her cue to leave. Heart beating like a trip-hammer, she turned and raced down the remainder of the stairs.

Once Buffy was safe, Remo bounded to the top of the staircase and, with a simple flex of his calf muscles, launched himself from the edge of the Pythia platform. He moved at an angle through the dwindling yellow smoke and, at the apex of his turn, his back barely brushing the vaulted concrete ceiling, he tucked his legs in close to his body and executed a flawless somersault, landing on both feet at the bottom of the stairs.

Remo stood face-to-stunned-face with Esther Clear-Seer.

"Tah-dah!" said Remo, throwing his arms out wide.

Esther Clear-Seer had no place to run. Remo barred her way. And all at once she knew in a sudden terrifying spark of blinding realization that this man was going to make her suffer for every evil she had committed in her life. Especially for the kidnappings.

It was the only time in her life one of her prophecies came true.

29

Harold Smith and the Master of Sinanju caught up with Remo at the main gates to Ranch Ragnarok. He had sat the still-unconscious Buffy Brand against the nearest guard tower. Beside her, staring blankly into the forest, was Lori Cole.

Smith left the door to his rental car open and, ignoring Remo, stooped to examine the Cole girl.

"Sorry, Smitty. Her mind's gone," Remo said vaguely. "Buffy should pull through, though." He continued fiddling earnestly with something in his hands.

"Mark Kaspar and Esther Clear-Seer?" Smith asked.

Remo shook his head. The look on his face told Smith not to press the point. He began loading the two women in the back of his car.

Chiun had sidled up beside Remo, and fell to watching the young man as he worked.

"You are well," the Master of Sinanju said, his eyes unreadable, his tone deceptively casual.

Remo nodded. "The prophecy was told in Old World terms, but it was intended for the New World. It wasn't Sinanju and Greece. The 'East' was Sinanju, but the 'West' meant America.'' He looked up from his work. "I am the prophecy."

Chiun nodded.

"I have always suspected there was something fundamentally wrong with the legend of Tang. He is remembered as a dullard. Perhaps history has been too kind to him."

Remo sensed that Chiun was about to have another go at the ancient scrolls of Sinanju with a quill pen and a bottle of Wite-Out. Before then, Remo had one more thing to do.

"We should leave," Smith said, straightening from the back of the car. The girls were safely strapped in, ready to be dropped off at the nearest hospital. "The state police are arriving in Thermopolis. We should be gone before they begin making inquiries."

"Right behind you, Smitty," Remo said. He turned a small knob and squinted in confusion at what was an unplanned response.

"What is that?" Smith asked, nodding to the knapsack in Remo's hand.

"Just something I picked up from one of the bunkers. Did you know this place was loaded with explosives and gasoline?"

"I was aware of that."

"It's kind of convenient," Remo said. His tongue jutted between his thin lips as he made a final adjustment on the contents of the knapsack. "There," he announced proudly.

Smith peered inside the small bag. "Remo, that is a timer-detonator," he said worriedly.

"Yup. I filled the Pythia chamber with enough explosives to take out half the state. It should take care of the bunkers, as well. But I'm not so hot with gadgets. So I suggest we get out of here. Fast.''

And with that Remo pulled the knapsack closed and flung it deep into the Ragnarok grounds. It soared through the air until it was nearly a speck in the clear blue sky. Only Remo and Chiun saw it drop neatly through the open skylight of the Pythia Pit.

They were back in the rental car, Smith behind the wheel, and driving rapidly down the dirt access road when the first explosion rocked the ground beneath them. This was rapidly followed by others that soon became one long percussive wave of shuddering rumbles and thunderings.

A tiny hail of black pebbles pelted the roof and hood of the fleeing car as the Wyoming prairie collapsed and ignited in leaping monsters of searing flame.

"You may cancel the submarine vessel, Emperor Smith,'' Chiun said thoughtfully from the passenger's seat. "Now that all dangers have passed, the House of Sinanju stands ready to serve your mighty throne.''

From the back seat, beside Buffy Brand, Remo snorted loudly. Smith, uncomfortable at perpetuating the lie, nonetheless nodded stiffly as the car plowed out onto the main road beneath the flashing amber light.

Neither Remo nor Chiun was watching as a huge cloud of dirty yellow smoke belched high above the treetops behind them.

EPILOGUE

"Okay, that's it! That's it!" The supervisor was yelling at Nick Biel and Nick really didn't like it at all. His boss had been acting like a show-off ever since the bigshot had shown up earlier in the afternoon.

The entire area was charred black from the fires that had raged across the plains months before and Nick's backhoe was having a hard enough time getting in and out of the trenches that were the result of all the collapsed underground structures. The absolute last thing Nick needed was somebody screaming at him.

He got down out of the cab and walked around to where the supervisor and the mysterious bigshot stood. He was again struck by something familiar about the man. But he felt that way a lot. Last week he swore he had seen Bruce Willis at the mall.

He dismissed the thought and, following his supervisor's shouted instructions, got down on his ample belly and reached down into the collapsed wreckage of one of the buildings. He pulled a charred piece of corrugated tin out of the way and found the object below it. Just where the stranger said it would be.

Nick was amazed that it could have survived all of the explosions intact and he was even more amazed that someone would want something so filthy.

The man had thanked Nick's supervisor, and after he left everything had returned to business as usual. Nick had gone back to clearing away the building debris so that the environmental clean-up crews could get into the deepest bunkers.

All day as he worked, Nick kept wondering why the mysterious man looked so familiar. It wasn't until he was home in bed that night that the answer finally came to him. His union had urged its members to vote for the man during one of the past presidential elections.

He wondered what Michael ''Prince'' Princippi would want with a dirty old crockpot filled with yellow powder.

After the ashes of the great Reckoning, the warrior survivalists live by one primal instinct

JAMES AXLER
DEATH LANDS ®
Way of the Wolf

Unexpectedly dropped into a bleak Arctic landscape by a mat-trans jump, Ryan Cawdor and his companions find themselves the new bounty in a struggle for dominance between a group of Neanderthals and descendants of a military garrison stranded generations ago.

Don't miss out on the action in these titles featuring THE EXECUTIONER®, STONY MAN™ and SUPERBOLAN®!

The American Trilogy

#64222	PATRIOT GAMBIT	$3.75 U.S. $4.25 CAN.	☐ ☐
#64223	HOUR OF CONFLICT	$3.75 U.S. $4.25 CAN.	☐ ☐
#64224	CALL TO ARMS	$3.75 U.S. $4.25 CAN.	☐ ☐

Stony Man™

#61910	FLASHBACK	$5.50 U.S. $6.50 CAN.	☐ ☐
#61911	ASIAN STORM	$5.50 U.S. $6.50 CAN.	☐ ☐
#61912	BLOOD STAR	$5.50 U.S. $6.50 CAN.	☐ ☐

SuperBolan®

#61452	DAY OF THE VULTURE	$5.50 U.S. $6.50 CAN.	☐ ☐
#61453	FLAMES OF WRATH	$5.50 U.S. $6.50 CAN.	☐ ☐
#61454	HIGH AGGRESSION	$5.50 U.S. $6.50 CAN.	☐ ☐

(limited quantities available on certain titles)

TOTAL AMOUNT	$
POSTAGE & HANDLING	$
($1.00 for one book, 50¢ for each additional)	
APPLICABLE TAXES*	$ _____
TOTAL PAYABLE	$ _____
(check or money order—please do not send cash)	

To order, complete this form and send it, along with a check or money order for the total above, payable to Gold Eagle Books, to: **In the U.S.:** 3010 Walden Avenue, P.O. Box 9077, Buffalo, NY 14269-9077; **In Canada:** P.O. Box 636, Fort Erie, Ontario, L2A 5X3.

Name: _____

Address: _____ City: _____

State/Prov.: _____ Zip/Postal Code: _____

*New York residents remit applicable sales taxes.
Canadian residents remit applicable GST and provincial taxes.

GEBACK19

Under Attack!

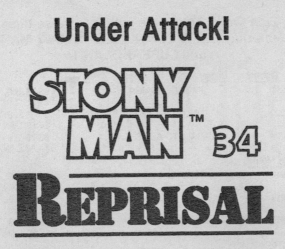

STONY MAN™ 34

REPRISAL

In a brilliant conspiracy to restore the glory days of the CIA, a rogue agent has masterminded a plot to take out Company competition. His stolen clipper chip has effectively shut down the Farm's communications network and made sitting ducks of the field teams. With Phoenix Force ambushed and trapped in the Colombian jungle, and a cartel wet team moving in on Able Team stateside, it's up to Mack Bolan and the Stony experts to bring off the impossible.

Available in April 1998 at your favorite retail outlet.

James Axler

OUTLANDERS™

PARALLAX RED

Kane and his colleagues stumble upon an ancient colony on Mars that housed a group of genetically altered humans, retained by the Archons to do their bidding. After making the mat-trans jump to Mars, the group finds itself faced with two challenges: a doomsday device that could destroy Earth, and a race of Transhumans desperate to steal human genetic material to make moving to Earth possible.

In the Outlands, the future is an eternity of hell....